Nicla's Story

Arnaldo Aranci

ISBN 979-8-218-22836-1

To my parents, Nicla and Tony, who sacrificed everything for us, and whose romance inspired this story.

Acknowledgements

I would like to thank Michael Biagioli, Carol Aranci Buongirno, and Mary Ann Knight for their invaluable hard work in editing this book.

I thank Jennifer Papa, Lisa Stamidis, Mary Giangrande, and Richard Pershan for their encouragement to undertake and complete this journey.

I also thank Eric Knight for his help in guiding me through the publishing process.

To my cousin Flavia, with whom I shared many beautiful Italian summers of my childhood and who told me the story of the Blue Prince, I offer, *Mille grazzie, bella*!

And finally, boundless thanks to my wife, Annmarie, for her love and support in helping me bring this book to life.

Chapter 1

The sky would be black with them soon. By the hundreds they came - the American planes. Then the bombs would begin to fall. Nicla was making her way home with bags in both hands when the sirens began to wail. Her pace quickened as she saw others darting for homes with cellars. The Americans were trying to dislodge the German army from her town and its commercial harbor. The Italians and Americans were allies now, but the bombs killed indiscriminately. Nicla could sense from the waxing drone that the planes were getting closer.

She picked up her step. Too far from home. She would have to make it to a bomb shelter. Two more blocks. Livorno was an ancient port city of narrow streets. A canal wound its way between tan, stucco walls and terra cotta roofs. Some called it Little Venice.

Although Nicla was preoccupied with outpacing the roaring harbingers of destruction, she couldn't help noticing odd details along the way: an overturned vendor's cart - its contents, mussels, and sea urchins, strewn across the road. A cat gingerly sniffed at the black bristles of the urchins.

The earth began to vibrate beneath her feet and deep shock-waves compressed the air around her. The pulses bunched closer together. Bombs were falling on the harbor. Clutching her bags, she broke into a run. There was *il Municipio* - the town hall. The basement was a bomb shelter. She stumbled through the door, bumping against the frail backs of an elderly couple making their way in.

"*Mi scuzi*," she entreated, adjusting the shawl on the older woman.

"*Vai, bella*," the woman replied with a hand on Nicla's shoulder. "Go pretty. You are still young. Don't lose time with us."

Nicla dropped her bags and helped the couple down the stairs. The blasts outside increased in frequency and intensity.

The shelter wasn't more than some wooden benches set in rows, church-style. Sometimes the local priest would lead prayers if he made it there during a raid. That day, there were only a handful of people. Against the back wall, sat a mother with her 12-year-old daughter's head buried under her arm. Facing them was a younger boy, the brother, who danced a taunting jig and occasionally poked his sister. A thundering bomb strike caused him to leap onto his mother's lap. The three embraced. Plaster dust floated down on them from the ceiling.

That one was very close, Nicla thought. She looked down the end of her bench at a gaunt, little man in a long coat, curled on his side. He was sleeping through the bombardment. Nicla was fascinated by the way different individuals handled war. The old couple was holding hands. A woman in black massaged her rosary beads mouthing silent prayers, never pausing for the shaking of the room. Her shopping bags waited dutifully at her side.

Bags! Nicla realized she had left her own bags at the top of the stairs. She bolted off the bench, only to be knocked off balance by another seismic shock.

"Wait!" cried the old woman. But Nicla was at the top of the stairs. A rat was tugging at the loaf of bread poking from the end of her toppled bags.

"*Bestia!*" she screamed, throwing her shoe at the wretched op-portunist. Of all the things she detested about bomb shelters, an encounter with its most ubiquitous denizen was the vilest. They gave her chills. She couldn't look at them. But she was not surprised at her willingness to confront the repulsive creature. Those bags contained her family's meager dinner. Besides, many things people did to survive the war were much more surprising to Nicla, and more heroic.

Breaking off the tainted end of the bread, she gathered her bags and turned to make her way back down the stairs. But the explosions were tapering, the sirens waning. It was time to go.

Outside, Nicla encountered a scene of quiet, creeping back to life. It was like a normal morning. But there were surreal touches. Smoke rose in the sky down by the harbor. A German motorcycle and side car raced past, swerving to avoid potholes, and lifting onto two wheels in the process. One of its passengers grabbed his helmet to keep it on his head.

Shouts began to emanate from around the corner. Making her way home in that direction, Nicla found an apartment building with its face sheared off. An errant bomb had landed in the street. The crater bore silent, gaping witness. She looked up. Broken pipes like stalactites, and wires like strange vines, hung here and there where walls had been. On the third floor, a bald man, fully clothed in a black vest and tie, scratched his head as he peered over the edge of the floor - now a precipice. His wife, arms on her hips, called him back in belittling tones. On the second floor, dinner was still cooking on a stove in an empty apartment. Nicla wondered when the occupants would attend to it.

Off to the other side of the road, a boy lay on his side clutching his leg. Nicla saw no wounds. He couldn't have been close to the bomb when it hit. Surely, he would have been killed. An old man standing next to the boy, turned and shook his fist at the invisible foe that had receded down the road. "*Disgraziati*! Miserable Germans!"

Nicla concluded that the boy had come out after the attack. The German motorcycle and side car must have clipped the boy's leg as they veered to avoid the bomb crater.

Seeing the boy attended to, Nicla continued home. She was only nineteen, but she had seen enough tragedy and experienced enough heartache for a lifetime. Outwardly she had the fresh look of a young girl. Her light brown hair bounced silky on her shoulders. Her eyes were hazel. And though her face was still soft and beautiful, a pursed brow and stony stare were the premature gifts of war.

There was a photo of Nicla taken in happier times. She was on the beach, not far from where she was walking. Her expression was that of shy embarrassment, knowing that her beauty was being admired by her lover, but also captured for whoever might come across the photo. When she looked at that picture during the war, she wondered if she were the same person anymore.

Claudio had taken the photo. Nicla was sixteen then. Claudio was eighteen when he laughed and held the camera, encouraging her to turn to him. For Nicla, her first romance had been full of excitement, knowing looks, and blocking out the rest of the world. The town was their realm and they presided over it. But here she was, walking alone through a town that had become a somber host of war. Gone were the shine and promise of adventure that each unexplored lane or unvisited café had offered.

In her romantic reverie, the streets and corners had slipped by, and now, in the dreary present, she was almost home. She rounded a corner to find a disturbing sight. There, in front of the three-family dwelling in which Nicla's family resided, was the German motorcycle and cart that had passed her before. What could they be doing in front of her home? It was strange and frightening. It was trouble. Everywhere the Germans went was trouble. The pained look of the injured boy floated into Nicla's mind, rising from the wake of the terrible vehicle facing her home.

Wary, but driven by protective instinct, she entered the house. A German sergeant was carrying Nicla's sewing machine toward the door. A soldier was holding back Nicla's mother as she uttered a stream of obscenities. Nicla's father vainly pleaded with his wife to desist. Nicla threw herself at the soldier, trying to pry his arms from her mother.

The sergeant at the door barked something loudly in German. It was a tone that did not invite challenge - not without consequence. To emphasize the gravity of his intent, he freed one hand from the sewing machine, unholstered his pistol, and pointed it at the women. All movement and sound stopped for several, long seconds. Then the sergeant shook his head in disgust, said something dismissive and walked out with the sewing machine.

Thinking they would be taken prisoner, or even shot, all eyes in the family turned to the remaining soldier. He was glaring at Nicla as he adjusted his helmet, which had been displaced in the tussle. As he walked past, his backhand found Nicla's cheek. She fell against the wall. Her father lunged at the soldier.

"No! *Babbo*, please!" she begged and threw her arms around her father. "Remember the Pratos!" she whispered in his ear. The Pratos were neighbors who had harbored Jews. They were taken, along with the Jews, and none had been seen again.

As she felt his fury abate, Nicla released her father and ran out the front door. Her sewing machine was precariously balanced on the hood of the sidecar, held there by the miscreant who had treated her so cruelly. The sidecar and the bike to which it was tethered raced away.

Shaken, angry, and perplexed, Nicla wondered why on earth they had come for her sewing machine. She could not imagine. Perhaps some German officer, growing fat on Italian food, had split his britches. But they could have found any seamstress to mend them. Clearly they were looting. The antique machine was worth something for sure on the black market. Perhaps it was just their luck to find it in Nicla's house.

Or perhaps, she thought, some neighbor had told the pilferers about the sewing machine. Although Nicla had seen selfless heroism in those troubled times, she had also witnessed people overcome by the instinct to survive. They would trade information for a bag of flour. She couldn't fault them. It was only human weakness. It didn't matter, anyway. The machine was gone, and with it, their livelihood.

Chapter 2

Nicla reentered the house looking at the floor despondently. "I'll just have to sew by hand. I can still keep up."

"Your face!" cried her mother, rushing to Nicla's side. The vestige of the encounter still glowed on Nicla's cheek. "Let me see." She held Nicla's head.

"I'm alright, Mamma." Nicla took her mother's hand from her face and kissed it. She brought her mother over to the kitchen table and sat her down.

"I'm well enough to go back to work," declared Nicla's father. "They'll take me back at the dock." He had been injured when a pallet crushed his leg.

"No, that leg is still not healed." Nicla's mother beckoned her husband to the table with an outstretched arm. She took his hand. "Please, my *Principe Azzuro*. You can't risk going back until you're better." The name, *Principe Azzuro,* or Blue Prince, in Italian folklore was analogous to Prince Charming.

Nicla gazed fondly on her parents, admiring the deep love they had formed over the decades. At the same time, she knew that the family had been barely scraping by on sewing income alone. Although many people brought their garments to the Conti home for Nicla and her mother Silvia to repair, sewing by hand would take too long. It would not be enough to sustain them. She wracked her brains for an idea.

"The Contessa has a sewing machine!" she exclaimed, "I saw it once when I was dropping off clothes."

The Contessa Finzi lived in a villa on the small mountain of Montenero.

The next day, Nicla set off on foot for Montenero. As she left her apartment building, she encountered her little brother. He was twelve, thin from a meager wartime diet, but tan and sinewy from doing what all young boys in Italy do - playing soccer. He was kicking a ball against a building, playing some game with his own rules. Apparently, he achieved some milestone, for he let out a cheer. On the next kick, however, the ball bounced off Nicla's leg and into the street.

"*Ma dai*! Come on!" he exclaimed plaintively, both arms out, as if pleading with a referee, "I was setting a new record."

Nicla picked up the ball and handed it to him. She kissed him on his forehead. This was the baby of the family. When he was an infant, she had played with him and cared for him like her own, living doll. But she loved him like no girl could love a toy.

"*Sei fortunato*. You're lucky," she reassured him, "School is out. You have all summer to beat your record. Where are your friends anyway?" Seeing he was too angry to reply, Nicla smiled. *If that were my only concern*, she thought. She caressed his soft hair and bid him, "*Ciao`, bello.*"

She began walking through the streets of Livorno toward Montenero, which was just outside of town. She passed by different shops - the butcher, with his plucked chickens and skinned rabbits hanging in the window. The offerings were sparse now. Gone was the prewar surfeit of prosciuttos and other delectables adorning the glass.

There was more of everything before the war. Flags flew. Trucks rolled down the street bearing speakers extolling the accomplishments of *il Duce* - Mussolini. It was infectious, Fascism. The people had swallowed it whole during good times, welcoming with salutes and song the sower of the evil seed. Their present misery was reaped in death and privation.

Nicla passed *il bar*, the café, her favorite place in the city. The air around it always redolent with the fragrance of sweet pastry and coffee. The sun seemed to shine brighter on that corner - on the little tables and chairs decorating the sidewalk. The bartender, in his white jacket, would be snapping the cap off an *analcolico* - a tiny bottle of bright red bitters, or serving a flaky torta alongside a demitasse of aromatic coffee. How could one not be happy in that atmosphere?

But the idyllic vision was corrupted by two German officers sitting at a table outside the café. They were not old, and they cut rather sharp figures in their uniforms. Were it not for the visceral hatred Nicla had for these outfits, she might have thought the two handsome.

"*Guten Morgen, Fraulein,*" the dark haired one bid her.

"*Buon giorno, signorina,*" the other attempted in Italian, not rolling his R's. The soft, guttural pronunciation reminded Nicla of a French accent. Again, something that would normally have enchanted Nicla, but now revolted her. She walked deliberately; her gaze fixed straight ahead. The officers chuckled and made some other comments in German. Nicla paid no heed.

She had hoped to catch the *filobus* to Monte Nero. The *filobus* or "wire-bus" was the middle step in the evolutionary chain between trolley and modern city bus. It had rubber tires like a bus but retained the two arms that reached up to electric wires. The lifelines of the city, they sizzled with electric vitality. The occasional sparks that flashed when the contact poles bounced against them always fascinated Nicla. When she was younger, they frightened her. Now, in these listless days, she wished she could reach up and draw some life from the parallel purveyors of energy.

Much of the *filobus* lines had been destroyed by American bombardment, but Nicla could still catch the bus that ran from the outskirts of the city up to Montenero. So, she continued her trek in that direction. Eventually, she arrived at the gas station owned by her Uncle Fiore.

"*Ciao`, bella!*" he called, looking up from a car he was working on."

"*Ciao`, Zio!*" she replied, making the detour onto his lot. Zio Fiore was always happy to see her. He was full of life. From childhood, she could recall how he made her laugh. He would dance a jig or stand on his head against a wall. One of her earliest memories was holding both his hands and performing a somersault. He still brought a smile to her face.

"Where are you going?" he asked, wiping his hands on the rag hanging from his grease-stained overalls.

"I'm going to catch the *filobus* to Montenero."

"You're in luck. Save your money. I have a new *Topolino* I just finished working on. It belongs to a banker. I'll take you in it."

Topolino was the nickname the Italians had given to the Fiat 500. It meant "little mouse." It was aptly named, as it hardly fit two people and bore a close resemblance to its moniker. Fiore took her by the hand, and they squeezed into the diminutive vehicle.

They rattled along with the windows down and the tiny engine humming. It was sunny, hot, and dry - typical for the Italian summer. In the city, the car passed stucco walls baking in the sun. The only respite for these languishing barriers was the occasional shadow cast by vines climbing over from gardens within.

Behind some particularly high walls was the cemetery. Nicla pictured the mausoleums and statues that reminded her of a ghostly Roman city. There were relatives resting there. Some sent there too soon by the war.

She thought of her cousin, Fortunato. He had been riding a bike on a lonely, country road when he died. His misfortune was being passed by a convoy of German trucks as it was strafed by an American plane. His body was brought back to town by a farmer on his way in with his crops. The crops were sold, and Fortunato's body was planted in the cemetery. Looking out the window of the car, Nicla pondered. From the day we crawl, we spend our lives pushing ourselves up, away from the ground, only to yield ultimately, to its inexorable pull.

"Have you heard from, Vivi?" asked Uncle Fiore, steering the *Topolino*. Vivi was Nicla's older brother. He was an Anti-Fascist and was with the Partisan resistance. Civilian fighters such as Vivi found sanctuary from the Germans in the hills of Montenero.

"No. I haven't heard from him for almost a year now."

"That doesn't mean anything. It's just too dangerous for him to visit you. He's protecting the family. I'm sure."

"I know. But the Partisans are going too far lately. They blew up that bridge. It worries me. If they start killing Germans, you know what they do." Nicla was alluding to the well-known reprisals the Nazi's made upon citizens.

"Vivi knows how to take care of himself, and he knows these hills. He'll be alright." Fiore turned his attention back to the road. He didn't ask about Nicla's boyfriend, Claudio. He didn't want to upset her. Like thousands of other young men, Claudio had been drafted and gone off to war with the Italian army. Nicla hadn't heard from him since.

Reaching the outskirts of the city, the landscape began to resemble the classic Tuscan countryside. Umbrella trees - Italian stone pines, like giant broccoli plants, lined the road. Dark, green plumes of narrow cypress dotted the amber Tuscan hills and pointed to the sky. She looked up at that blue canopy. It was so clear and beautiful. How could bombs rain from it? Soon she'd be in the mountains and the specter of bombardment would lay far behind in the city.

"How do you know the Contessa will have work for you?" Fiore asked over the hum of the engine.

"I don't. I need her sewing machine more than her business."

"You were always *la furba* - the smart one."

"Not smart enough to beat you at anything, *Zio*."

"You beat me at cards, don't you?"

"*Scopa* doesn't count." Nicla pushed his shoulder. "You let me win at that."

"You were smart enough to know I'd give you a ride if I saw you walking." Fiore grinned. He had her. She smiled and looked out the window.

They were getting to higher elevations and Nicla could look down upon a spectacular vista. There were rolling hills leading back down to the city. These were only interrupted by the occasional red, clay roof. The port city of Livorno, like a magnet, had pulled hundreds of these roofs into a cluster of terra cotta on the coast.

From Montenero, Nicla could pan her eyes along the horizon. Nothing but turquoise-blue ocean stretched over the edge of the earth to places she could only imagine. The crystal sky accompanied its conjoined partner over that precipice. It fascinated her. She would have gladly followed the early explorers in pursuing that ever-advancing line of demarcation.

"You can drop me off in the square." Nicla's head was half out the window. "I want to stop in the church first."

"You want some help from above?"

"Yes, and to pray for an end to this cursed war."

"You're right. Good girl. You pray for that..." Fiore's voice trailed off, contemplating, as he drove, the uncertainty of all their futures.

When they reached the summit, Nicla could see more mountains to the north. So distant were they, that the atmosphere between her and these majestic peaks was opaque and almost tangible. Although it was summer, the mountains were streaked with patches of white. But it was not snow. White Carrera marble adorned their slopes. These were the Apuan Alps - part of the Apennine chain that forms the spine of the Italian peninsula. It was from these mountains that Michelangelo's David made his way to Florence, locked in a block of marble, to be freed by the artist's chisel.

"Here we are," Fiore announced as the metallic purr of the engine finished reverberating through the pastel-blue sheet metal of the Fiat, "When should I come back for you?"

"I'm not sure when I'll be done. I'll come home on the *filobus*." Nicla kissed her uncle on the cheek. "*Ciao`Zio*."

"*Ciao`, bella*."

As she stepped from the car, Nicla was greeted by a Madonna sculpted in relief on a stone wall. The Virgin and child were clad in blue, red and gold. They were within a miniature, Greco-Roman temple projecting slightly from the wall. This was the *Madonna di Montenero*. She was the patron saint of Tuscany, and her likeness was found all about Montenero. Nicla wondered why the Virgin looked so forlorn. Could she foresee the loss she was destined to endure? Nicla took solace that in her own heart, she could still hold onto hope for Claudio and her brother Vivi.

"I'm coming to visit you," Nicla told her adoptive mother. She made the sign of the cross and turned toward the Virgin's more famous home – *Il Santuario della Madonna di Montenero*.

The air was lighter and fresher on Montenero. There was always a cool breeze from the ocean below. The courtyard of the Sanctuary was raised like a mesa above Montenero's cobblestone streets. It was accessible by a short flight of stairs hewn from grey stone. Nicla had ascended these steps on her knees as a schoolgirl. She thought back to that ritual. It was performed one hundred days before graduation - a time full of hope. Now she climbed the stairs with a resigned gate and a future circumscribed by the exigencies of war.

She entered the church and passed into one of its galleries. The walls were teaming with votive offerings to the Virgin. They were quite disparate. There were some that would be expected - crutches and canes relinquished by the healed. Others were more unusual. There was a medal which had saved a soldier in the First World War. It bore an image of the Virgin along with a dent from the bullet it had thwarted.

The article that had always captured Nicla's attention most was a Turkish outfit made for a little girl. It was red and covered with ornate gold designs. Small red slippers completed the glittering ensemble. Nicla was taken not only by its beauty, but she was also fascinated by the story behind it. The girl that had worn this dress was a well-to-do Italian girl who had been kidnapped by Turkish pirates. The girl's brother had rescued her and brought her home in these clothes. It was a story that Nicla had played out in her imagination when she was younger. In Nicla's version of the tale, it was *il Principe Azzuro*, the Blue Prince, who came to her rescue.

Now, a simple reunion with Claudio would dwarf any rescue from pirates. Even news that he was alive would lift her from the unbearable anxiety that lurked just below her preoccupation with surviving. Her mind sometimes wandered to morose images of Claudio's life ebbing away on a battlefield. Was he in Russia as rumored about the young men from her town? Perhaps he was in one of their prison camps.

Moving into the chapel, Nicla took out her handkerchief and covered her hair. She took a seat in a pew towards the front. Behind the altar stood an immense and striking piece of Baroque art. Its focal point was a painting of the Madonna. Bursting from around the painting, like rays of intense light, were enormous, golden shafts of sculpted wood. Marble cherubim and clouds swirled among the golden rays reaching up to colorful frescoes in the dome. The whole piece seemed to be rising to Heaven.

To Nicla, the majestic scene represented the glory of God. Despite the inexplicable randomness of the war, Nicla still believed in God. There was something eternal the war could not touch. It was love. And love was from God. The deep, abiding love she had for her family, even the intense romantic love she felt for Claudio - these were God's miraculous gifts. They would endure through separation. Nicla kneeled and prayed for the safety of those through whom God had manifested this love. She also prayed that the Contessa still had a sewing machine.

Chapter 3

T he road to Contessa Finzi's villa began at an opening in a stone wall. Nicla wound her way by foot up the narrow, dirt drive. The grounds seemed a bit unkempt. There were vines growing on a statue of a curly-haired little boy and bushes protruded into the road.

"*Ciao*!" came a voice from behind Nicla.

She recoiled; hands raised at the figure emerging from behind a bush. "*Dio Mio!*" she exclaimed breathlessly, "you could have killed me from fright."

Nicla recognized him as the grandson of the Contessa. He was about two years her senior. His name was Luca. He was strong and fit, but he displayed a slight limp. It was the vestige of a car accident that as a young boy had claimed his parents. Although the disability had kept him from many happy pursuits of other boys, it had spared him from conscription.

"What brings you here?" he inquired. "Doesn't Alberto bring the clothes down to you?"

Luca knew of Nicla. He had occasionally been with Alberto, the chauffeur, when he dropped off clothing for Nicla to mend. Sometimes, for alterations that had to be measured on the Contessa, Nicla was brought up to the villa.

"The Germans took my sewing machine," Nicla explained. "I was wondering if there is still one in the maid's room."

"What? They took your sewing machine!" Luca shook his head. "That's a rogue operation. Things must be starting to unravel for them. Maybe it won't be long before the Americans get here."

"God willing. I'm just trying to keep my family fed until they do,"

"Come," Luca motioned with his head, "I'll take you to Grandma."

They continued up the drive, past more lonesome statues besieged by verdant predators. Obviously the gardener was no longer in their employ. Suddenly, two large dogs came snarling across the lawn towards them. Nicla pushed against Luca, grabbing his shirt sleeve. She grimaced but did not make a sound.

"Romolo! Remo!" Luca ordered, pointing to the ground. The dogs sat obediently. "They're my hunting dogs." Lovingly, he pet the dogs named after the mythical twins who founded Rome. Statuettes of the boys beneath the she-wolf who suckled them were popular souvenirs. The irony of naming canines after the legendary human brothers was not lost upon Nicla.

"Maybe Romolo and Remo can make a new Italy after the war, like they made Rome." Nicla bent to pet them.

"No, they're not political animals. And they're not leaders. Watch how they follow us. *Vieni!*" he commanded and turned toward the house. The dogs followed but Nicla stood her ground. Luca turned back to her. "Are you coming?".

"Not on your call."

"What? You thought? No. I was talking to the dogs."

"I know." Nicla smiled.

Relieved, Luca returned the expression. They continued their walk.

"I don't think I've seen you in town lately," Nicla commented as they approached the main residence.

"It's a little embarrassing, someone my age, not being in the army, or at least with the Partisans."

"But you have a good..." Nicla's voice trailed off.

"My leg? Yes, good excuse, but it doesn't make me feel any more useful. My country is going to shit, and I have nothing to offer. One of these days, I will. Anyway, here's the house. I'll bring you in to *Nonna*.

The interior of the Contessa's home was spacious. A cool breeze from the ocean floated through large windows which were swung open. The Contessa was sitting on a sofa before a small coffee table in an ornately decorated room. She looked up and saw Nicla enter. "*Vieni, cara*. Come dear," she entreated, motioning with her hand to the space next to her on the sofa.

The Contessa was a tiny lady in her seventies. She wore horned-rimmed glasses and had a beauty mark on her cheek. "Luca, have Alberto bring coffee for this pretty girl and me."

"Yes, *Nonna*." Luca gave a mock bow. He returned her smile as he rose and left the room.

"He's handsome, isn't he?" the Contessa asked Nicla with a glint in her eye.

"Yes, Contessa," Nicla replied with a hint of a smirk.

"Ah, you catch me playing matchmaker. Well, I tried. You probably have a boyfriend in the army like all the other girls. What's his name?"

"Claudio."

The Contessa looked her over. Nicla sat up straight and strong. In the Contessa's judgement, this was no façade. She sensed Nicla's inner fortitude. It reminded the Contessa of herself.

"Well, I'm sure you'll see Claudio again soon. As for my grandson, I think he's too angry for romance. He's full of grand plans and ideals. I think I hold him back more than his leg does." She sighed. "I raised him after the accident. Now, he feels he owes me, even though he would never say it." She sat pensive for a moment, then her expression livened. "So, my dear, are you here looking for some sewing work?"

"Yes, Contessa." Nicla told the story of her pilfered sewing machine. The Contessa was aghast.

"Of course, you can use the one in Luisa's room. She couldn't sew much anyway. That's why we always hired you for the more difficult assignments. You know, we haven't seen Luisa in two months. I'm worried about her. She went into town and didn't come back. I hope she's alright. I like to think she met someone nice."

The Contessa took Nicla's hand. "If you need more work, you can do Luisa's job - at least until she comes back. It's a little cleaning and some cooking. Naturally, sewing as well."

"Could I bring some sewing jobs from my other customers to work on here?"

"On my time?" The Contessa recoiled dramatically, then smiled. "Of course, you can, my treasure. You'll have plenty of free time. How much work do you think I have for you around here, anyway? Besides me, it's just Luca and Alberto." As if on cue, Alberto entered with coffee.

"I was young once too, you know," the Contessa declared as she raised her demitasse, "And I had a Claudio, like you. His name was Daniele." She took a deep breath, looking off in the distance. "My mother didn't like him because he came from a poor family. There was no war for him to go off to, like your Claudio - just other lands and excitement. I can't say I blame him. My family was so proper and boring. But he did me a favor. I met my husband shortly after he left." She put her cup down in a dignified manner. "We had a wonderful marriage."

"It must have been terrible to lose him," added Nicla sympathetically.

"Yes, imagine losing my husband, my daughter, and son-in-law, all in that accident. Thank God, Luca was spared. I only got through it because I had him to raise. Oh my, he was a handful! But now... he is the one who dotes on *me*."

When they finished their coffee, the Contessa took Nicla by the hand. "Come, *bella*. Let's look at that sewing machine." She took Nicla by the hand and led her down a long hall.

Luisa's room was as fancy as the rest of the villa. Nicla thought back on meeting Luisa years before. Luisa was about ten years older than Nicla. That a servant like Luisa slept in such a beautiful room always impressed Nicla. When Nicla had come to make alterations for the Contessa, she sensed an air of condescension from Luisa. Nicla didn't begrudge that in her. They were both commoners, and if Luisa wanted to play the lady for a moment, good for her.

Nicla looked around the empty room. It made her sad to think Liusa had left such comfort behind. She couldn't imagine her doing better elsewhere. The sewing machine was still there.

"So. Will you work for me?" asked the Contessa. "You can stay in this room."

This startled Nicla. She had never thought of staying there. "Oh, no. I mean, I want the job, but I have to stay with my family. They need me."

The Contessa looked at her proudly. "You're a good girl. That's fine. Alberto can bring you back and forth. He needs to get out more."

Nicla was almost speechless. "You're so kind, Contessa. Thank you."

"Think nothing of it, my dear. It will be nice to have another female around here. Come." She took Nicla by the hand again.

As the Contessa was leading Nicla back down the hall, Nicla turned and gazed at a tall hutch against the wall.

"You like the knickknacks?" asked the Contessa.

"Yes... but..."

"Go on. You have a question."

"Wasn't there a door here?"

"You noticed that didn't you? Tell me. If you didn't already know about the door, would the hutch seem out of place to you?"

"No, Contessa. I never would have guessed."

"Good. But now I have a dilemma. You're too smart to leave it at that, aren't you? And I'm not going to make up some story that you will see right through." She gazed at Nicla with her head tilted to one side. Finally, she took Nicla's hands in hers. "Alright. I've known you and your family for years. You're good people. I can trust you." The Contessa turned and called down the hallway, "Alberto, come here."

"Yes, Signora," Alberto replied dutifully on his arrival.

"Move away the hutch."

"Signora!" he gasped.

"It's alright, Nicla is to be trusted."

Alberto looked at Nicla and back at the Contessa, who nodded encouragingly.

"Yes, Contessa." He began to slide the hutch along the wall. It moved quite easily, thanks to some small wheels artfully recessed beneath it. The removal of the hutch exposed a door. Alberto opened it.

As the Contessa led Nicla down the stairs, she turned and eyed Nicla with anticipation. There, before them, lay a treasure trove - all manner of art and luxurious objects: vases, urns, and candle-holders made of gold and other precious metals. There were paintings, tapestries, and jewelry boxes. Nicla turned to the Contessa, dumbfounded.

"A few more knickknacks, eh?" remarked the Contessa, enjoying her own joke. "Come upstairs. I'll explain, my dear."

Chapter 4

N icla and the Contessa were sitting at a table in the kitchen. Alberto, wearing an apron over his black pants and white shirt, was arranging some prosciutto and melon slices on dishes at a counter.

"Most of those valuables belong to friends," the Contessa informed Nicla, "But some of the pieces are mine. I'm sure you noticed that things look a little bare around here."

"You're protecting those things from the NAZIs, aren't you, Signora?"

"Yes, my smart young lady. First the Italian government started confiscating - I should say looting, from the Jews. Many of those things in the cellar belong to my Jewish friends. Once Mussolini fell, and the Germans moved in, they started pilfering from anyone - all the fine art they could get their greedy hands on."

"My sewing machine was a piece of fine art to me."

"Yes dear. Nothing is off limits to them. Did you notice the painting of the crucifixion of Jesus down there? It's a Giotto. It was an altarpiece in a church. A friend of mine who knew the priest had it driven here all the way from San Gimignano in the back of a coffee delivery truck. It's a good thing the rest of the

Church was painted with frescos. The NAZIs haven't figured out how to chisel those of the walls, yet."

Alberto placed the dishes of prosciutto and melon before the Contessa and Nicla.

"Thank you, Alberto." The Contessa smiled. Alberto bowed slightly and went back to his work at the counter. "He's a better cook than Luisa was. Such a good man." She looked at him affectionately. "Thirty years he's been with us. He never questioned taking over the cooking." She turned to Nicla. "He looks good in the apron, doesn't he?"

"Yes, Signora," interjected the stoic butler, never looking up from his work at the counter.

"What happened to your Jewish friends, Contessa?" Nicla asked.

"Some of them were able to get out of Italy before things got bad. Others have disappeared. Most of them told me, should anything happen to them, to use the valuables to help our cause."

As the Contessa's words trailed off, Luca entered the kitchen. "What's this about our cause?" he asked. "That is a topic upon which I've pontificated much and effectuated little. Continue please."

The Contessa and Nicla offered blank looks. After a few stammers, the Contessa began, "I was saying... Nicla will be working for us. Yes... just a little cooking and sewing. And-"

"You showed her, didn't you?" interrupted Luca.

After a sheepish look, the Contessa gathered herself. "And what of it? It's my prerogative to share my secrets with whomever I please." She folded her arms.

Luca came around behind the seated Contessa and put his chin on her shoulder. "Oh, *Nonna*, you're beautiful when you're indignant." He kissed her cheek. "You can't keep a secret can you?"

She playfully pushed him away. "Go. Sit down. Eat. You think you're so smart, you never have to eat?'"

Luca took a dish from Alberto and turned to Nicla. "Now what will you do when the German's torture you for Nonna's secret?"

"I'll tell them to *vaffanculo.*"

Luca was taken aback not only by Nicla's vulgar epithet, but by her deadpan delivery. She had gotten the better of him. "I like this one, Nonna. But I shall never cross her."

Nicla turned to the Contessa. "Pardon my language, Contessa. I have great anger toward the Nazis."

"Quite understandable, my dear. I wish my station allowed me the luxury of such frankness. You'll be a breath of fresh air around here."

They ate and talked for some time. At one point, Luca stood up and announced he would let the Contessa and Nicla plot the ouster of the Nazis on their own while he went out hunting.

Nicla admired him. Despite his undertone of bitterness, she could sense a strong and undaunted spirit.

It was decided that Alberto should drive Nicla to and from the villa daily. Nicla would go home in the late afternoon to help her mother around the house. She would also be allowed to bring other customers' sewing to the villa to mend in her free time using the Contessa's machine.

For the remainder of the day, Nicla did a little sewing and cleaning. It became clear however that the Contessa wanted Nicla more for some company than her labor. That suited Nicla fine, as the Contessa was a colorful storyteller. She seemed to be reliving her own youth as she recounted tales of trysts and betrayals. Nicla thought it interesting that the rich had the leisure time to engage in such pursuits. She had more pressing obligations. But she did think back to when life was more carefree, before the war. She and Claudio had spent time as if it were in endless supply.

Later in the day, when it was time to return home, Nicla was seated behind Alberto in the Contessa's car. It was a cream-colored, 1930 Isotta Fraschini, with a low top, elongated front end, and sweeping fenders. Nicla had never been in such a vehicle.

Its chrome grill was adorned with lightning bolts. They flashed diagonally across the gleaming façade and bespoke not only the power under the hood but that of its owner.

Nicla felt odd sitting alone in the back of this rolling opulence, but allowed herself a moment to imagine she was the Contessa's daughter. Perhaps she was being driven to a rendezvous like those recounted by the Contessa.

They were rolling slowly down the drive of the villa when Luca emerged from a stand of small pines. He had a hunting rifle slung over his shoulder and his dogs beside him. Alberto brought the car to a stop as Luca approached the window. He addressed Nicla. "You're coming back to hear more of Nonna's stories - I mean to work - tomorrow?"

"Of course. The stories are better than the pay. Why do you ask? Are you afraid I'll learn something about you?"

"What could there be to tell about me? That I hunt?"

"How ordinary." Nicla looked out the other window with a blasé turn of her head.

Luca was flummoxed at his inability to get the best of this pretty seamstress. He took hold of the door handle. "Alright, Alberto, I'm afraid I'll have to take over from here."

"*Signore?*" Alberto was bewildered.

"It's fine." Luca opened Alberto's door, "Here, take my rifle and the dogs back to the house for me."

Alberto, being accustomed to Luca's impetuous behavior and having been his frequent hunting companion, simply nodded. He called the dogs to follow as he turned toward the house. Meanwhile, Luca hopped into the driver's seat of the Isotta. "Shall I proceed, *Signorina?*"

"Yes, boy," Nicla fought back an impish smile.

"Boy? Now you've gone too far."

"To town, please."

Luca grinned and began driving.

The way to Nicla's home in the city required them to pass through the square on Montenero. As they drove, the road leading to the square began to swell with townspeople. At one point, Luca could proceed no further. He struggled to see around the corner. "I hope this is not what I think it is."

Nicla could not wait to see. It was clearly something unusual. She bolted from the car and headed for the square.

"*Signorina!* Stop!" Luca abandoned the car and pursued her. She was well ahead and out of sight. Luca saw German soldiers along the road motioning citizens toward the square. The people moved along in marked trepidation. A woman was holding a handkerchief to her mouth. An elderly man squeezed his wife's hand as much to steel himself as to support her. But they all continued. And each time the people slowed, a menacing gesture of a soldier's weapon caused them to quicken their pace.

As Luca pushed through the throngs and rounded the corner, he found Nicla frozen before a specter they had both heard of but never witnessed. On top of a makeshift scaffold were four citizens accused of aiding the Partisans. Among them was a middle-aged woman with a kerchief on her head. One by one, nooses were being fit around their necks by a German soldier at the direction of an officer. The victims stoically complied.

Nicla wanted to turn away, but she was transfixed by the resignation of the woman on the scaffold. *Scream! Run!* she thought to herself. *Better they shoot you!* she almost shouted out.

Then it began. It was too horrible to watch. She turned to find Luca at her side and buried her head in his chest. But even with her hands over her ears, Nicla could not avoid hearing the collective gasps of the crowd as each of the four souls was prematurely rent from this life by the NAZI evil.

"Come *Signorina*," Luca comforted. He directed Nicla back to the car with an arm around her shoulder. "I will take you home."

They were coming down from Montenero in the Contessa's car. Nicla sat in the front seat with Luca. She was in shock from what she had witnessed in the square. As she looked out the window to the ocean, her mind drifted back to happier days. She and Claudio would sit on the rocks that rose from the turquoise sea. The waves would crash and rush between the weathered stones. All manner of swooshing sounds gushed from the crevices as the water swirled in and receded. Nicla would be hypnotized by the sounds and the soft spray. She had wanted to melt into the ocean and lose herself in it. That was when she was happy - before the war. How she wished to go there now and leave behind the terrible thing she had just witnessed.

She remembered watching from the rocks as Claudio and the other young men played a fantastic game on a large steel buoy. A twenty-foot pole stuck straight up from the top of the buoy. Crossbars on the pole created a sort of ladder. A score of young men would latch onto the ladder until their weight tipped it down to the ocean's surface. Claudio would sit on the top rung and the others would let go of the ladder.

Slowly at first, but with increasing speed, the ladder with Claudio atop would rise like a giant arm from the ocean. At its zenith, Claudio would launch himself across the blue sky. Swinging his arms back like an eagle, then forward, he would disappear into the water like a javelin.

Swimming over to Nicla on the rocks he might ask, "What do you think?"

"Your feet were a little apart."

Claudio would grab Nicla and pull her squealing into the churning blue water. They would surface in each other's arms.

"Signorina?" It was Luca. "Are you all right?" Nicla found herself back in the front seat of the Contessa's car.

"Yes. I was just resting."

"Good. You need it. That was a terrible thing to experience."

"I'll be alright. You've been very nice."

"It's nothing. You'll be home soon with your family. That will help you feel better."

Luca was right. Family was a comforting thought to Nicla. After the spectacle in the square, she could not wait to hold each of them. But this also made her think of her brother Vivi with the Partisans. The poor people in the square were hung for simply assisting the Partisans. She prayed for her brother.

The car passed through the fields leading back to downtown Livorno. Golden bales of rolled hay dotted the green Tuscan countryside. Cows grazed lazily. The pastoral scene belied the darkness pervading the city ahead.

Finally, their car entered Livorno proper, and Luca brought it to a stop at an intersection. Beside them, parked along the sidewalk, was a NAZI staff car. Its top was down. In the rear seat was an officer with a girl next to him. Her head was tossed back, and her wavy, brown hair bounced as she laughed. How the girl could delight in their company, Nicla could not imagine. At that moment, the girl turned and met eyes with her. The smile drained from the young woman's face. It was Luisa, the Contessa's former maid.

Nicla would not forget the look in her eyes. Yes there was shame and embarrassment, but it was also a helpless look - so different from her expression of a moment before, when she was playing the fawning consort. It was as if Luisa was reaching out from a web in which she was trapped. Before Nicla could comprehend any of this, the Contessa's car lurched forward.

"Did you see that?" she asked.

"Yes." Luca looked straight ahead. There was sadness in his voice. "And I won't tell *Nonna* about it, either. That's what you want, that I not tell her, correct?"

"Yes. How did you know?"

"I knew you wouldn't want to hurt *Nonna*. Better she goes on wondering what happened to Luisa, than find out about that. But

I also thought you might feel sympathy for Luisa." He turned to Nicla. "You do, don't you?"

"I think it's disgraceful, but yes, I feel sorry for her in a way. I can't imagine what drove her to that. She had a nice job working for your *nonna*. What happened?"

"Something drew her away. I don't know what. She had no family to turn to. She seemed fine living with us. When she didn't come back from town that day, I knew it couldn't be good."

Soon they arrived at Nicla's building. From behind their car came a shout, "Halt!"

Luca looked in the mirror. He saw nothing. "Stay calm. We're not doing anything wrong. I have a lot of connections with the police... if that's who it is."

He continued to scan the area. Suddenly, from below the front of the car rose a darkened figure. It was Nicla's little brother, Matteo. He was brandishing a broom stick for a rifle. "Get out with your hands up, NAZI!"

Luca, recognizing his role in the game of ambushed NAZI officer, ducked below the dashboard and rolled out of the driver's door. A firefight ensued with Luca wielding his thumb and index finger as his Luger pistol and Matteo his broomstick rifle. There was much crawling around the car and popping up for wildly aimed shots.

Nicla sat in the car and watched with a growing smile. Finally, Luca succumbed to a well-placed shot to the heart. He collapsed with his hands drawn to his chest. Nicla thought his death throes worthy of critical acclaim.

Matteo crept slowly toward the supine figure. After verifying the demise of his enemy, he stepped over Luca's cadaver toward the car. *"Che bella macchina!"* he exclaimed running his hand over the sloping fender. "Can you take me for a ride?"

"Matteo!" Nicla reproached, getting out of the car, "Show some manners."

"It's alright." Luca came to his feet. "You like her, eh? I'll take you for a ride one day. That is... if your sister approves." He smiled at Nicla, doing his best to conceal his limp as he moved back to the driver's door. "But now I must be going. I'm sure your sister has had enough of me for one day."

"She has? I think you're fun." Matteo reloaded his broom stick and raised it at Luca who was now behind the wheel.

"*Buona sera, signorina,*" Luca bid Nicla with a nod as the magnificent machine pulled away.

Matteo dropped to one knee and loosed some parting shots. Nicla stood pondering the unforeseeable events of that day and what they might portend.

Chapter 5

The days passed. For all the disruption the war visited on the rest of the Italian people, Nicla's days were almost routine now. Alberto would pick her up in the morning with a *"Buon giorno, signorina."* She would climb in the back of the grand vehicle clutching some clothes to sew for her customers. The ride up to Montenero was sunnier, the air flowing through her hair fresher - made so by the lifting of one more burden from her shoulders. Her family would not starve. Even Zio Fiore bestowed his blessing upon her new arrangement by waving each time she passed his garage like a noble lady in her coach.

Daily thereafter, at the villa, Nicla occupied herself with housework and some sewing - what she could accomplish between the Contessa's stories. These would sometimes conclude with epilogues such as, "Needless to say, the gardener was dismissed and the girl was sent on a long vacation," or stern admonitions, "That's why you should never stare at the Duke's nose. He's been quite sensitive about it ever since."

Sometimes a rather interesting character made his appearance at the estate. Nicla would usually find him sitting in the parlor having coffee with the Contessa. He was referred to simply as Signore Montanini. Although his name meant "little mountains" in Italian, he was tall and slender. His narrow mustache and expensive suit completed a sophisticated look. To Nicla, he appeared to be in his mid-forties. Other than a nod from him as she passed, Nicla knew nothing about him. For all her gossip about other nobles and high-society types, the Contessa never told Nicla much about Signore Montanini.

"He's an old friend of the family," was all Nicla heard of him from the Contessa. Still, Nicla thought there was something more to Signore Montanini than the Contessa was letting on. Other than this bit of mystery, things were uneventful at the villa.

One day, as Nicla walked outside the house to hang some laundry, Luca drove up in the car. "It's time for a driving lesson," he called from the open window.

"Who told you I need a lesson?"

"Oh. Very good," he smiled, "I'm glad to hear it. Take me for a ride, then." He swept his hand in a panoramic gesture. "It would be nice to enjoy the scenery for a change and let someone else drive." He tried to hide his enthusiasm in calling her bluff. Hailing from the city and moreover, being a woman, it was beyond a safe bet for Luca that Nicla could not drive as she intimated.

"I would love to, but unfortunately, I have these clothes to hang." She lifted her basket slightly and began to turn away.

"I only thought that you would like to take a break from your labors and-"

"Move over." Nicla put down the basket and came round the driver's side.

With great alacrity and barely hiding his glee, Luca slid to his right. The engine was still running.

Nicla grasped the steering wheel and craned her head as she looked around the car's dash.

"Well? Shall we?" Luca asked after more than a few moments.

"Alright...let's see..." Nicla haltingly reached for the shifter, looking at Luca for some affirmation that this was indeed the proper first step.

Luca shook his head, then nodded toward the clutch on the floor.

"Is this right?" Nicla put her foot on the brake instead. Luca winced anticipating the car would buck and grind while being shifted into gear. But rather than put the car in gear, Nicla looked at Luca with an odd smile.

Suddenly, her foot jumped from the brake pedal and onto the clutch. She shifted confidently into first gear, released the clutch, and the car surged forward. Second, third gear – deftly she piloted the vehicle down the drive. Leaning forward, ignoring Luca's stunned expression, all Nicla could see, feel, and enjoy was the power she had over that vehicle. It was exhilaration like she hadn't experienced since the war began.

She had to swerve to avoid Signore Montanini's vehicle coming up the driveway. After righting the car and coming to a stop, she proudly turned to see Luca's reaction.

"How?" was all he could muster.

"My Uncle Fiore, the one with the garage. He taught me. My parents never knew. Why would they suspect? Me being a *girl*," she added sarcastically. "My *Zio*, he always encouraged me. He told me I could do anything."

"Apparently, he was correct."

"Where would you like to go, sir?" Nicla put her hands back on the wheel.

"Oh, far be it from me to give orders. You're well in command. Please. Lead on."

"Very well." Nicla knew exactly where she wanted to go.

They drove through the winding and sometimes steep roads of Montenero. Occasionally a curve would offer a vista of the hills and ocean below. But enjoying the view while driving was dangerous. The right edge of the road offered little more than a low curb between the car and a precipitous drop. Straying too far to the inside risked an invisible oncomer around the bend. Luca marveled at Nicla's navigation of the mountain gauntlet.

They arrived at the square in Montenero. It was enclosed by the sanctuary of the Madonna, some shops, and a café. As they stepped from the car, they were greeted by looks of astonishment from two old men on a bench. Luca was well known around Montenero, as was his usual driver, Alberto. The sight of this unknown person driving Luca was startling on several levels, not the least of which was her gender.

"My chauffeur was drafted," Luca announced to the elderly pair, shrugging his shoulders as he stepped backwards.

"Your chauffeur is an old man!" retorted one of the men. "Maybe they'll draft us next!" The two men laughed.

Luca had already joined Nicla in crossing the square toward the café. They sat at one of the small tables outside. The building and the umbrella provided just enough shade to keep them out of the bright, midday sun. They ordered coffees. Nicla took hers simply, with latte. Cappuccinos, named after the *cappuccia,* or hoods, worn by Cappuccian friars were only available in the bigger cafés down in the city of Livorno.

"How is my driving?" Nicla asked.

"Oh, fairly good. You were riding the clutch a bit, at times. You could use a few more lessons."

"I see. Well, I should be getting back to my laundry. It's sitting in that basket next to the drive. What will the Contessa think?"

"She'll be happy we went out together."

"I have a boyfriend."

"I know. I was just referring to *Nonna's* eternal optimism regarding my romantic prospects."

"I should think someone in your position would have no problems. Why aren't you engaged to some nobleman's daughter?"

"You mean, besides my leg?"

"I never even considered that. Why would I?"

Luca studied Nicla. "Alright. So, you want to know why there is no *principessa* in my life?"

"Yes."

"Have you seen the type of girls that noble upbringing creates? They're so stiff and proper. I have yet to meet one that could let down her guard and have some fun."

"Or know how to drive?"

"Exactly. But I wouldn't say you know how to drive. You know how to make the car move. It's another thing to *drive*."

"And I suppose you know how?"

"I try. But not in that boat we came here in. I have an Alfa Romeo. I keep it in that barn at the far end of the property. Unfortunately, I *can't* take you for a ride in it."

"Why? The Germans might confiscate it?"

"No. It's only a one-seater. Have you seen one? It has no fenders - like a cigar with wheels - a real racecar. I'll let you try it someday. If you think you can handle it."

Nicla let that challenge go as the waiter arrived with some pastry. She looked out at the view across the square. Even in the shade of the umbrella, the sun insisted on being noticed, heating the cicadas in the trees to an incredible buzz. A tiny lizard clung to the wall of the café. These *lucertole* were everywhere in the summer.

"When I was little, my brother Vivi taught me to catch those." Nicla pointed out the tiny creature for Luca.

"I suppose he didn't tell you what happens when they are caught?"

"No." Nicla knew what Luca was driving at. When she had first captured one, she learned to her horror that they have the shocking ability to detach their own tail and leave it behind. Worse, the dismembered appendage continues to wriggle in the would-be captor's hand.

"I'll bet he enjoyed your reaction when you caught one."

"Yes, he was very amused... until I feigned passing out. He became quite upset then."

Luca sipped his coffee and looked at her with narrowed eyes. *Would this girl ever let herself be bested?*

Nicla looked away trying not to smile. She realized she was having fun and feeling quite carefree. She hadn't felt this way since before the war. It didn't seem quite right to be there with Luca. She and Claudio had sat at this very café and laughed. They would take the funicular up from the city.   The small train car would ascend the hills of Montenero pulled by a cable between the rails of the single track. Ancient stone walls bordered both sides of the narrow passage. Grape arbors and fig trees tantalized in backyards just beyond reach.

The part of the ride that always frightened Nicla was when the other funicular car, tethered to the same long loop of cable, approached them on the single track. A head-on collision seemed certain. To avert disaster, the cars would have to simultaneously reach the spot where the track split in two for a few meters, then bowed back to a single track again. To Nicla's wonder, they always did. The cars would narrowly pass each other. As the other car went by, Nicla and Claudio would see other lovers returning from romantic journeys. The couples would exchange knowing smiles.

"You've finished your *dolce*?" asked Luca.

"Hmm? Sorry, I was just thinking."

"You were thinking of happier times, I'm sure." He tossed back the last of his coffee and looked out across the mountain, "*My* good times were so long ago, I can hardly remember them."

Nicla thought that life must not have been so easy for this rich boy, losing his parents and being left with a leg that would serve neither his zest for adventure nor his need for a purpose.

"You were looking out at the ocean." Luca motioned with his head. "That's what you need - some time on the water."

Chapter 6

Luca was at the wheel of the Isotta, with Nicla at his side. It was a bright, clear morning and they were coming into the city of Livorno.

"I really have a lot to do for the Contessa. I don't have time for this," Nicla protested half-heartedly.

"Nonsense. Did you see how happy she was when I told her we were going somewhere together?"

"You shouldn't lead her on so."

"Yes, I get the message. You have a boyfriend. But this is business. I need a first mate for my excursion. It's big job running a yacht."

Nicla hadn't seen many yachts around Livorno, especially since the war started. In fact, much of what had been docked at the port was destroyed by allied bombing or confiscated by the Germans.

"Look at that," Luca muttered in astonishment as they turned a corner. What had been an apartment house was now a pile of stone - some of it in the street.

"Poor things," Nicla lamented referring to whoever had occupied the dwelling. "I should hate the Americans for this."

"You know it's the British too, don't you? Either way it's necessary to drive the Nazis out."

"How does *this*, help?" She waved her arm at the destruction.

"It's insane, isn't it? We must be two kilometers from the port. The allies call it high-altitude, precision bombing. Bunch of propaganda. If they were any less precise, we wouldn't be safe even on Montenero."

Luca navigated the car around the rubble. They came out on a street that ran along the canal. Cutting a grand arc through Livorno, the canal sprang from the port and found its terminus there as well.

The moment Luca parked the car, Nicla bolted to look over the canal wall. Well below the level of the street - perhaps fifteen feet, it lay. Stones formed its high walls. Nicla took in the vista of the emerald waterway lined with small, wooden boats.

Luca joined Nicla at the wall. "It's beautiful, isn't it?"

"Yes," Nicla leaned over the stones. "I could stand here all day."

"We have a boat to catch."

"I didn't know we had a schedule. By the way, I don't see any yachts down there."

"Oh, it's quite a vessel. It will keep you busy as first mate. Come on." Instead of moving toward the stone stairs going down to the canal, Luca walked across the narrow street. Nicla held her ground, puzzled.

At the door of an apartment building, Luca turned and beckoned. "This way to the dock."

Nicla did not understand but followed. She arrived at the door as it opened. They were greeted warmly by a stout, little lady in an apron. "Luca!" she exclaimed, extending her arms upward to the taller, young man.

"Ada." Luca bent and kissed her on each cheek.

"It's been so long. Come in." She pulled Luca by the hand.

"I know. I'm sorry. Any word on Donato?" Luca referred to Ada's son in the army.

"No. I just pray and take life one day at a time."

"He'll be fine. He's the most resourceful person I know. He'll find a way home. You'll see."

"Yes," Ada brightened, "You two got in and out of more than one *pasticcio* when you were little." *Pasticcio*, the Italian word for pie, is the idiom for a mess – a fitting metaphor for the jams the boys had gotten into.

"Do you think Donato would mind if we took the boat out?"

"You know how we feel about you. You're like a brother to Donato. And you're like my second son." Ada paused and looked beyond Luca to Nicla near the door. "And would my second son be bringing home a daughter-in-law for me?"

"No. She's...This is Nicla."

"*Piacere*," Nicla greeted, offering Ada the two kisses obliged in Italian receptions.

"*Bellina!*" declared Ada as she held Nicla's two hands and admired her from head to toe. She turned to Luca. "Yes, go." She pushed him toward the back of the apartment. "I won't make you squirm with a lot of questions. It's a beautiful day for two beautiful young people. Go." She gently guided Nicla as well. "*Vai, bellina*. Enjoy!"

Luca led Nicla down the stairs below Ada's place. Nicla wondered where they were going. "Aren't we supposed to be going on the canal?"

"Shush!" Luca led onward.

They came out into a basement that was more of a tunnel. Nicla looked up at the curved, low ceilings. "Are we in the catacombs?"

"No. There are no maritime objects in the catacombs." Luca pointed to the fishing paraphernalia hanging on the walls. "Besides, we removed the skeletons of the ancient Christians, so you don't have to worry."

Nicla smiled and followed.

Luca opened two wide doors. The sunlight poured in. Nicla stepped out into another world. Before her was the canal - peaceful, sea-green, but opaque and inscrutable. Rising high on both

sides were the ancient canal walls. Nicla saw, here and there between the stones, a few tufts of grass whose seeds had somehow
found purchase. She thought how resourceful Mother Nature is.

"*Buon giorno*," came a greeting from a stocky old man with a
wide face. He wore baggy clothes, and a flat cap. Sitting next to
his boat, he was mending some fishing tackle.

"*Buon giorno*, Eugenio," replied Luca, "Were you already fishing
this morning?"

"He who sleeps does not catch fish," countered Eugenio. His
thick fingers worked dexterously at tying off a rig. "Looks like good
fishing for you, too. Yes?" He looked up at Nicla with a smile.

"Just a little trip," Luca replied as they moved on. He turned to
Nicla. "We must make a good couple, don't you think?"

"Where is your ship, Captain?" Nicla redirected.

Luca guided Nicla to what could barely be called a dingy, floating
next to the stone walk. It sported a tiny outboard motor that
looked more like an electric eggbeater with one spindle.

"Your yacht, I presume?" Nicla asked smirking.

"Oh, she's quite seaworthy. Donato and I weathered many a
squall in this little lady."

"What about the ladies you took out on her? How did they
fare?"

"We kept them safe from pirates."

Nicla thought of the Turkish slippers and the girl captured by
pirates. "Did you play the Blue Prince and save these girls from the
sea monsters you invented?"

"The sea monsters are real. The Blue Prince is the fairytale."
Luca got into the boat and reached out his hand. "Are *you* in need
of a Blue Prince?"

"No. I can do fine on my own." Eschewing Luca's hand, Nicla
stepped into the little craft. She felt the water give under her weight
and push back, as if it were testing the newcomer's balance. She
grabbed Luca's hand and sat down quickly. Just as hastily, she let
go.

"Instead of the Blue Prince, perhaps a pair of sea legs would serve you better." Luca tried not to chuckle.

"Are you getting in?" Nicla asked impatiently.

"Immediately, *Signorina*!" Untying the small vessel, Luca hopped in and moved to the stern. Nicla was amazed at how nimbly he moved without rocking the boat. One would never have guessed at any issue with his leg.

Nicla sat on the front bench facing the rear. She watched Luca give two tugs on the cord of the little motor. It sputtered to life. He sat in the rear holding the handle as they pulled away into the middle of the canal.

They moved slowly past other little boats tethered alongside the waterway. Looking up, Nicla surveyed the buildings that lined the streets above the canal. They added to the feeling of depth. She was gliding through a Tuscan fiord of pastel stucco, green shutters, and grey stone.

"Beautiful morning. My favorite time to be here," Luca announced over the soft putter of the motor. Nicla nodded and leaned back, eyes closed, enjoying the sun on her face. Her hair shone.

Luca took the opportunity to admire her beauty. Nicla opened her eyes. Luca turned slightly, but not in time. He feigned innocence looking beyond Nicla to the arched bridge they were approaching. As much as she wanted to rebuke him, Nicla fought back a smile. It was nice to have a handsome young man appreciate her. It reminded her of the way Claudio looked at her.

Around each bend was some nuance. Ancient doors and gates decorated the stone walls of the canal. They looked like they belonged in the Colosseum - as if gladiators or lions would be loosed upon their opening. Two boys were leaning over the edge of the stone walk, dangling a string. They were pulling up a crab. Nicla imagined it appearing from the murky depth. The canal was beautiful but impenetrable.

"What are you thinking about?" Luca broke her pensive gaze.

"The canal. I wonder how deep it is. It makes me a little uncomfortable."

"Like haughty people?"

"No. I can figure them out pretty quickly. Take you for example. I can see right through you."

"Oh, really? What do you see?"

She leaned forward as if to peer inside him. "You're as clear as the sea out there," she motioned over her shoulder with her head, "I can see starfish and coral way down in your soul."

"Some sharks and eels, no doubt?"

"No, you'd like me to think that. But you're kinder than you let on. I would say there's even some nobility in you. And not the kind you're born into."

Luca was taken aback. He thought he had put on a good front. Who was this poor city girl divining his inner self?

They were approaching the last bridge over the canal. Beyond this span lay the crystal ocean. The corridor of buildings began to open, and the horizon grew. Nicla turned to enjoy the expanding vista. On the bridge, she could make out the helmets of two German soldiers. As the boat approached, she could see they were bearing automatic weapons. She turned back to Luca with a concerned look.

"We're fine," Luca assured, "They're looking for saboteurs."

"What?" The boat was passing under the bridge now.

"They're guarding the port. Just smile at them when we come out."

As they emerged, Nicla looked up. One soldier was looking down almost nostalgically at the couple in their little boat. Nicla thought he might have a girlfriend back home with whom he had gone boating. The other soldier flashed a perverse grin and began raising his weapon at Nicla.

Luca rose slightly and leaned in front of Nicla. He smiled and waved to the soldiers, muttering what seemed like a greeting but consisted largely of profanity. The soldier who had been enraptured in thoughts of love, shoved his comrade, causing him to lower his weapon and catch his balance. The dreamer reprimanded his sadistic partner, who chuckled and shouted something in German at the couple pulling away.

"I have to turn away from the docks and make for the ocean, quickly. That's what they're looking for." Luca sat back down. "Are you alright?"

"My heart is pounding." Nicla tried to compose herself. "That's the second time I've had a gun pointed at me." She looked out at the ocean. "Maybe I'll get used to it before the war is over."

"And before the war is over, I'm going to do something to get the NAZIs the hell out of here." Luca took a breath and tried to relax. Touched by her melancholy turn, he sought to bring up Nicla's spirits. "Look, here's *la Fortezza Vecchia.*"

They were gliding by the steep, banked walls of an ancient fortress which rose right out of the water. The immense stronghold had a zigzag shape from several enormous bastions which projected outward into the harbor. One could imagine soldiers of olden days on the ramparts, firing cannons at invaders. The immense edifice had been standing sentinel for the port since the early 1500s.

"When Donato and I were little, we tried to climb it," Luca proclaimed.

"No! Come on!"

"Yes. We pretended we were pirates. We threw a rope with a grappling hook up there." He pointed to where the first level of wall ended, and another section rose.

"You actually tried that?"

"Yes, and once we climbed to the top of that first section, it was too far to throw the rope up to the parapets. On the last try, I lost my grip on the rope and it fell down into the water." Luca demonstrated with fumbling hands. He grabbed the tiller again. "So, there we were, stuck on that little ledge. We were afraid to jump. Look how far out the walls slope. It would take quite a leap."

"How did you get down?"

"I can't tell you how long we stood there. We each told the other one to jump first. Then, all of a sudden, Donato took a deep breath and dove - headfirst! I thought he was going to die. When he came back up to the surface, it gave me courage. It shamed me, too. So, I said a quick prayer, closed my eyes and jumped. I was more religious then - nimbler, too."

By "nimbler," Nicla knew Luca meant more than the agility of youth. The incident must have transpired before Luca's tragic accident. Nicla began to feel compassion for Luca.

Sensing this, Luca sought to change the subject. "You're supposed to be my first mate on this vessel. Have you set a course for *Molo Nuovo*?"

"Yes sir. It's that way." Nicla pointed.

"Very good. Please relay that to the helmsman and we shall proceed."

Nicla concluded that the helmsman and captain were one in the same on this ship. She closed her eyes and turned her attention to soaking in the sensations of the sea. The air was salty and fresh. She could feel the warm breeze of *il Libeccio* - the southwest wind that could bring sudden tempests. But on that day, it washed across her skin like a salve. Ahead lay the great landmark of the port, *Molo Nuovo*.

Chapter 7

Opening her eyes, Nicla could see *Molo Nuovo*. Not just a breakwater as its name implied, *Molo Nuovo* was a massive structure looming before them. Over a kilometer long, it looked like a monstrous castle wall, placed in the ocean by a king who never finished the rest of his citadel. It had been commissioned by the Grand Duke of Tuscany in the 1800s to protect the harbor from the gales of *il Libeccio*. Because of its sweeping arch shape, it was more properly named *Diga Curvilenea*. The irony of the locals referring to it as the New Breakwater (*Molo Nuovo*), lay not only in its age, but in its resemblance to something built by the Romans.

Luca cut the engine and the little boat glided up to a stairway that descended into water. The steps had been cut into huge marble blocks that formed the base of the *Molo*. Luca hopped out and tied the boat to a post. "I think you're becoming more of a celebrity passenger than a first mate. The captain ties the boat off for you."

Having learned her lesson back at the canal, Nicla took Luca's hand and disembarked. "I've never been here. It's even bigger than it looks from the shore."

"You haven't seen the seaward side? I think you'll be surprised. Come. There's a lot to explore."

They walked along the landward side of the great sea wall. Nicla could feel the permanence of the great marble blocks on which they tread. She looked up at the large rectangular stones woven up to the sky in an impenetrable barrier. To her, she was walking on a piece of antiquity that future generations would visit.

"Do you think this could crumble someday, a thousand years from now?" she asked. "Like parts of the Colosseum? They probably thought that would last forever."

"Nothing lasts forever."

"I know some things that do."

"You're not going to talk about love, are you?"

"No. I meant the sun." She leaned back and smiled. "And the ocean," she took a deep breath, "and... there will always be cynical people."

"Hmm. You don't miss a chance to take a shot. Let's go on top of the wall."

They walked toward one end of the giant edifice. At this point, the immense wall curled like a conch shell, wrapping around a spiral staircase carved into the stone. Luca and Nicla ascended within the stone enclosure.

"It feels like we're in a castle." Nicla's words echoed off the stones.

"How about now?" Luca announced as they came out on top of the wall.

There before them was a sight that reminded Nicla of the Great Wall of China. The top of the wall formed a road that stretched into the distance. It was bordered by low parapets.

Nicla turned in a circle to take in the view. She could see the city of Livorno and the hills of Montenero as its backdrop. She surveyed the rocky coastline and beaches where she and Claudio had enjoyed the crystal-clear water. Far beyond, in the hazy distance, were the Apuan Alps with their white marble caps.

She turned to look out at the ocean and saw how vast the horizon was from this vantage point. The sea breeze ruffled her hair. "It's wonderful!" she exclaimed. Turning back to Luca, a strand of light-brown hair fluttered across her face.

"Wonderful," Luca concurred, reaching out to brush Nicla's hair from her face. At that instant, a capricious breeze intervened to move the wayward strand. Luca's hand froze an inch from Nicla's forehead. "Even the wind..." he decried under his breath and dropped his hand.

Nicla, sensing what had just taken place, sought to relieve Luca's embarrassment - if not her own. "*Andiamo*! Let's go see *il faro*!" This was the lighthouse at the far end of *Molo Nuovo*.

"Of course, *Signorina*."

They walked along the top of the grand wall. Nicla pirouetted occasionally, enjoying the panorama, and reveling in the freedom she was experiencing. They reached the lighthouse. It was constructed from the same stones as the wall from which it rose. It looked more like a turret in a castle than a lighthouse. Looking down from the wall, Nicla could see two German soldiers posted at the entrance.

"They're guarding the door," Luca pointed out, "They wouldn't want any saboteurs going up and damaging the beacon. Can't have their supply ships running aground during a storm - even if *il Libeccio* would cooperate with us."

"Why aren't they up here on the wall, too?" Nicla leaned over to look at the armed men. "They usually are. Now I wish I had some dynamite. But we'd be shooting ourselves in the foot. The Germans will be gone eventually. We'll need the lighthouse for *our* ships, then."

Nicla sat on the parapet near the tower. "I used to watch this lighthouse at night from my house. We lived on the third floor on Via Magnini. I never imagined being this close to it." She leaned a hand against the stones of the lighthouse. "You know what my parents used to tell my brother about this when he was very small?

"What?"

"That it was *il carbonaio* and he was looking for naughty boys to take. They would say it when my brother wouldn't go to sleep." *Il carbonaio* was the Italian boogeyman. He was, as his name "the coalman" suggested, so black that he could not be seen in the dark.

"I always wondered about that story," Luca pondered. "How could kids go to sleep if they're afraid of *il carbonaio*?"

"I know. My parents are old-fashioned. But after my father left the bedroom, I would sing Matteo a lullaby. That worked much better.

"I should think so."

"After he fell asleep, I would go over to the window and watch *il faro*. I could see the beam. It looked like an arm. It would reach out to the city - like it was touching the houses." Nicla reached out her arm and swept it toward the city. "Then it would reach our house and flash in my eyes. It felt like *il carbonaio* was looking right into our bedroom!"

"I could see *il faro* from Montenero, too."

"What did you think of it, when you were little?"

"After the accident, *Nonna* told me it was my parents watching over me."

"Really?"

"No. Sorry. It was too good of a story not to try on you."

"Oh, you *mascalzone*!" Nicla pushed Luca with both hands. She looked askance at him. "You know what? I think you *were* telling the truth. And now you're trying to be the strong man and cover up something sweet that you let me see. You forget. I can see through you." Nicla squinted her eyes.

"Yes, I forgot. I'll give you another chance. What am I thinking now?" Luca leaned forward slightly, offering Nicla a better view into his eyes.

"Hmm." Nicla stroked her chin. "I see. You're madly in love..." Luca's eyes widened.

"With yourself!" Nicla concluded.

Although he was let down, Luca appreciated the girl who was turning out to be every bit his equal in wit. "*Buona battuta.* Good shot." He conceded. "But you're not the first person to say that to me - that I'm in love with myself."

"You mean I'm not the first *girl* to say that."

"No. I've gotten that from male friends, too. Is it a crime to be confident?"

"It's no crime. You should be confident. You're obviously a gifted *imbroglione*. You convinced me to come out here alone with you." Nicla paused. "But you're also a gentleman, so I feel safe."

Once again, Luca was baffled. He felt rejected but praised. He shifted gears. "Let's go over to the seaward side - on the rocks."

The ocean side of *il Molo* was more of a traditional breakwater. It resembled a narrow island made of huge stones. Luca and Nicla carefully made their way down to where the rocks met the water. They removed their shoes and put their feet in the water.

"I forgot how good this feels," Nicla declared as the water splashed on her ankles. "I have to taste it." She reached down, dipped her hand in, and brought it back cupped to her mouth. She tasted the crystal-clear brine. It brought back such good feelings and memories associated with the ocean. She felt a connection to something deep inside her. You could not grow up in Livorno and not feel part of the ocean.

"That's a strange habit." Luca furled his brow. "I love the ocean, too." He took off his shirt. "And here's how I make love to her!" He dove in.

Nicla was left with her mouth open. Luca came to the surface and threw back his shock of black hair. "What? You never saw a man jump in the ocean?"

"You still have your pants on."

"If you weren't here, I wouldn't! Besides, they'll dry when I get out."

"You said you were making love to her," Nicla nodded toward the water. "That's no way - with your pants on!"

"You're right." He turned toward the open sea. "Forgive me my dear!" he called out. "I shall return to be with you when we can commune in a more dignified manner."

He spun around and swam to Nicla. She was looking down at him from the rocks, smiling. She did find him very entertaining. He pushed himself up, half out of the water at her feet. She also noticed that shirtless, he cut a striking figure. At that moment, a rogue wave crashed over his back. It pushed him closer to Nicla and splashed on Nicla's dress.

She leaned forward. "Your jealous lover sent you a message."

"You're right. She is not one to trifle with. I better get out." Luca pulled himself out and sat next to Nicla. He called back toward the sea with hands cupped round his mouth, "Don't be jealous! She's just a friend!"

The word "friend" struck Nicla. It was the first time Luca had verbalized that she wasn't simply his employee. But then there was the other word he used - "just." It saddened her a bit.

"*Can* I call you friend? A good friend?" Luca asked.

"Yes. Thank you. You've been very kind." She looked over his face. His expression was deeply earnest, and it was indeed kind. She had misjudged him by his arrogant façade. And now, she allowed herself to acknowledge something she had thought dangerous to contemplate – she was attracted to him. While she still loved Claudio, she looked at Luca, and thought: *This could be someone's Blue Prince.*

A hum started to rise in Nicla's ears. She wondered if it were her emotions warring with her reason. "Do you hear that?" she asked still holding Luca's gaze.

"I do." He turned and looked seaward. "It's an air raid!" He jumped to his feet. Sirens began to crank in the city. "We should be safe if we take the boat farther out. They're going to hit the harbor."

"My father!" Nicla exclaimed. "He's home! His leg is broken, and he can't walk." She turned to face the city. "I have to go to him."

"What? He has a broken leg?"

"He went back to work and got hurt again. Come on. We have to leave."

They hurried back to their boat as the din of the aircraft grew louder. Once launched, they puttered as fast as the little motor would take them.

"This is not wise. It's dangerous to head in!" Luca shouted over the roar of the planes . "Won't your mother help him get to a shelter – or your brother?"

"She'll be at the market at this time of day. Who knows where my brother is. Hurry, please." Explosions began to erupt from the harbor. Plumes of black smoke rose into the sky.

Suddenly, before them, a tremendous hole opened in the ocean accompanied by a loud sucking sound. A spray of surf shot up as the hole closed. It was a wayward bomb. The tiny craft rose precipitously and fell into the trough. Water spilled over the bow.

"God save us!" Nicla cried out, pushing her wet hair off her brow.

"It's alright. We're steady now. Almost there."

As they reached the canal, Nicla turned to Luca. "Let me off. I'll run home. The car is too far from here. Please stop!"

Luca knew she was right. He also knew he could not keep up with her on foot. He pulled the boat over to the first stairway in the canal. Nicla hopped out and ran up the steps. "Get to a shelter!" she called from the street.

"I'll get the car and meet you!" Luca pulled away in the dinghy and headed up the canal. Explosions thundered as bombs meant for the harbor hit civilian dwellings. Above the parapet, Luca saw the heads of townspeople scampering for refuge as the sirens wailed. He thought Nicla's actions were an exercise in futility. She could never arrive home in time to make any difference had fate chosen her father. But Luca would have done the same in Nicla's position.

The bombardment continued as Luca navigated the canal. He realized this was not just an attack on the port. It was also an attack on the city's infrastructure, and it was coming in waves. Arriving at the dinghy's berth, Luca hurriedly lashed it to a stone mooring post and made for the nearest stairway. He was stopped by the sight of a boy huddled against the canal wall. He was barely ten years old and frail. The boy looked up momentarily, then put his head back on his drawn-up knees.

"Do you need help?" Luca asked.

"Make it stop." The boy covered his ears.

"Where are your parents?" Luca shouted over the explosions.

"Dead."

Luca sat down next to the child and put his arm around him. The boy put his head against Luca's chest.

"Who do you live with?" Luca asked.

"My uncle." The boy cringed at another explosion, "But he's out fishing."

"It will be alright. I'll stay with-" Suddenly a tremendous detonation resounded through the canal. The two huddled as debris hurtled over the wall above them and down into the canal. Brick and stone cascaded onto the walkway, into the water, and upon the boats moored alongside. The sound of stone striking stone and hollow wooden hulls rang out. The tiny vessels rocked wildly. They pulled on their tethers as if trying escape the destruction raining down. The debris also smashed against the wall across the canal. Had Luca and the boy not been against the leeward wall of the canal, they would surely have been killed.

After several other close strikes and many agonizing minutes, the explosions waned. The bombardment ceased.

"There. It's over," Luca reassured. "Will your uncle return soon?"

"Look!" The boy pointed. "Here he is." A boat was pulling up to the berth before them.

"*Ciao*`!" Luca saluted the man in the boat. He turned to the boy. "And *ciao*` to you *amico*." He rubbed the boy's head.

"*Zio*! This man helped me!" the boy cried to his uncle in the boat.

Luca had already begun to bound, as best as his leg would allow, up the stone stairs. "It was nothing!" he called turning at the top of the stairs. "He's a brave boy!"

The uncle stood dumbstruck, with hands on his hips as Luca disappeared. The boy jumped into his uncle's arms.

In the street, Luca was faced with a scene of utter devastation. Several of the houses along the via had been reduced to rubble. A few people were returning from bomb shelters and others were coming out of buildings. Calls for loved ones rang out.

Luca found the Isotta and climbed in. He had to get to Nicla, but the street had become a maze of debris. As he maneuvered the large vehicle through the ruins, he witnessed firsthand the terrible scourge of war. A husband frantically dug through rubble seeking his soulmate. A girl, her clothes tattered and face smudged, sat with her back against half a wall, clutching her doll. A boy, perhaps her brother, sought to console her inconsolable loss. Other sights - victims being carried and rushed to hospitals - Luca could hardly bear to look upon. *They're going to kill us all before they liberate us*, he thought.

Around one corner, a woman emerged in front of Luca's car. He stopped abruptly. She was white with dust, like a Geisha, and stumbled around the car like a walking corpse. "Are you alright?" he asked as she walked by his open window. She continued on, muttering, with unseeing eyes. Luca watched in the mirror as she was enveloped in the arms of a man running toward her. It was such miracles within the chaos that gave Luca some hope that this hell could be endured. And he hoped that Nicla had been blessed with a happy reunion. But with this much damage to the city, he was worried for her.

His car reached Nicla's quarter, and he turned down her street. He could not see far. The neighborhood had received its share of the terror from above. And then he saw what he had feared. Nicla's small apartment building had been hit. It was demolished. In the street, huddled together on their knees were Nicla, her mother, and brother. Their unearthly shrieks pierced Luca's heart. Death had visited Nicla's home.

Chapter 8

A fter her father's death, Nicla and her family were taken in by
Nicla's uncle, Fiore. They lived together in the small house
next to his gas station. The Contessa had invited all of them to
come live at her villa, but Nicla's mother had declined. It was
a decision made out of pride. Living under the Contessa's roof
would give Silvia a sense of indebtedness. Besides, she needed to
be in the city to stay in contact with sewing clients.

At the villa, Nicla moved lifelessly through each day. Her father
had been close to her, and his loss was great. It was hard to find
anything to lift her spirits. Claudio's return seemed too remote
and uncertain. Hope was something upon which she could wager
no more. Fate, it seemed, had tipped its hand.

Everyone around her could see Nicla's depression, but none
could pull her from it. The Contessa continued with her stories.
She tried to tell the funnier ones, to no avail. Nicla would smile
dutifully, but clearly her mind was elsewhere. Although the Contessa offered to lighten her chores, Nicla wished to be kept busier
than ever. Lost in monotony, she was anesthetized.

Even the Contessa's stoic friend, Signore Montanini, was moved
by Nicla's despondence. One afternoon, he and the Contessa were
sitting on the sofa in the parlor. Nicla had been summoned before

the Contessa for some trifle. "This is the girl I was telling you about," she whispered to Montanini. "Poor thing."

"Contessa...Signore," Nicla addressed them respectfully.

"The Contessa told me about your father. *Mi dispiace*," Montanini offered his condolences.

"Grazzie, Signore." Nicla appreciated the sentiment but was slightly taken aback. Of all the times she had seen Montanini around the villa, this was the first instance where he proffered more than a nod. Furthermore, he spoke with a foreign accent, but she couldn't place it. He had, however, succeeded in lifting her momentarily from her gloom - if not in spirit, in intrigue. She went about the rest of her day imagining from whence he might hail and what could be his business at the villa.

Luca's interaction with Nicla had also changed. His haughty bravado was gone, replaced by earnest concern.

"Are you alright?" he asked, leaning into her sewing room one morning.

Nicla turned from her machine but remained seated. "I'm fine. Busy as always." She managed a faint smile.

"Is there anything I can do for you or your family?"

"Thank you. No. You've done enough. Paying for the funeral was very kind. You and the Contessa have been so generous and understanding."

The sun from the window was shining through Nicla's light-brown hair, turning it a golden hue. Her hazel eyes sparkled. Luca marveled for a moment, then regained his train of thought.

"Why don't you take a break? Would you like to go for a ride in the Isotta? It's a nice day."

Somewhere inside, part of Nicla wanted to accept. It would be wonderful to forget her troubles and enjoy the glorious day beckoning outside her window.

"I've got a lot of work to do." She motioned to some clothes on the bed. "I can't."

"Oh. I see. Very well. But please, you mustn't work so hard. It's just that... well, you've been through a lot..."

"It's alright, Luca." Nicla rose and walked to him, taking his hand in hers. "I know you're concerned. I truly appreciate it. But I've got to work through some things in my mind - on my own." She squeezed his hand and went back to her work.

Luca was at a loss. He turned and walked away. He did not know how to deal with Nicla's present state, nor did he have the confidence to try. Ever since the day of the bombing that took Nicla's father, he had felt a failure. In her hour of need, he could not accompany her on her desperate flight to find her father. He was inadequate. And perhaps Nicla had reached the same conclusion. The fact that none of this even occurred to Nicla, that she held him in the highest regard, and that her emotional isolation was purely self-imposed, was beyond his grasp.

In the following weeks, their paths would cross. The exchanges became briefer. Their misperceptions of each other were self-fulfilling. Luca saw Nicla's detachment as judgment. Nicla saw Luca's perfunctory greetings as a loss of interest.

One afternoon, the Contessa called Luca into the parlor. Nicla was already by the Contessa's side. "I need you both to run some errands for me."

"*Nonna*, really?" Luca rolled his eyes.

"Yes. I need some very specific things. Nicla can pick them out. You can drive her."

"Alberto can drive her."

Nicla feigned indifference, but Luca was beginning to hurt her.

"Alberto is not up to it, today," the Contessa declared. "And I want someone brave to protect my sweet one here." She took Nicla's hand. "Things are getting less orderly in town now that the Americans are getting closer."

"That is not true." Luca protested. "You know-"

"Tut!" The Contessa held up a finger. "No more of that. Now, it's all settled. I have given Nicla instructions on where to go and what to get." The Contessa caressed Luca's cheek. "Go on. Do this little kindness for you *Nonna*."

Luca and Nicla rode into town in the Isotta. They were both seated in the front. It was particularly hot. Even the breeze coming in the windows felt warm. As they descended from Montenero, Nicla noted how the fields had regained their golden hue of summer. A lone falcon was soaring, riding the breeze high above and ahead of their car. *Does she know war?* Nicla thought. The falcon banked and the sunlight flashed against her white, under feathers. That such a beautiful creation could be mimicked in creating machines that brought death seemed perverse to Nicla. *Then again*, she thought, *that's what the falcon brings to her prey - death*. Still, the soaring bird was a beautiful sight to behold.

"I wish I could fly like that falcon," she spoke dreamily.

Luca looked upward. "I don't doubt that you could. Put your arms out and I'll speed up. Go on. Try to catch the wind." He accelerated slightly.

Nicla turned to him with an astonished smile. "That's the old Luca. Where has he been?"

"Why? Where did I go?"

"Please be serious. You haven't been yourself - not for a while."

Luca sighed. "Alright. It's a lot of things - the war, my place in this whole thing, and..." he turned to Nicla. "You know what? It's nice to see *you* smile for a change."

"You're changing the subject. I was asking about you."

"It's hot. We'll stop and get a cold drink in town. Maybe I can explain then. Look! The falcon is diving." The bird of prey had pinned back its wings and plummeted beyond some trees. "Goodbye mouse or whatever she was after. Your falcon is not so pretty to her prey, is she?"

"She's just doing what she has to do to keep her family alive."

"At least she *can* do something about it," Luca noted wistfully.

Nicla knew his frustration. But she didn't know how to pivot from the subject in a way that was not banal. There was silence for some time.

"Who is Signore Montanini, really?" Nicla asked.

"An old friend of the family."

"Yes. I know that part. What does he do? Where is he from?"

"He's an art dealer. I think he's Swiss. Why do you ask?"

"He's very mysterious if you ask me. He has a funny accent."

"He's been all around the world. I think his parents moved a lot when he was young. I bet he doesn't even have a mother tongue."

"Does he have business with the Contessa's artwork?"

"You mean her treasure trove in the basement? Yes. He helps her sell some pieces. Maybe that's why he seems so mysterious to you. One must keep these things close to the vest you know. The NAZIs are always looking to pilfer art."

"And sewing machines," Nicla added in disgust.

"That was a unique occurrence. I had never heard of such a thing. Are you sure they didn't just follow a pretty girl to her house?"

"No. They were there when I got home. And you just called me pretty. Do you realize that?"

"I thought you had a sister."

Nicla enjoyed his retort. She had to smirk. "*Boun Detto.* Well said." She looked out the window. "Let's enjoy the countryside."

They continued their descent from the relative safety of Montenero and the countryside, into the war-torn city of Livorno. Once there, they made a few stops for the Contessa: picking up some material for a dress, a cake from a *pasticcieria*.

"Pull over here, at the tobacconist." Nicla pointed.

Luca obliged.

Nicla continued, "The Contessa wants us to pick up an antique cigarette case they're holding for her. It's strange isn't it? She doesn't smoke. Does she?"

"No, not that I know of. Maybe it's a piece for her secret treasure trove. She said 'antique,' didn't she?"

"Yes, but it seems a trifle compared to all the big pieces down there."

"Well, maybe it's a gift for Signore Montanini. At least love is blooming *somewhere* in the villa."

"Good for her, a younger man even. Well, she's free to fall in love. I on the other hand -"

"Look!" Two German soldiers were stepping briskly up to the tobacconist's door. "They don't look like they're going to pick up cigarettes."

"Maybe they're in a hurry." Nicla hoped.

"I don't like this."

After a minute inside, the soldiers emerged with the tobacconist between them. They were moving with the same dispatch with which they had entered. The tobacconist's expression alternated from forlorn to wincing as he was jostled by his unwelcome escorts.

"That's terrible," Nicla whispered.

The trio receded around a corner.

"Stay in the car." Luca instructed firmly.

"What?"

"When I get out, slide over to the driver's seat. If anyone comes in the shop after me, drive back to the villa."

"Are you crazy? Why?"

Luca had already exited the vehicle.

Nicla watched Luca walk calmly into the tobacconist's shop. She moved behind the wheel without taking her eyes off the storefront. Her heart raced. What seemed like much longer than a minute passed. She turned and scanned up and down the street. Looking back out the driver's window, her heart stopped as a hand reached for the car door.

It was Luca.

"Get in!" she hissed.

"Relax." Luca stepped into the car.

"What's gotten into you? They could have come back for something." Nicla looked around again.

"I got it." Luca tapped the front pocket of his pants. He looked out the window and back. "You want to see it?" He removed a silver cigarette case from his pocket. It was engraved with an image of the sun that had a face like a human. Triangular rays around the sun formed a compass rose.

"You risked your life for that! A cigarette case? I can't understand you."

Luca looked around out the window once more. "I think we're fine here. But no use tempting fate any further. Let's go."

"Where?"

"To the café on Piazza Micheli. Come on. Let's see you drive again."

The café was situated on a sunny piazza which offered a view of one of the marinas near the port. Nicla and Luca sat at a small table outside. They were close enough to the harbor for Nicla to see one wall of *la Fortezza Vecchia* and the great, cylindrical tower that rose from it. The tower resembled the more famous one in nearby Pisa, only this defensive tower was much stouter, to stand stalwart against would-be conquerors from the sea.

"I can't stop thinking about the tobacconist." Nicla looked out toward the ocean. "Why did they take him? What's going to happen to him?"

"Maybe he's connected to the Partisans somehow. Perhaps he funnels money to them. Maybe they found out he's Jewish. I don't know." Luca shook his head. "As to what's going to happen to him... Please. Let's change the subject. Let's pretend we're here before the war."

"Pretend? Is that what you were doing when you went in that shop - pretending your life wasn't in danger?"

"Screw the Germans. I'll do what I please."

"I'll do what I please? Where is this coming from?"

Luca leaned forward. "I've been kept too safe - too far removed from this war. Oh yes. I have a valid excuse." He stuck out his leg. "So here I am, contributing nothing. It's humiliating. I need to put myself at risk for my country, like the Partisans." He nodded toward Montenero. "You see what I've resorted to? Useless gestures! For what? A cigarette case? It's pathetic." He threw the silver case on the table.

Nicla glanced at the silver sun looking up at her, but she was more concerned about Luca who had turned and was gazing up to the hills of Montenero.

"I've been thinking about it for some time," he grumbled. "Now I know."

"What is it?"

"I'm joining the Partisans."

Chapter 9

L uca disappeared from the villa shortly after his proclamation to Nicla. She had hoped at the café that it was a momentary lashing out and would pass. But one day, he did not come back from hunting. His dogs were found never to have left the premises. This was cause for much concern. The fears of all in the household were confirmed when the Contessa found his note on the coffee table where she so often spun her tales. Her shriek pierced the house. In the note, Luca begged her forgiveness and commended her to the care of Nicla and Alberto. He assured that he would be back when the war was over. There wasn't much more.

In the weeks that followed, Nicla settled back into the routine of her position. The atmosphere at the villa was bleak. The Contessa had no stories to share. She refused to take her coffee at the table where she had read, what was for her, the unspeakable news. Instead, she sat with Signore Montanini out on the *terazza*. They did not present the same picture together that they once created in the parlor. It was as if they had traded affects. The once sober Montanini was almost convivial juxtaposed with the Contessa's now sullen humor.

Nicla happened to pass the two while carrying some laundry.

"Look, here is someone to cheer you up." Montanini signaled with his coffee cup. "*Vieni!* Come here, *Signorina.*" He turned to the Contessa. "The girl is a great comfort to you, isn't she?"

"Yes. My *tesoro* - my treasure," replied the Contessa.

Montanini fixed his gaze on Nicla. "The Contessa says you're very loyal."

Nicla wasn't sure if he was admiring or trying to size her up in some other way. She gave a polite nod. "*Grazzie, Signore.*" She bowed slightly. "*Grazzie,* Contessa."

Montanini continued. "You also have your own sewing clients in town, yes?"

Nicla was becoming uncomfortable. "*Si Signore.* Alberto brings me to make deliveries."

"Yes. I know." Montanini picked up his cigarette and took a long draw without breaking his stare. One eye squinted slightly.

Trying anything to avert her own eyes from Montanini's gaze, Nicla looked down at the table. There, next to an ashtray, was the silver cigarette case with the sun engraving.

"You like my cigarette box?" He picked it up. "It was a gift from the Contessa. Nice piece isn't it?" He held it out briefly for Nicla, then slipped it into his jacket. "You had a disconcerting experience picking it up, I was told."

Nicla turned and looked at the Contessa, then back at Montanini. She wasn't sure what to say about it.

"You needn't be shy about it. You showed a lot of composure under the circumstances. A very dependable girl, I should say." He sat back, puffed his cigarette again, and blew smoke in the air with a finality of having passed judgment upon her.

At a loss for what he was driving at, Nicla struggled for a polite response.

"Nicla," the Contessa broke in, "you must be getting tired holding that laundry." She turned to Montanini. "George, let the girl go." She touched Nicla on the arm. "Go on dear. You may leave now."

"*Grazzie*, Contessa. Excuse me, *Signore*."

Nicla was relieved to escape Montanini's scrutiny. He had paid her no attention previously. She couldn't fathom this newfound attentiveness or the keenness with which he expressed it. She went back to her chores feeling uneasy.

Several days later, Nicla was working in the kitchen with Alberto. It was approaching midday, and they were preparing *pranzo* - their biggest meal. Nicla was cutting some octopus, which had been cooked earlier and was now cool. It was to be tossed with some boiled potatoes, parsley, and lemon.

"Luisa was a nice girl, but you're a much better cook." Alberto dislodged a lemon seed with his knife.

"Grazzie, Alberto. I only know a couple of tricks."

"Where did you learn this one, signorina? It is *proprio speciale!*"

"I *had* to learn this one. Claudio used to bring home octopus when he went fishing with the mask and fins."

"Did you ever go with him when he fished like that?"

Nicla smiled with a furrowed brow and cocked her head. "How did you guess?"

Alberto shrugged and continued cutting lemons. "You are not one to miss out on some adventure. I've seen you drive the Isotta."

Nicla continued to marvel at him with one hand on her hip and the other holding a plate of octopus.

Alberto raised his head momentarily. "You asked Claudio if you could go along, underwater fishing, didn't you?" He went back to chopping some parsley.

"Yes. As a matter of fact, I did ask to go along with him."

"What was it like?"

"It was wonderful." A faraway look overtook Nicla. She envisioned swimming by Claudio's side on the surface of the crystal water. "I remember how the sun made designs on the ocean floor."

"You held hands?"

"I didn't know you were there."

"It's a perfect picture - two young people swimming side by side." Alberto glanced at Nicla, who now had both hands on her hips. "Oh, very well..." he yielded. "Did you catch *il polpo*?"

"Yes, and it's funny how we did. I noticed some crab shells on the bottom, and I pointed. Claudio dove down, took his spear, and thrust it into the sand next to the shells." Nicla made a forceful motion with one hand toward the floor. "Then the sand came alive."

"The sand came alive?"

"It was *il polpo*. He was the same color as the sand. The crab was its last meal."

"I like crabs, too. I shall watch where I leave the shells."

Nicla smiled. "That wasn't the end of it. *Il polpo* grabbed hard, all up Claudio's arm with its tentacles. It wouldn't let go." She ran her fingers up her arm and squeezed. "When we were back on the surface, Claudio said he was going to bite it between its eyes to make it let go."

"Ugh. *Disgustoso!* Did he?"

"I told him I wouldn't kiss him for a week if he did. So, he took a knife from his waistband and used that. The poor thing went limp, but it left little circles all over his arm from the suction cups." She shook her head and rubbed her arm.

"And?" Alberto asked eagerly.

"And what?"

"Did you kiss him?"

"Alberto, please."

At that moment, the Contessa walked into the kitchen. "What's this about kissing?"

"Nothing, *Signora*," Alberto replied nonchalantly. "Can I be of service?"

"I need to see Nicla. Come with me, dear." The Contessa put out her hand. "Alberto, I'll need you too."

The Contessa led them down the corridor to the tall hutch that hid the entrance to the basement art cache. "I have a new piece that I want you to see."

On command, Alberto rolled away the hutch and opened the door. The Contessa beckoned Nicla to follow down the stairs.

Nicla's curiosity was more than piqued. What new item would be so special as to merit an invitation to this secret place? She hadn't been there since the Contessa revealed it. As she descended, Nicla looked about. Everything was just as remarkable as the first time she had laid eyes on it. There was even an impression of more opulence, but she couldn't discern what had been added.

When they reached the bottom of the stairs, the Contessa turned to Nicla. "I'm somewhat conflicted regarding this new addition. I want to know your opinion."

Nicla was discomforted by this. She couldn't understand why the Contessa would have reservations about a piece of art. Perhaps it was stolen, or the subject matter was taboo. Nicla's mind flipped through the possibilities. The Contessa led onward.

They approached a corner formed by a tall, medieval painting of Christ on the cross and a nude statue of the goddess Harmonia. Nicla, though intrigued by the mystery, was apprehensive. She paused and allowed the Contessa to round the corner first. The Contessa turned to encourage Nicla, who looked for a signal of assurance. A nod and come-hither motion emboldened her. Nicla rounded the corner. There was Claudio.

Chapter 10

Nicla burst into tears and flung her arms around Claudio. She buried her head in the side of his neck. They held their embrace until Nicla leaned back and looked him in the face.

"I can't believe it. How?" She wiped tears from her eyes. Claudio looked to the Contessa who was dabbing her own eyes with a handkerchief.

"You two have a lot to talk about. I'll leave you alone." The Contessa proceeded up the stairs.

Nicla turned back to Claudio. "My head is spinning. I don't understand. What are you doing here?"

"I'm with the Partisans."

"How can that be? You were in the army. I thought you were in Russia?"

"I *was* in Russia. It was a disaster. The guns they gave us didn't work in the cold. When they brought us back after the surrender, there was chaos. The Americans pressed some of our units into their service. Some were commandeered by the *Germans*! I wasn't waiting around to end up with the Germans. I deserted and made my way back here...Now I fight the Germans with the Partisans."

"My God. How did you find me here, at the villa, in this room?"

"Don't worry about that. Let me look at you." He leaned back with his hands on Nicla's waist. "Beautiful! Let me hold you again." He picked her up and whirled her around in his arms. Nicla let out a joyful shriek and he put her down. They kissed.

Nicla took his hand. "Can we go outside? We can sit and talk on the *terazza*."

"No. We must stay down here. The Contessa was not happy that I put you all in jeopardy like this. I came in late last night and she insisted I stay down here. I fell asleep on that sofa over there. I can't believe I slept at all, much less this long."

"But how did you know to come *here* to find me?"

"Come. Let's sit. I'll tell you." Claudio led Nicla to an antique sofa upholstered in red velvet and framed in ornately carved walnut. "This probably belonged to royalty." He stroked the cushion. "Well, it made a fine bed for an outlaw last night."

As Nicla sat, she couldn't believe her eyes. She tried to soak up Claudio's image. He was not the same boy who had been torn from her happy life. He was leaner, his features more chiseled, but he had the same head of dark hair, brushed back. He pulled up a stool so that he could face Nicla on the couch.

"Wait!" Nicla exclaimed. "Do you know anything about Vivi?"

"No. I don't. He must be with another brigade."

"What about Luca?"

"He's fine. He's with us." Claudio gave her a sideways glance. "Are you very concerned about him?"

"Yes. His family saved us from starving."

"That's all?"

Nicla pursed her brow and studied him for a bit. "I don't like what you're implying."

"I'm sorry. I know what that wolf was like before the war. Don't let his leg fool you." Claudio leaned forward and took Nicla's hands in his. "But I know you. And I know I can trust you. Forgive me."

Nicla folded her arms and looked away from Claudio. "Well. I don't know..." Finally, she turned back. "Alright. I don't blame you for being jealous. Luca *is* handsome."

"Very good. I deserved that. What about me? How do I look?" He stood up and held his hands out, palms up.

Nicla rubbed her chin. "Older."

"That's it? Older? I would think-"

Nicla jumped from the couch and threw herself into kissing him with such zeal that they nearly fell over. Eventually, Claudio regained his equilibrium and composure. "I see you prefer older men."

"Well. You don't have any grey yet." She ran her fingers through his hair. "But you'll do."

They heard the hutch being rolled away at the top of the stairs. Alberto appeared, descending with a large tray. On it were a bottle of wine, two glasses and several dishes.

"*Signore*," Alberto addressed Claudio, "would you mind pulling that ottoman over here?"

Claudio positioned the ottoman in front of the sofa. Alberto laid the tray on the antique tuffet.

"Is this satisfactory, *Signorina*?" Alberto asked.

"Of course, Alberto. Thank you."

"I will return with *il secondo piatto*." Alberto was referring to the main course which the Italians call the second plate. He gave a slight bow and left them.

"*Polpo!*" exclaimed Claudio admiring the plate of octopus and potatoes.

"Yes. I made it. It's like I knew you were coming."

"And you made it just like you used to - only I didn't catch it. Who cares. Let's eat." Claudio sat on the stool and ravenously set upon the seafood dish. Nicla sat in disbelief over the serendipitous reunion of octopus and Claudio.

After much gustation and pronunciations of Nicla's culinary prowess, Claudio took a large swig from his wine glass and leaned forward. He became serious. "How have you been, really? I heard about your father. I'm sorry. He was a good man."

"It's been hard. But I've been busy with work here and with Mamma. I don't have a lot of time to be depressed."

"You're strong. I always knew you could get through anything. Remember the time I fell off my bike and hurt my shoulder? You stood in the road and stopped that car like you were a policeman."

"Someone had to take charge. You were just lying there crying."

"I was *not* crying. A little groaning, yes. What do you expect? My collar bone was broken! Anyway, that guy had no choice but to take me to the hospital. I think you would have pulled him out of his car and driven yourself if he refused."

At this point, Alberto appeared with the next course: *frutti di mare* - fruits of the ocean. Called such because of its assortment of clams, mussels, and other bounty of the sea.

"More seafood!" Claudio exclaimed with much zeal. "I feel like I'm living back in the city. We fugitives don't get much of this up in the hills. Did you make this too?"

"No. This one is all Alberto." She turned to Alberto with a smile. "You really are quite a cook for a chauffeur."

"If you say so, *signorina*." Once again, he bowed and exited.

And once again, there ensued much consumption and extolling of the cook's expertise. When Claudio had loudly sucked the last mussel shell dry, Nicla broached what she had been biding her time to ask. "What is your connection to the Contessa?"

"The Contessa helps us."

"How does she help you?"

"In several ways, actually. Look around. When she sells one of these pieces of art on the black market, she gives the money to the Partisans. She helps us buy weapons."

"So, Signore Montanini *is* an art dealer?"

"Yes and no. He helps sell the art. And I suppose he has some experience with it. But that's just a cover. He also gets us intelligence on German troop movements and ships arriving in the port. He's really with the American OSS."

"OSS?"

"He's a spy."

Nicla slapped her knee. "I knew there was something strange about him!" She stood up. "So that's his accent! He's American." She was pacing now. "I *thought* he looked like Clark Gable with that little mustache."

"Another older man fixation?"

Nicla glared.

Claudio continued, "Listen. Only the highest levels know about him. You must keep this to yourself. We can't afford for him to be discovered."

"Of course. But there's more to this, isn't there? How do you, a Partisan soldier, know about an American spy?"

"My squad leader took me aside. He told me Montanini was asking about you - could you be trusted, and things of that nature."

"Me?" Nicla was becoming alarmed. "What do they want with me?"

"They want you to work with us." He put both hands on her shoulders. "They want you for a *staffetta*."

Nicla was in shock. She knew what a *staffetta* was - a female courier in the Italian resistance. The *staffette,* as they are referred to in plural, would run messages and supplies between the Partisan resistance fighters in the hills and their citizen collaborators in towns. Nicla also knew that many *staffette* had been captured, tortured, and publicly executed.

"*Staffetta*? My God. This is all too much." Nicla became weak in the knees. She sought the support of the sofa. Sitting with a faraway look, she pondered the overwhelming responsibility and the peril it entailed.

"Nicla, please." Claudio lowered himself to one knee and took her hands. "I want you to refuse."

Nicla broke from her trance and turned to Claudio with troubled eyes. "How can I say no?"

"Easy. You tell Montanini it's too much for you. You have your mother and little brother to support. You can't risk it. *I'll* tell him if necessary."

"Is that why you came here - to dissuade me?"

"Yes! They'll be furious with me back in my unit, but I snuck out to talk some sense into you before you made a foolish decision."

"Foolish?" Nicla stood up and walked a few steps from Claudio. As she contemplated the weight of the decision before her, she found herself absently gazing at a painting. In it, a girl wearing a ruffled petticoat carried a basket up a hill. The grass was swirling in the wind. A wolf crouched in the grass.

As the painting came into focus, something else became clear to Nicla. She turned back to Claudio. "Yes, Claudio. You're right. I shouldn't make a foolish decision. I'm making the only decision my conscience allows me to make. I am going to say yes."

"No! Nicla! This is insanity."

"If it will help the resistance, you, my brother, or even Luca, I'll do it."

"But it's not necessary. They can find someone else."

"No. I'm sure they picked me because I'm in the right position to help."

Seeing his despair, Nicla sat down next to Claudio. "But it's more than that for me. It's something I've been feeling for some time now. It's difficult to put into words. I'm tired of this war dictating what happens to me. I need to take some control. I need to at least *feel* I have some influence over my destiny."

"If the Germans catch you, do you know what they do to make you talk?"

"Stop. I've made up my mind. You know me when I make up my mind."

"Yes." Claudio dropped his head. "I do."

After sitting for some time in a disconsolate state, and several more appeals to her better judgment, Claudio rose, and took Nicla in his arms. "Now it's not only the Germans I have to deal with. I have to worry about what's happening with you."

Nicla took Claudio's face in her hands. "Think of it this way. It's like we'll be fighting together."

"I want to be angry with you." He shook his head. "I can't believe I'm saying this, but I'm proud of you."

Nicla threw her arms around him and squeezed. "I knew you would understand." She pulled him back over to the sofa. "Let's not discuss it anymore. We don't have that much time before you have to leave, do we?"

"No. At nightfall, I leave under cover of darkness."

"Then let's talk of happy things."

They reminisced for hours about times before the war - innocent times when being with each other occupied all their thoughts and filled them with thrill and anticipation. At some point, Claudio attempted to recreate one of those times on the sofa.

"Stop! Alberto could come back," Nicla cautioned, mustering all her willpower, and fixing her dress.

"But look where I sit." He tapped the luxurious sofa. "I am the king. And Alberto has been ordered not to disturb us. Come, my coy courtier. The king beckons you to his royal sofa." He pulled her close.

Breaking free, Nicla stood up and snatched a golden candlestick from atop an ornate credenza. Putting on her most regal air, she pointed it at Claudio. "You've got it wrong. I'm the queen and you are a royal suitor from another land. How rich are you?" She brandished the candlestick. "What have you brought me as an offering?"

"What do you mean?" Claudio waved expansively around the room. "I bring you a room full of treasure."

Nicla turned and took a gold chalice from the credenza. "Not enough. Bring me some wine, too." She held out the goblet.

"Careful. That cup is so ancient, it may have been used by Jesus - or at least some pope or bishop." Claudio leaped from the couch and knelt before Nicla. "Why don't you knight me instead?"

"Very well." She pretended to drink deeply from the cup. "So, you want to bamboozle the drunken queen into granting you a higher station in life? Well, didn't you already claim to be royalty?"

"I am. I'm your Blue Prince aren't I?"

"Oh yes, *mio Principe Azzurro*. Well, you must save me from peril first. Let's stick to knighthood for now." As Claudio maintained his kneeling stance, Nicla proceeded to tap each of his shoulders with her newly adopted scepter. "Arise, Sir Claudio."

"And now am I worthy to ask for your hand?"

"Physically, yes, you may take my hand. Whether you are worthy of my heart, show me first what you have brought from far off places."

Claudio led her about the basement, pointing out works of art and other treasures. For each he invented a fanciful story. "This ivory carving is from a sultan whose daughter I almost married."

"Oh really? Is that your attitude toward commitment?"

"She had beautiful eyes, but when she removed her veil... let's say I had a change of heart."

They continued this way, walking and talking. Time slipped away. As the hour drew near for Claudio's departure, there were several attempts at leaving, but each resulted in falling back into each other's arms. Finally, it was Alberto's appearance that forced the issue.

"You don't have to say anything, Alberto." Claudio held up his hand. He turned back to Nicla. "Let's make this quick and less painful. *Ciao, bella*. Remember. Be careful. *A Dio.*" He gave Nicla a quick, tight embrace and bolted up the stairs.

"*A Dio!*" Nicla called after him. She sat on the sofa and began to sob.

Chapter 11

It was several days before Nicla was approached by Signore Montanini. During that time her head spun trying to grasp what had transpired. It was shock enough finding Claudio in the basement and then having to let him go. She also had before her the grave new responsibility of becoming a *staffetta*. What would she be asked to do? How dangerous would it be? These questions occupied Nicla's thoughts as she went about her daily routine. The Contessa could provide no answers. She simply said that Montanini would give the details.

The day arrived when she heard his car come up the drive. Nicla's heart began to beat faster. Montanini was sitting at the kitchen table when she was called in. To Nicla, it seemed an odd place to meet a guest.

"Sit down, dear." Montanini smiled as he indicated the chair next to him. Nicla complied. Montanini continued. "I know you are aware of the nature of this meeting." His Italian was noticeably imperfect now that Nicla was cognizant of his role. "I want to be sure you know what you are getting yourself into."

"You want me to carry messages, don't you?"

"Yes."

"I know what would happen if I'm caught, Signore Montanini. I've thought it through, and I want to do it."

"Very well then. Let me tell you how you can serve the cause."

"Respectfully, Signore, I don't see how it's your cause."

Montanini recoiled slightly.

Nicla continued. "I know you want to motivate me, and we share the same goal. I appreciate that. But we Italians have a cause. You have a war to win."

Montanini sat back and nodded. "Understood." He reached in his jacket pocket and took out the cigarette case that Nicla recognized. Removing a cigarette, he tapped it on the table and lit it. "I feel I should tell you. I am an American, yes... and proud to serve my country. But I *am* Italian. Granted, Montanini is not my real name, and I was born in the US, but my parents were born here in Italy. How do you think I learned to speak Italian? It was my first language as a child."

He took out his wallet. "I want to show you something." Producing a wrinkled photo from the wallet, he leaned across the table and laid it before Nicla. It was of an elderly couple dressed in black and standing very formally. There were three children sitting and standing in front of them. "My grandparents are still here in Italy. They live an hour down the road in Grosseto."

Montanini picked the picture back up and beheld it fondly. "When we liberate Italy, I'm going to visit them." Putting the photo and wallet back in his jacket, he looked earnestly at Nicla. "I can't say I have the same feeling you do, Nicla. You lived through this misery. But defeating the Germans means more to me than you think."

"I'm sorry. I misjudged you."

"No need for an apology. I would think the same in your position. Who is this foreigner pumping me up to do his dirty work? Correct?"

"Something like that, yes. But tell me Signore. In your occupation, is it wise to have your grandparents' picture on your person? What if you are discovered?"

Montanini smiled. "There's no address. And even a Swiss art dealer has grandparents."

They both smiled. Then Montanini became serious.

"Now, regarding your role in all of this, you will continue to make your deliveries to your customers. However, you will have some new clients. They will be our civilian collaborators. There will be messages to me hidden in pockets of the clothes they give you. I may give you messages to sew in hems and deliver back. These people provide us with vital information about German activities down by the port."

"Like the message that was in that cigarette case?"

"You figured that out, didn't you? I thought you did. You are very observant." He gave Nicla a look of admiration. "I'm sorry about that. Generally, that is not our procedure - sending unsuspecting individuals to carry intelligence."

"Then why did you?"

"A few days before, we lost a girl."

"What happened to her?"

"We don't know. She was probably taken for interrogation. That's why we had to rush. We didn't know if she would lead the Germans to the tobacconist. If you ask me, they must have used some other clues to figure out the tobacconist's role. I know our girl would not have divulged it, no matter what they did to her. Oh, I'm sorry. I'm frightening you."

"It's alright. I told you I knew what I was getting into." Nicla put on a brave front, but Montanini could see she was overcompensating.

"I think you should know," Montanini added, "the Contessa knew nothing. I asked her to have the cigarette case picked up. I figured she'd send Alberto and the less they knew the better. She was very angry when she realized she'd put her grandson and you in harm's way."

Nicla's thoughts turned back to the Tobacconist being led away: *Thank God we didn't arrive at the shop a few minutes earlier when the Germans showed up.* "Tell me Signore Montanini, if Luca or I opened the case, would we have found the message?"

"Probably not. It was on pieces of paper rolled up in several cigarettes. Tobacco was stuffed at both ends. But don't worry." He waved the cigarette he was smoking. "This isn't one of them." He took a drag, making the end glow.

Nicla marveled at the lengths to which they had gone in hiding the message. The importance of the role she was assuming was becoming clearer. She looked at Montanini with steely eyes. "What can I do?"

Chapter 12

Alberto continued to drive Nicla to town in the Isotta to make her usual pickups and deliveries. Then it came time for Nicla's first rendezvous with one of Montanini's contacts. The Isotta pulled up to one of the apartment buildings that fronted the canal. It was next door to where Nicla and Luca had embarked on their excursion to *Molo Nuovo*.

Nicla sat looking at the front door. She struggled to chase from her mind the images of the Tobacconist being taken away and the civilians being hung in the square on Montenero. She turned to look at Alberto.

"Just like any other pickup," he reassured her.

She took a deep breath and nodded, searching his eyes for some courage. She turned and got out of the car. As she approached the building, she became hyper-aware of her surroundings. Everything around her reverberated with intensity. If an ant had crawled across the sidewalk, she would have heard it. She strained to get as much out of her peripheral vision without swiveling her head and looking suspicious.

As she reached for the door clapper, her heart was racing. She didn't think she could wait more than a few seconds for an answer. Thankfully, the door opened promptly. A light-haired woman in her forties, with a powerful but feminine build, stood with a puzzled look on her face. "You're new," she announced somewhat disappointed.

"Yes." Nicla was anxious to get her goods and leave but surprised at the woman's reaction. "You weren't told about me?"

"No. They don't tell us much - just times." She adjusted her tight dress with one hand. Nicla noticed that the woman's other arm, holding the door, was thick and strong. "Anyway," the woman softened a bit, "I'm sorry. I would ask your name, but I'm not supposed to."

Suddenly, the woman smiled and touched Nicla's shoulder. "Laugh like we're old friends," she ordered Nicla through a grin, "and don't turn around. There's a pair of German soldiers walking by. I'm going to nod at them." She did so, nonchalantly. "Now you can turn around toward them."

Nicla obeyed robotically.

"Look like you're mildly curious," the woman continued. "That's right. You've seen them a hundred times. Now turn right back around to me."

"Are they going?" Nicla's eyes were frozen, wide open, and she could barely breathe.

"Yes..." The woman's head did not move, but her eyes followed the soldiers up the street.

She turned her focus back to Nicla and looked at her up and down. "You're too pretty. I was worried they were going to come up and talk to you. Being conspicuous isn't good in this game. But being pretty may come in handy. You might use it to your advantage. Anyway, come in." She moved slightly away to offer Nicla space to enter. "I would have asked you in, before, but I didn't want to look like we were avoiding those soldiers."

"I really should pick up what I have to and be going. Alberto is in the car waiting." Nicla motioned.

The woman leaned back into the doorway. "*That* car? Are you *trying* to attract attention? Well..." She looked sideways at Alberto in the car window, who gave a slight bow of his head. "Alright," she concluded. "It might work. The pretty servant girl doing the rich lady's errands - that's as good a cover as any. Come in."

Her arm now locked in the woman's firm grip, Nicla had no choice. She was led to the kitchen table. Seated there was an older man who looked familiar.

"This is my father."

"*Piacere, Signorina,*" he greeted her with a knowing smile.

Nicla was trying to place him.

"You're here nice and early," he continued. "He who sleeps-"

"Does not catch fish," Nicla finished his sentence. Here was the little man she met on the canal with Luca. Only now, he was not wearing his flat cap. His bristling white hair, cut very short, made him look older.

"This time, *you* are the fish," he continued, "You will have to swim low, under the nets, so as not to be caught."

"Oh, she's swimming low alright," the daughter proclaimed with hands on her hips. "You should see the car she came in – with a chauffeur too! She might as well be on the roof of the car banging pots and pans."

Nicla gave her an icy look. "Alberto has been driving me around for months and we haven't been stopped once."

"Relax." The woman pushed Nicla's shoulder, knocking her off balance a bit.

Nicla rebounded quickly, raised her chin, and straightened her shoulders.

"I'm only joking." The woman assured. "You'll get used to me. I'm a little rough, but I'm trying to help you. We are all in this together."

The old fisherman addressed his daughter. "I believe this girl is as tough as you. The Partisans should give her a gun and take her up in the hills with them. The war would be over soon."

Nicla turned to him. "You bring in more than *fish* from the port, don't you?"

The man looked at his daughter with raised eyebrows. "She's bright, too. Isn't she, Caterina?"

"*Babbo!* My name.*"

"Don't worry. This one won't crack under interrogation. Besides, it's obvious she knows more about us than she lets on." He turned to Nicla. "I wager you remember my name too - from when you met me on the canal. Isn't that so?"

"Yes. It's Eugenio."

"Good. You're honest, too." He leaned back, putting his arms behind his head. "Tell me. What did you mean, I bring in more than just fish?"

"Well, since you go out fishing past the port every day, I thought you would notice what the Germans were doing and could report it. That's the information I'm picking up, isn't it?"

"Good thing you don't work for the Germans!" His broad face broke into a smile revealing a significant gap in his front teeth.

The daughter picked up a small pile of clothes from the table where Eugenio sat. "Here is your pickup. There are messages scrolled up and sewn into the hems of the brown pants."

Nicla grasped the clothes in her arms taking note of the brown pants. For the first time, she felt the weight of her new responsibility and an odd dichotomy. Nestled in the mundane was vital information that could turn the tide of war.

"There are rumors about a particular Partisan fighter." The old man spoke alluringly. "I believe he may be your boyfriend, Luca."

"Luca is not my boyfriend."

"Oh, sorry. You were together that day on the canal, and I thought..."

"What have you heard about him?" Nicla tried not to sound anxious.

"They call this person *la Lucertola*. The Germans can't catch him. He escapes and leaves them holding his tail. You know, like the little -"

"Lizard." Nicla interjected, recalling her brother's childhood prank. "Yes, I know what a *lucertola* is. Why do you think it's Luca?"

"Because, it is said *la Lucertola* limps." He paused, studying Nicla for a reaction. She did her best not to show one.

"That's the beautiful irony of it," he continued. "Here is a man who is lame but strikes quickly and stealthily like a *lucertola*. You know that German train car of munitions that blew up in the station last week? They say that while some Partisans drew the German guards down the track, *la Lucertola* snuck under the train car and planted the explosives."

Nicla tried to imagine Luca doing this. Recalling his impetuous dash into the tobacconist's shop, she pictured him under the train car, his hands working furiously while shots rang out in the distance. He had finally found his way of risking it all for the cause. She felt a sense of satisfaction for him. The shame and frustration he had placed on himself must be behind him. Still, she feared terribly for him.

"You'd better be going now," the daughter advised. "I don't like that limousine attracting attention in front of our place any longer." She put both her hands on Nicla's shoulders and looked in her eyes. "You can do this."

"Convince yourself they're just clothes to mend," Eugenio counseled. "If you believe it, the Germans will believe it."

As Nicla stepped out of the front door, she felt fear like she never had before. It was a frightening new world. The sensory overload she had felt approaching the building was amplified a hundredfold coming out. Now she had the evidence in her hands, which if discovered, could lead to unthinkable torture. Further, there was the awesome responsibility for the message she carried. Lives depended on it; she was sure. She walked to the car with a humming in her ear and a slight dizziness that made her feel as if she were about to faint.

"Are you alright?" asked Alberto as she sat down beside him.

Nicla looked straight ahead. "Let's get away from here."

Chapter 13

B ack in her sewing room, Nicla worked at undoing the stitches
that formed the hems of the brown pants. Her hands shook
as the edges of the scrolled papers began to show.

Taking one out, she unraveled it. It was very small. She wondered if she should read it. She might be captured and tortured to
divulge its contents. The thought terrified her. Examining it, she
was relieved at the cryptic nature of the minute writing. She could
never remember it. There were almost no words. The word *an-
coraggio* appeared in several places. There were also numbers that
were clearly hours of the day. She concluded it was information
regarding the goings on at the docks.

Soon after, Nicla found herself sitting next to the Contessa on
the sofa in the big room where they had first met. On the other
side of the coffee table, Montanini sat in an armchair.

"This is very good." He flipped through the tiny papers Nicla
had given him. "Very good, indeed." He looked up at her. "You
did well."

"Of course." The Contessa patted Nicla's knee. "Now that's
enough, George. I don't see why you should involve her further.
She's a young girl with her whole life ahead of her. This war will
be over soon enough without her."

"You're free to stop anytime," Montanini reminded Nicla. "You know that don't you?"

"Yes, I know." Nicla turned to the Contessa. "You've been like a second mother to me. I can never thank you enough. Please forgive me, but this is something I must do. I need to pay for my freedom. I want to earn it. Then I can say it's mine and no one gave it to me."

The Contessa gazed at Nicla lovingly and stroked her cheek. "I understand, dear. I wouldn't be where I am if I let life sweep me along with the current." She adjusted the shoulder on Nicla's dress. "And I never depended totally on any man - not even my beloved husband, the Count. He knew I needed freedom to... as you put it well my dear, *earn* some victories for myself. He was wonderful that way."

Nicla beamed. "*Grazzie*, Contessa. I hope I make you proud of me."

"There is no question of that, *bella*." The Contessa sat up straight as if to steel herself. "Now, let's see how Signore Montanini can help you show your mettle." She squeezed Nicla's hands and turned back to Montanini.

"I'm going to give you some additional notes, from me," Montanini began. "You are to sew them, along with the notes from the fisherman, back into the hems of the pants. I want you to take the pants and other articles of clothing to the square here on Montenero. Since it's not far, you are to walk. There's no need for the car to attract more attention than necessary. You will find two old gentlemen-"

"Sitting on a bench," Nicla interrupted.

"They're a fixture, aren't they?" Montanini rubbed his chin.

"Like the sanctuary. I've never gone there and not seen them."

"That's why we use them. It will not seem out of the ordinary. We generally don't like these sorts of public exchanges, but when I need to get information to the Partisans immediately, I turn to those two. I have no time to set up a rendezvous elsewhere."

Nicla was astounded that these old pensioners were part of the resistance. She also concluded that this was intelligence of great importance if it needed to be dispatched with such urgency. She felt her anxiety begin to grow again. "When should I leave?"

"How fast can you sew?"

Not long after her meeting with Montanini, Nicla found herself on the road to the center of Montenero. She was on foot and carried her small bundle of clothes against her body. It was the same road on which she had witnessed the townspeople propelled by German soldiers toward the square and forced to witness the hangings of the Partisan collaborators.

She had been with Luca then. Now alone, she felt that she might be walking toward her own execution. The day was so beautiful, the air light. To her flank, gaps between homes gave Nicla a view of the ocean below the mountain. She could see Molo Nuovo and recalled her outing there with Luca. Now, the ocean was calm and smooth. Its only blemish was the dark silhouette of a German supply ship making its way toward the port, purveying sustenance for the despised occupation. This instilled in Nicla some resolve, but it did not allay her fears.

Some children ran past her laughing and chasing each other. It reminded her of her little brother and her responsibility to her family. Perhaps it was selfish of her to risk her life so. If her mother only knew what Nicla was up to, she would be furious - if she could even believe it.

Seeing the children playing brought Nicla back to her own childhood. She pictured herself among them. Although they had surely known hunger and lacking, in that moment, war did not exist for them. Nicla wished she were so carefree.

Her contemplation was disturbed by a faint rumble from down the road behind her. As it increased in volume, Nicla knew it must be a German military truck. She had seen them moving everywhere about Livorno. They had flat beds, with bench seats on each side where soldiers sat facing each other. Sometimes these trucks were covered with a canvas top. Other times, they were open, exposing the minions of NAZI oppression and violence. Nicla knew well the growl of these frightful vehicles.

Stepping to the side of the road and trying to hold her gaze forward, Nicla's heart crept up into her throat. *They see so many girls walking along the road, why would I be noticeable?* She tried to calm herself.

As the truck passed, it slowed somewhat. It was of the uncovered variety. Nicla tried not to look, but she could hear the soldiers in high spirits, laughing and talking. Glancing up for a moment, Nicla saw one soldier take note of her. He turned and shouted to the driver. The truck stopped. To Nicla's horror, the soldier hopped down and stood looking straight at her.

Nicla, now in a state of mortal terror, sought to remain upright and walk on legs that felt like jelly. The soldier placed himself in her path. He was young and blond. Doffing his soft military cap, he bowed and attempted an introduction in Italian. Nicla made out only his name, Karl, and the word *signorina*. He turned and gestured gallantly toward the truck as if offering Nicla a ride. Casting her eyes downward and shaking her head, Nicla attempted to pass around him.

The soldier, having none of her evasion, swept Nicla up in his arms. She closed her eyes and gripped the clothes she carried as he swung her up into the grasp of another soldier on the truck. Karl leapt back into his place along the bench, and the receiving soldier joyfully dropped Nicla on Karl's lap. A chorus of approval rose from the soldiers. After a shout from Karl, the truck rumbled onward.

Nicla squirmed to break free, but she did not dare use her hands for fear of letting go of the clothes. Her wriggling served only to delight her company. The soldier across from her leaned forward and reached out to Nicla. Apparently he was offering to carry the clothes for her.

Nicla's recoil induced him to make a grab at the pile. His hand found the brown pants containing the messages sewn in the hem. Nicla yanked backward, but his grasp was firmly on the end of one leg.

Nicla was in a state of panic. The hem was sewn loosely to facilitate extraction of the messages. It would never hold against the tug of this brute. Her eyes gaped at the seam, frantically hoping it would not tear. She had to relinquish.

As the soldier took the pants from Nicla, she pleadingly tried to explain they were for her grandfather. The only word the soldier latched onto was *nonno* - grandfather. He stood and held the pants against his waist as if to try them on for size. Making some joke in German while bellowing "*nonno!*" he spun around for his laughing comrades. Then he tossed the pants toward the front of the truck.

Nicla dared not show her desperation. The pants made their way through several hands before being tossed back whence they came. Just as the flying garment was about to meet Karl's raised hand, the truck dropped into a large pothole. The trousers sailed out of the back of the truck.

Nicla watched in horror as the pants landed in the road and receded. She dropped the rest of her clothes and threw all her might into breaking free from Karl. She snarled and fought like a wild animal. The pants were almost out of view. She wheeled and slapped Karl in the face. Karl recoiled holding his face. A roar of laughter and satirical reproaches were directed his way. Nicla reached for the tailgate.

"*Halt!*" boomed a voice from the forward end. The truck stopped, along with all merriment. Nicla took her hand off the tailgate. A tall soldier rose from his seat and strode past the now silent men. Reaching Nicla, he put his hands on her shoulders.

"Entschuldigen Sie, Fraulein," he spoke softly as he gently maneuvered past her casting a glare at Karl. Gracefully, he hopped down from the truck and reached up for Nicla. Instinctively trusting him, she placed a hand on one of his broad shoulders and all but fell into his arms. He lowered her to her feet.

Straight away, he turned and trotted down the road to retrieve the pants. Nicla sought to compose herself. On his return, he barked up at the men in the truck. They hastily put together the scattered garments and handed them off the back of the truck to Nicla. The tall soldier completed the pile in her hands by adding the trousers, which he had done his best to fold.

A tear fell down Nicla's cheek. She looked downward, embarrassed. *"Grazzie."*

The soldier lifted her chin. *"Du bist mutig."*

Nicla was at a loss. She searched his face, which, like his words, was inscrutable to her.

He pointed to her. *"Tu,"* he managed in Italian. Then he made two fists and tapped his chest in a show of strength. *"Tu...Couragiert,"* he finished in German.

"Ah... Coraggiosa?" She pointed to herself in disbelief.

"Ja. Tu Coraggiosa." He managed with a heavy German accent.

Some derisive calls began to emanate from the truck, which the soldier quieted with a scowl. He directed his attention back to Nicla. *"Auf Wiedersehen, Fräulein."* Slowly he stepped past her, holding her gaze as he returned to the truck. He leapt aboard, and the truck pulled away.

Nicla stood watching the truck disappear over the next hill. She remained there for more than a moment. She was reeling from what had transpired. Part of her wanted to turn around and return to the villa. This was work for someone stronger. But at the same time, she was angry, and it increased her resolve to rid her homeland of this menace. She was somewhat disappointed in herself for having cried, but her tears had not been seen by her tormentors - only the kind soldier.

"Courageous," he had called her. She knew what he meant. She had held her own on that truck. She did not break down. The soldier recognized it and now she did.

She walked onward, no longer on weak legs. Her thoughts, however, turned from pride to confusion. She had hated all the German soldiers. But the kindhearted soldier challenged that. Back home in Germany, he was undoubtedly someone's Blue Prince. A girl was waiting and worrying for him as Nicla was for Claudio. Perhaps the message Nicla was delivering for the Partisans would bring about his death. It was a disturbing confluence of fates. It was not strange for war, however. She knew this.

Nicla passed the wall bearing the miniature shrine to the Madonna of Montenero. She recalled the last time she had stopped here. It was just before going to see the Contessa in search of a sewing machine. So much had happened since then. Claudio had returned and gone from her life. Luca had entered and done the same. Her father died. Still, she had not heard from her brother Vivi.

"I'm trusting you," she spoke to the Virgin with child. She thought of Mary at the foot of the cross. "Your heart was pierced. Please. Ask God to spare me such pain. Pray for me. And for what I must do. See..." She held up the pile of garments in her hands. "I have another burden. Give me the strength." She freed one hand and made the sign of the cross.

Nicla soon reached the center of Montenero. The sanctuary of the Madonna was across the square. She saw the café where she and Luca had coffee. At their usual places on a bench, were the two old gentlemen. They were dressed nicely with linen jackets and ties, and though their outfits were clean, they were noticeably worn. One of the elderly gentlemen was frail and taller than his counterpart. He had a newspaper neatly folded over his crossed leg. The shorter one sported horned rimmed glasses which were sturdy like his build. He was winding a pocket watch. Nicla looked about furtively. She approached.

"*Ah. Signorina. Buon giorno,*" greeted the shorter one, stopping mid-wind to appreciate Nicla's beauty.

"*Buon giorno,*" replied Nicla perfunctorily. She glanced about the square again.

The taller gentleman pointed to Nicla's pile of clothes. "Do you need directions for your delivery, *bella*?"

"You know she doesn't need directions around here," corrected the shorter gentleman, "This is the girl that used to drive around with Luca. Isn't that true, dear?" His face gleamed up at her in admiration.

"*Si, signore.*" Nicla spoke quickly. She didn't want to linger any longer than necessary.

The short one searched Nicla's eyes. "Those clothes are for us, aren't they?"

Nicla nodded.

"Which article holds the messages?"

"The pants," she whispered almost inaudibly. At this point, Nicla was ready to toss the clothes on their laps and walk away.

"Relax," assured the taller man, "they are just pants. That's how you must think. You are giving them to your grandfather." He nodded toward his bench mate.

"And you're her *great*-grandfather!" retorted the shorter one. "He's obviously older than me, isn't he?" He glared at the tall one. "Now, hand me the clothes and give your *nonno* a kiss. Make it look good for the German officers who just sat down at the café behind you."

German officers! A jolt coursed through Nicla's heart. She robotically did as she was told, bending to hand over the clothes and kiss the short one on the cheek. She stood back up, stiffly, worrying what the Germans behind her might have noticed.

"You old scoundrel!" exclaimed the taller one. "There are no Germans at the café! Don't you see she's already nervous? He's incorrigible, *signorina.*"

"Best to really play our parts," claimed the short one. "She should kiss her *nonno*, don't you think?

Nicla wished she could find some levity in that. But only getting back to the villa would reduce her anxiety. "I've made my delivery. I must go now, *signori*. Good day." She turned and began to walk away.

"*La Lucertola* is gaining quite a reputation around here," the short gentleman called to her.

Nicla froze and turned back. "What do you know about Luca?"

"I only know what we hear," replied the short one. "No more than you, likely. I just wanted to see if you had heard of his... as the French say...*nom de guerre?*"

"I have. And I don't care for it."

"Oh?" He tilted his head and his voice rose slightly in pitch. "You're worried for him, perhaps?"

"That's my affair."

"Good for you, dear!" Interjected the taller one. "Tell him to stop nosing into your life. The old fool lived his life already." He opened his paper and feigned reading.

"What are you talking about? I just asked a question."

"You're always prying with the young folks. Especially the *signorine*."

"*You* say that to *me*? What about the waitress?"

The tall one lowered his paper. "What waitress? You mean Teresa?"

"Ah ha!" The short one held up a finger in triumph. "You call her by name."

"What else should I call her?"

Nicla was already halfway across the square, wondering if the Partisans would get their message.

Chapter 14

Over the next several weeks, Nicla was called upon by Montanini to make several more "deliveries," as he called them. These were bundles already prepared for her. They looked like baskets of food with a towel draped across the top. Since she hadn't been asked to sew any messages into anything, she concluded there must be some important objects already hidden in the baskets. She hoped they were not weapons.

The destinations for the deliveries were buildings situated along the canal in the city. Alberto drove her in the Isotta. Invariably, she was surprised by who opened the doors to accept these conveyances. They were very average looking people. Nothing outwardly attested to their role as Partisans.

One such delivery occurred late in the day. It was to be made on Nicla's way home for the evening. Alberto pulled the Isotta up alongside a building that Nicla recognized. It was Ada's home, where Luca and Nicla had embarked on their outing to Molo Nuovo.

Nicla got out of the car and took the basket from the rear seat. "It's heavier than usual. What do you think Montanini put in here?"

"I don't know, Signorina," replied Alberto. "But don't take long. Ada likes to talk and it's close to curfew."

Nicla knew the Germans enforced the sundown curfew strictly and that Alberto had to drive past checkpoints on his way out of the city.

"I'll be right back." She smiled to reassure Alberto, who was looking somewhat on edge. She strode confidently up to Ada's door. The repetition of these drop-offs had inured her somewhat to the inherent danger. Becoming conscious of this, she felt pride. A few weeks earlier, she would have been trembling.

Ada did not answer the door when Nicla knocked. Turning to look back for Alberto, Nicla found herself face to face with a German soldier.

She gasped. Her body stiffened. The soldier sensed something in her recoil. He looked down at her basket and back at Nicla. She struggled to project nonchalance. He squinted and turned his head slightly, studying her face - too long for Nicla to bear. Finally, he motioned to her basket with the rifle still strapped over his shoulder and said something in German. Nicla's mind was spinning.

Behind the soldier, she noticed Alberto had left the car and was approaching the soldier from behind. He removed a small handgun from his chauffer's jacket and was holding it low and close to his body. Nicla knew she had to act. She put down the basket and laid one hand gently on the soldier's cheek. Placing her other hand behind his waist, she pulled him close.

The soldier smirked slightly. He moved a hand to Nicla's lower back. She tilted her head enough for her hair to fall forward and tossed it back again. Behind the soldier's back, she motioned for Alberto to desist. He replaced the gun in his jacket but kept his hand on it. The soldier put his other hand behind Nicla and pulled her tighter. He began to move his face closer to hers.

"Nicla!" It was Ada calling from her doorway. The soldier scowled and looked up. Ada had her hands on her hips. "What are you doing flirting with that soldier?"

Understanding none of Ada's admonition, the soldier barked back at her in German. Ada rejoined in equally disparaging tones. The soldier pushed Nicla aside and stepped toward Ada who began to backpedal into her apartment. The soldier advanced with deliberate steps. He was unaware that hugging the wall just inside the doorway was a man with a rifle pointed at the height of an average man's head.

As the soldier reached the door, the sound of a motorcycle racing down the street caused him to whirl about. Nicla turned also. It was a sidecar cycle. It stopped in front of Ada's home. The driver was the soldier who had slapped Nicla when they took her sewing machine. She turned her back in horror so as not to offer him the opportunity to recognize her.

Clearly, the soldier's penchant for looting remained. An entire leg of prosciutto was strapped across the sidecar. His comrade at Ada's door turned to approach the motorcycle. As he passed Nicla, he stopped and squatted next to the basket. Nicla held her breath. He pulled back the cloth cover and placed his hand in the basket. Alberto's hand tightened on the pistol in his jacket.

"Ah!" he exclaimed raising his eyebrows and glancing up at Nicla. "*Was ist das?*" Slowly, he pulled his hand out of the basket and held up a large wedge of Parmesan cheese. Reaching in with his other hand, he removed a loaf of bread and stood up. Alternating, he held each to his nose and savored their aroma.

"*Danke, Fraulein!*" He waived his newfound gastronomic gems at Nicla and hopped into the sidecar. The tandem sped off leaving a cloud of fumes.

No one moved for several seconds. Nicla looked at Ada in the doorway and then to Alberto. Finally, she threw herself to her knees by the basket and peered inside. There was only bread and cheese. She was baffled. Gazing blankly at the remaining edibles, she became aware of a second cloth beneath them.

She moved some of the food over and pulled back the fabric. The bottom of the basket was lined with bundles of explosives wrapped in plastic. She looked up at Alberto. He shook his head. She turned back to look at Ada in the doorway, but she was no longer there. Several feet back into the house a dark figure holding a rifle looked back at Nicla. It was Luca.

Nicla nearly blurted out his name, but Luca raised a finger to his lips. She jumped to her feet and started for the door. Catching herself, she wheeled around and picked up the basket. It seemed to weigh much less now as she turned excitedly for the door. Flying through the entrance, she did not grasp the risk she took in tossing the basket to the floor. She was ecstatic.

"Luca!" She threw her arms around him. "Thank God you're alright." She put all her strength into her grip, as if he were about to vanish from among them again. When she became conscious of the others in the room, she stepped back and regained her composure. "Your grandmother is all but sick worrying about you!"

"Just *Nonna*?" He tilted his head.

"Well... all of us. You know. Alberto is not the same since you left."

"Alberto?" The realization sent Luca abruptly toward the door. Opening it, but staying back in the shadows of the apartment, Luca beckoned Alberto.

Standing by the Isotta, Alberto looked up and down the street and walked briskly to the door. "*Signore!*" His face shone as he reached for Luca's hand. He shook it with both of his. Luca's face beamed as he added his other hand as well.

Nicla was surprised. This display of warmth was a minor, but touching, breach of decorum she had never witnessed between them. Sadly, she had no time to take pleasure in it. She would have enjoyed teasing them about it at another time.

"Luca," she interrupted firmly, "what are you going to do with whatever that is in that basket?"

Letting go of Alberto's hands, Luca turned and stepped toward Nicla. The smile left his face and he spoke flatly, "The explosives? I'm going to add them to the pile already in the little boat on the canal. You remember the boat we took out to Molo Nuovo?"

"What?" Her face was twisted in disbelief. She turned to Alberto. He was equally dumbfounded.

"I'm going to float it down the canal, right up to that supply ship in the harbor, and blow a hole in it." He looked about for a reaction. All were nonplussed, save for Ada, who apparently knew about the plan. "You all don't seem to have much flair for the dramatic."

"This is crazy." Nicla had a hand to her forehead. "You'll be killed before you get near it."

I won't have to get too near the ship. The explosives are wrapped and waterproof. Once I get out in the harbor, I get out of the boat and swim up to the ship." He pantomimed a few one-handed strokes. "I attach the charges to the hull, set the fuse, and swim away. They'll never know I was there."

"You won't even get to the harbor." Nicla was shaking her head. "How will you get past the guards on the last bridge over the canal?"

Luca face lit up with surprise. "You remember them, don't you? That one bastard pointed a gun right at you. Don't worry, your boyfriend has that covered."

"Claudio? What are you talking about?"

"Yes. Your Claudio, along with a few other Partisans. They're going to divert the guards from the bridge. I have to give him credit. His part is probably more dangerous than mine."

"Oh no. No." Nicla felt lightheaded. This was beyond belief for her. "You're all going to get killed." She desperately grasped for some reason with which to dissuade him. "It won't work. There are a hundred ways it can go wrong. Even if it did work... what if you kill some Germans? They'll execute one civilian for every one you kill. You know that."

"Not likely. At the waterline, the blast will just flood the cargo hold. The small crew will calmly abandon ship. It will be disabled, maybe even list into the channel and block other ships. Some spoiled weinersnitchel, but no one killed."

"But why? The Americans will be here soon enough. It's inevitable. They're already past Rome. What difference will one supply ship make? Is it worth your lives?

"If we stop one bullet in the hold of that ship from reaching the barrel of a German gun, that would be enough. Maybe we'll save your brother from that bullet."

Nicla was taken aback by the mention of her brother, Vivi. All of this was racing through her mind and happening too fast. She turned to Alberto. "Talk some sense into him, Alberto. Please!"

"*Signore*," Alberto addressed Luca in a calm tone.

Luca held up his hand and walked over to him. He placed it on Alberto's shoulder. "Alberto, you are the man who taught me to ride a bike when I was small. Then you taught me to shoot and hunt... to train the dogs... and drive a car." He squeezed Alberto's shoulder. "You've been like a father to me."

"*Signore*."

"Not *signore*. I want you to call me Luca. At least here - now. And I want you to give me your support for what I'm about to do."

Alberto gazed for some time upon the brave man whom he had practically raised from a boy. "Yes, Luca," he choked out solemnly. "You have my support. Just as you always had."

"Alberto! Have you gone mad too?" Nicla shouted. "Does anyone see the insanity in this?"

"You're forgetting," Luca held up a finger. "I am *la Lucertola*. I always get away." He ran his fingers like a scampering lizard.

"Yes. I know." Nicla acknowledged, "We are all proud of you. But how many lives does a *lucertola* have?"

"I don't know about lives, but the *lucertola* can leave a few tails behind before it's done." Luca paused and looked down at his leg. "Maybe I could leave this leg behind." He tapped it. "I'd like to grow a new one that works a bit better."

Nicla was on the verge of tears. "What about Claudio? Please. Call it off for him. For me!"

"Yes, Claudio," Luca mused, a hand on his chin. "Don't worry about him. He can handle himself. I must admit that. I've seen him in action. He'll be fine and back to you soon. Besides, it's too late to call it off. He's going to be there by the bridge at nightfall. And speaking of the time, you better be going. You and Alberto need to be off the streets by curfew. And we all need to be out of Ada's house." He turned and smiled at her. "Now," he held out his hands to Nicla, "come here and wish me luck."

Nicla rushed over and buried her cheek against Luca's chest. He leaned down and whispered in her ear, "I should have kissed you at Molo Nuovo."

Nicla looked up with tears in her eyes. She whispered back, "Someday, you will be someone's Blue Prince. *A Dio*," she commended him to God's protection and turned away.

Chapter 15

The ride to Zio Fiore's house was quiet. Nicla and Alberto were lost in thought. Each feared for their loved ones, and neither wished to burden the other with doubt.

Alberto pulled the Isotta in front of Zio Fiore's garage. They sat in silence for a few moments. "What will become of them?" Nicla asked gazing straight ahead.

Alberto turned to her. "Luca is very resourceful. He will find a way back. I know it."

"And Claudio?"

"I don't know your boyfriend." Alberto looked forward again. "From what I saw of him in the basement at the villa, he struck me as someone strong and determined – like Luca." Alberto paused for a moment. "Your Claudio also has a powerful reason to survive. They both do. Hold onto that, *Signorina*."

Alberto drove away and Nicla entered the small house next to Zio Fiore's garage. Her little brother and Zio Fiore were at a table set for four but sized for two. Her mother Silvia was at the stove.

"You're just in time, *Bellina*," her mother announced, stirring a sweet-smelling preparation in a large frying pan. "I'm making *la francesina*."

The aroma of sauteing onions, tomatoes, and olive oil came sizzling up from the pan. They were infusing their flavors into some shredded beef. *La francesina* was one of Nicla's favorite dishes and it is unique to Livorno.

"The butcher traded me a beef shin for some sewing I did for his wife." Silvia shook the pan by the handle. "First, I boiled the meat nice and slow, all afternoon. It's so tender, it fell apart with the fork." She began to stir in some scrambled eggs. "It's almost ready."

"That's wonderful, *Mamma*," Nicla stated dutifully but absently, sitting down to the table. Silvia and Fiore looked at each other.

"Nicla, are you alright?" asked her uncle.

"Oh," Nicla started and tried to affect some normalcy in her tone. "I'm just a little tired."

"Are they working you too hard up at the Contessa's?" asked Silvia as she ladled the *francesina* onto each dish around the table. She barely had to lean, the table being so small. She kept her eyes on Nicla.

"No, *Mamma*. The Contessa is very good to me." Nicla turned to her brother and struggled for something to say. "Matteo, are you going to gather some more mussels at the reef tomorrow?"

"I just brought home *datteri* two days ago." He looked up momentarily from his voracious endeavors. "I'll catch some fish down by the docks. Mamma can make *cacciucco*." He wiped up some sauce and onions with a torn piece of bread. "Right Mamma?"

Fiore's eyes lit up at the mention of the renowned Tuscan fish stew. "Ah, *cacciucco*! As much as I look forward to that, you watch out down by the dock, Matteo," he pointed a fork at his young nephew. "It's thick with Germans." He scooped up a large dollop of *francesina*. "They don't like people getting close to their ships. And they don't give warnings before they shoot."

"Enough! Please!" Nicla bolted from the table and ran into the bedroom, shutting the door behind her.

Zio Fiore sat aghast, a forkful of francesina held before his open mouth. Silvia dropped the cooking spoon in the pan and followed her daughter. Matteo continued eating.

Silvia entered the small room which had been the bedroom of Fiore and his late wife. Since moving in with Fiore, Silvia shared the bed with Nicla. Matteo slept on a makeshift mattress on the floor. Fiore slept in the garage.

"*Bella di Mamma*," Silvia spoke softly to Nicla who lay face-down on the bed, crying in her pillow, "tell me. What is it?" She sat on the edge of the bed and placed her hand gently on Nicla's back.

"It's too terrible, Mother."

"Is someone hurt? It's not Vivi!" She grabbed Nicla's shoulders and wheeled her around.

"No! This has nothing to do with Vivi." Nicla saw the dread in her mother's eyes. "It's not Vivi." She squeezed her mother's arms.

"*Grazzie a Dio.*" Silvia made the sign of the cross. "Until your brother comes home, I die every time someone starts to tell me some news." She took a deep breath and exhaled. "Now. Tell me what is troubling you, *figlia mia.*"

Nicla sat all the way up. "It's Claudio. He's in terrible danger, Mamma. He's out there now, on a mission that could get him killed. I can't do anything about it, and I can't take it."

"How do you know about it? And how could you even do anything about it?"

Nicla realized she was on the verge of telling her mother about her role as a *staffetta*. There was no keeping it from her any longer. She spent the next hour telling Silvia everything – *Signore Montanini*, the deliveries, even the encounter with the German soldiers on the truck. Mostly, Silvia listened in utter astonishment. Finally, Nicla recounted the details of that night's mission.

"All this time..." Silvia hung her head. "I knew nothing. All you were going through, and I couldn't help you." She stroked Nicla's hair. "Mamma is here now."

Nicla hugged her tightly. She could now confide in someone who would understand her anguish. Silvia knew the pain of losing the love of her life and she knew Nicla's heart.

"How will I get through tonight Mamma?"

"Come. Let's go to bed. We'll get through it together." Silvia helped Nicla out of her clothes like she did when Nicla was a little girl. Nicla got into bed and her mother sat next to her. "Do you remember when you were little and I would put you to bed, I always put my ear against your chest?"

"Yes."

"Do you know why I did that?"

"You were listening to my heart."

"Yes. And do you know why? It's a miracle. Every beat, one after the other, tun-tun, tun-tun." She put her hand over Nicla's heart. "God keeps it going every second... minute after minute... day after day. No matter how much I took it for granted or was busy with silly things, He was there inside you, keeping my precious one alive with every beat. I was so grateful for each little tun-tun. When I was listening, you didn't know it, but I thanked God with such appreciation, it was beyond words. Someday, you will see - when you are a mother."

"That's very beautiful, Mamma. I do think of motherhood sometimes. I imagine making a family with Claudio. But right now, all I can think of is him out there in danger." Nicla began to rise again.

"I know." Silvia guided Nicla back down by her shoulders. "Listen. Remember when I would tell you stories to help you go to sleep?"

"Mamma, I'm sorry but-"

"Shh. Roll over." Silvia pushed Nicla over on her side and began to rub her back. "You remember the story of Buchettino?" Immediately, albeit reluctantly, Nicla was brought back to her childhood. As a little girl, she had been fascinated by the fable of the boy, Buchettino, who outwitted the ogre trying to catch and eat him.

"Mamma, please. I-"

"*Buchettino, Buchettino, dammi un fichino*," Silvia rhymed. "Buchettino, Buchettino, give me a fig." This was the ogre's entreaty to Buchettino who sat safely in a tree. The monster hoped to trick Buchettino into extending his hand so he could latch onto it. But Buchettino would only *throw* a fig down on the ground. So, the ogre would repeat his rhyming plea.

Nicla wanted to tell her mother that, as beautiful as this memory was, it would not assuage her anxiety for Claudio. But she could not. So sincere and touching was this loving gesture by her mother, that Nicla was moved to indulge her.

In Nicla's surrender, she allowed her mind to wander to the top of the tree with Buchettino. When Silvia reached the part of the tale where Buchettino fell for the Ogre's ruse, Nicla's eyes were beginning to close. She fought to stay awake. She wanted to hear her mother's voice like she heard it as a child. "Now I've got you!" Silvia spoke in the menacing tone of the ogre. Nicla felt again the wonder of childhood. But exhaustion from the day's events overtook her. She let go and drifted into a deep slumber.

Time passed as it does without awareness beyond the wall of sleep. Nicla did not hear her mother recount how the Ogre prepared the cauldron in which he would make Buchettino into his meal. Or how the boy cut his way out of the sack and replaced his body with some stones. Nor the ogre's rage at pulling a wet bag of stones from the kettle.

Nicla awoke with a start. It was daylight. She leapt out of bed and ran to the kitchen. She was shocked to find Alberto at the table being served by her mother.

"Alberto! What time is it? Have you heard anything?" She couldn't speak fast enough.

"*Buon giorno, Signorina*. I came to pick you up, but your mother came out to the car and told me you were still sleeping. She thought it best not to wake you."

"I asked him to come in," added Silvia. "Do you believe he brought coffee?" She held up a bag. "When was the last time we saw coffee?"

"I anticipated you would have trouble sleeping last night," Alberto explained, "so I came prepared." He held up his coffee cup.

Silvia cleared her throat to attract Nicla's attention while looking her up and down demonstratively.

"Oh." Nicla looked down at her nightgown. "I'll be right out." She turned to run for the bedroom. "Get the car ready! You have to tell me any news you've heard!" She disappeared into the room.

Chapter 16

N icla hopped breathlessly onto the front seat of the Isotta and closed the door. She turned to Alberto at the wheel. "What happened? Are they alright?" She almost shook him.

"*Signorina*. I know nothing. I spent the night at the villa and came here straight away."

"Let's drive into town! People must have heard something." Nicla bordered on desperation.

"So," came a voice from the backseat, "you *are* worried about me,"

"Luca!" Nicla wheeled around.

Luca was lounging with both arms stretched out along the top of the backseat. His legs were crossed, and he was barefoot. He was still damp from his mission at the harbor.

"Signore!" Alberto could not maintain his stoic affect. He spun to marvel at the apparition in the rear seat.

"Thank God!" Nicla was giddy. "Are you alright? Your feet! But how?"

"Let's see. Where do I start?" Luca stroked his chin. "The feet?" He held one foot out. "Not very proper for the son of a Contessa, eh Alberto? I had to take the shoes off. You can't stand on ceremony when you're trying to swim away from explosives on a relatively short fuse. Great way to drown before you even see your handywork take effect. Oh! And the explosion. You should have seen it. Boom!" He threw his hands in the air. "It was a sight. I had to turn and look even though I hadn't reached shore yet." He was leaning on the front seat, eye to eye with Nicla now.

"What about Claudio?" she asked anxiously.

Luca sat back and looked out the window. "A day ago, I might have been annoyed at that question. But Claudio is a good man."

"Is he alright?" Nicla's voice rose.

"I don't know. He and whoever else he was with, put up a hell of a fight with the guards on the bridge. I heard the shots trailing off into the city. He led those guards away so I could pass. I owe him my life."

"You don't know what happened to him?"

"No. He may be fine. The guards wouldn't have followed him too far away from the bridge. They would have to get back to their watch. When I get back with my brigade, I'll find out about him and get word to you through Montanini.

"Signore." Alberto was looking in the mirror having regained his professional comportment. "With regard to getting back, shouldn't we proceed immediately? I imagine the German's will be looking for the saboteur who damaged their ship."

"I suppose you're right, Alberto." Luca grinned unable to mask his pride.

"What if they set up checkpoints?" asked Nicla. "Would you be safer on foot, off the road?"

"I walked far enough from the port. I'm not walking all the way to Montenero. Here." Luca held up a blanket. "Fiore gave this to me."

"Zio Fiore?"

Luca chuckled. "Yes. Where do you think I slept for a couple of hours this morning? The garage is actually quite comfortable. Anyway," he shook the blanket, "if we see a checkpoint, I'll lie down on the floor back here, and you make sure I'm covered well."

"A blanket?" Nicla noted warily. "That's all that's between us and the hangman?"

Luca stroked his chin. He cast his eyes downward and nodded. "You're right. I shouldn't have. I've put you both in danger." He gazed out the window. "I wanted to impress you. I wanted to see you. It was selfish. I'm sorry." He reached for the door handle. "I'll find another way back to Montenero."

"Wait." Nicla grabbed his arm. "I have an idea."

The Isotta slowed down as it approached the temporary checkpoint. Two German soldiers with automatic weapons stood beside a motorcycle and sidecar. One soldier held his rifle at the ready while the other, with his weapon strapped over his shoulder, approached the car. Leaning in at the window, he looked over the driver and the couple in the back seat.

The soldier thought it suspicious that a young man would be the driver. Young Italian men were almost all in the military. But Luca was wearing Alberto's uniform and cap. He was also clean shaven – not a look the German would expect from the rugged Partisans hiding in the hills of Montenero.

"*Identificazione,*" the soldier demanded gruffly in Italian.

Luca reached in Alberto's jacket and pulled out a flimsy paper license. The soldier looked it over, then glared at Luca. Everyone in the car held their breath.

"*Nome?*" the soldier inquired.

"Conti, Viviliano," Luca replied.

The soldier checked his reply against the license. Luca hoped he looked close enough in age to Nicla's older brother, Vivi, whose birthdate was on the license.

The soldier peered in the back at Alberto and Nicla. They sat close together, holding hands. Alberto was wearing *Zio* Fiore's only suit. The soldier studied them. Nicla hoped they passed for father and daughter. She smiled, but inside she trembled. Alberto could feel her hand shake. The soldier asked something in German which neither understood. He waited for a reply, holding their gaze for what seemed an eternity. Finally, he spoke.

"*Continua,*" he ordered, handing back the license and motioning for his partner to let the car pass.

As they drove past the soldiers, Nicla squeezed Alberto's hand and looked straight ahead. Alberto took a handkerchief from Fiore's jacket and wiped his brow.

Luca watched in the mirror until they were far enough away. "That was a nice touch, having me shave. And when your brother gets back, thank him for the use of his license."

"If the Partisans carried identification, he would have his papers with him, and you would have been out of luck," Nicla noted.

"If the Partisan's carried identification, I would have had my *own* papers with me."

"They would have been soggy from your swim. Good luck explaining that." Nicla folded her arms triumphantly.

Luca accepted defeat and continued driving back to Montenero.

At the villa there was much rejoicing and many happy tears shed by the Contessa on the return of her grandson. She sat at the kitchen table with Nicla and him. Luca still wore Alberto's uniform. Alberto was at the stove, preparing an asparagus frittata. On Luca's admonition, neither Nicla nor Alberto was to mention his clandestine mission of the previous night.

"I still can't believe it," remarked the Contessa. "All this time, you left me here to worry."

"Forgive me, *Nonna.*" Luca stroked her arm across the table. "But with the Partisans, I finally felt I was doing something useful, instead of hunting and racing my car."

"Keeping me company isn't useful?" The Contessa held her hand to her chest. "Yes. You're right," she conceded. "This is no place for a strong young man whose country is occupied by pestilence."

"Thank you, *Nonna*. I knew you would understand."

"Then again," the Contessa's voice brightened, "There were other reasons to stay around the villa." She turned and lightly pushed the hair off Nicla's shoulder.

Nicla smiled demurely and cast her eyes downward.

"*La frittata di asparagi*," announced Alberto, still wearing Fiore's suit. He laid the dish of diced asparagus and eggs before Luca. A bit of stray olive oil, imbued golden-green from the asparagus, waited to be captured by a crust of bread.

"Beautiful, Alberto!" Luca set into the frittata with gusto.

"Ah. Now we're back to our happy life," concluded the Contessa. "And I heard the Little Flower on the radio say it won't be long before the Americans reach us."

The Contessa was referring to Fiorello La Guardia, the mayor of New York, whose weekly shortwave radio broadcasts, spoken in Italian, gave encouragement to the Italian people. His name, Fiorello, means little flower.

"The Americans! I'd better get ready to greet them." Luca rose from his seat. "And Alberto will be wanting this back." He ran his hands over the chauffeur's uniform. "Excuse me." He nodded to all.

The Contessa sighed and watched Luca walk away. She was trying to soak up every second of his presence. When he was finally out of the room, she turned to Nicla. "It's wonderful, isn't it, my dear?" The Contessa sipped her coffee.

"Yes, Contessa." Nicla's coffee remained untouched. She was preoccupied with Claudio's survival the night before.

"Listen, *Tesoro mio*," the Contessa began. "I have some clothes to be washed, especially that light-rose gown. You know, the one with the sash. The Duke is coming next week. And remember.

Don't stare at his nose." She held a finger up to her nose and winked.

"Yes, Contessa." Nicla gave a slight bow and walked out.

In the back of the Villa, Nicla stood behind a stone shed. She was washing clothes in a large porcelain sink affixed to the back wall. A washboard was hooked over the rim.

As she rotely slogged the wet garments against the corrugated metal, Nicla thought of Claudio. She imagined him near the bridge, shooting at the Germans and retreating down the street. She imagined the soldiers firing on him. Did he make it? Was he wounded and made a prisoner? Or worse?

As she struggled to resist thoughts of harsher fates, she heard a rumbling coming up the drive. She let the clothes slide into the sudsy water and stepped around the shed to see.

Two German trucks and a staff car were growling their way toward the main house. Nicla recoiled in shock and ducked back behind the shed. Her heart pounded. She peered around the corner. A group of soldiers jumped down from the trucks and trotted toward the front of the house, rifles in hand.

Nicla could not see the front door to the house from her vantage point. She heard shouts from the soldiers. Two officers walked up to the house.

Nicla's mind was in a whirl. Had someone divulged the details of the sabotage mission? Part of her wanted to run, but she couldn't. Luca was in there. She remained with her nose against the wall of the shed and one eye peering around the corner.

After ten long minutes, the soldiers reappeared carrying pieces of art toward the trucks. *The secret cache!* Nicla thought. *They came for that. It's not about the sabotage.*

Nicla watched as statues, rolled-up tapestries and large framed paintings were carried between pairs of soldiers and placed in the trucks. Her thoughts turned to Luca, Alberto, and the Contessa. What would be the consequence for harboring these goods? She prayed for their safety and waited.

Finally, the Contessa emerged flanked by the two German officers. She was escorted to their car. On the way, she would turn and gesture toward the house while saying something to the officers. It was clear to Nicla that she was pleading for Luca and Alberto. The officers paid her no heed. They were firm, but not rough. They showed her some of the deference one would expect from "gentlemen" officers toward a lady of noble birth, stopping to allow her to finish her exclamations, before moving her along. After being placed in the car, she alternated between dejection and renewed protests. The officers sat unmoved.

Nicla held her position. Four of the soldiers, done foisting the artwork onto the trucks, hopped onboard. Nicla waited in dread for the last two soldiers to come out. She was certain Luca and Alberto had been found. At this point, the best she could hope for was they would be escorted to the trucks as prisoners.

The rear door of the house opened. Luca stepped out. Behind him followed one of the soldiers. He was pointing a rifle at Luca's back. Nicla's breath left her. Reflexively, she ducked behind the shed. Collecting herself, she peered around the corner again, this time ducking lower.

To her horror, Alberto was being escorted in similar fashion by the other soldier. Looking at their faces, Nicla felt a terrible foreboding. They bore the resigned look that Nicla had seen on the citizens being hung in the square.

The soldiers stepped back and barked something at the men. Luca and Alberto stood side by side and faced the Germans. The soldiers had their backs to Nicla. They raised their rifles.

Nicla reached out toward Luca from behind the shed. Luca caught sight of her and quickly, almost imperceptibly, shook his head and looked away. Nicla pulled her hand back and covered her mouth. The soldiers raised their guns. Luca stood tall and put out his chest. He looked back at Nicla, held his chin up and smiled.

"*Feuern!*" shouted one of the soldiers.

Nicla threw herself behind the shed and covered her ears. It was too late. The peal of gunshots had already pierced her soul. This could not be happening. It was beyond her comprehension. She was numb. Instinctively, she began running away from the nightmare toward the rear of the estate, keeping the shed between her and the soldiers.

Blindly, she scraped through some hedges, tumbled down a hill, and found herself on all fours in a small meadow. She turned to see if the soldiers had followed. There was nothing. Still, she wanted to get out of this open space for fear of being spotted.

Off a way, she spied a villa that belonged to wealthy Jews. It had been confiscated by the Germans. The estate was now frequented by NAZI officers when they entertained. Rumor had it that some officers had even taken quarters there. She needed to get off the grounds undetected as quickly as possible.

Moving along the periphery, she made for a stable at the far corner of the property. As she came around to the front of the stable, she was confronted by a boy of about fourteen. He was standing in the arched doorway holding the reign of a beautiful, black stallion.

"What are you doing here?" he asked as he stroked the horse. Nicla's sudden appearance had startled it.

"Are there any Germans here?" she whispered.

"Yes. There are some soldiers in the house right now. I saw them go in with girls about an hour ago."

"Are there any outside?" Nicla tried to look beyond the stable.

"I don't think so. But a colonel is coming to ride this horse." The boy patted the stallion's shiny black coat. "He comes every week at this time. I get the horse ready for him, but I live over there, behind those bushes." He pointed beyond a hedgerow.

"Who do you live with?"

"My grandfather. He's the caretaker."

"Does he get along with the Germans?"

"No. The people that lived here were good to us. When the Germans took them away, *Nonno* said the Germans were devils... and some bad words I can't repeat because you are a lady."

Nicla stroked his hair. "Bless you." She kissed his cheek. Turning, she headed quickly for the grandfather's house.

"Stick around!" the boy called out. "I don't think the soldiers know the general is coming. It should get interesting!"

Nicla was already squeezing through the hedges.

Emerging from the bushes, she saw a small house with white-washed walls of rough stucco and a red clay roof. A man in his sixties, carrying a large watering can, was providing relief to some tomato plants in the bright sun. He wore a low-cut, tank shirt. White chest hairs climbed out at the neckline. He looked up, still bent in mid pour. Nicla was almost upon him.

"*Salve, Signore,*" she saluted him in a hushed voice.

The man stood up straight, startled but composed. "*Si, Signorina?*"

"Can you help me? I need to get back into the city."

"Are you alright?" He looked her up and down. The hem of Nicla's dress was torn and trailing on the ground. Bits of grass poked from her hair.

"Yes. I'm alright." Nicla looked back over her shoulder. "Please, can you drive me in your truck?" She motioned toward a small, flatbed pickup parked beside the house.

The man put down his watering can. "*Andiamo -* Let's go."

The little truck wound its way down through the narrow mountain roads of Montenero toward the city of Livorno. Nicla sat staring straight ahead. She hadn't said a word since entering the vehicle.

"*Mi chiamo,* Piero," the old man at the wheel introduced himself.

Nicla's eyes were fixed on some distant point. She was still numb from what had transpired minutes ago.

"*Signorina?*"

"Oh," Nicla started. "*Scuzi. Mi chiamo*, Nicla." She struggled to be cordial.

"What's wrong, *Signorina*? How can I help you?"

Piero's kindness cut through Nicla's stupor and unlocked her emotions. She burst into deep, choking sobs. He pulled the truck to the side of the road.

"It's alright," he consoled. "You cry." He lifted himself a bit to remove a handkerchief from his back pocket and offer it to Nicla. She took it in her hands, dropped her head into it and cried uncontrollably. Eventually, she caught her breath enough to thank him.

"I'm sorry, *signore*." She wiped her face and looked at him with pleading eyes. "How could it be real?"

"What is it, Signorina? What happened to you?"

Nicla thought for a moment. This man was clearly no German sympathizer. So, she began to recount her ordeal. The story was interrupted several times by Nicla falling back into crying. It was also interrupted by more than one honking car horn, as disgruntled drivers sought to pass the standing truck on the tight road.

"Have you no compassion!" Piero called out the window at one car.

The driver hurled an epithet.

"The rocks underwater know not the pain of the rocks in the sun," Piero mumbled. "We better get moving." He pulled the truck back onto the road and began driving. "Go on. Tell me more."

Nicla continued. When she mentioned being in the employ of the Contessa, Piero interrupted, "You worked for the Contessa?"

"Yes. I was her seamstress. I also did housework for her."

Piero took his focus off the road and turned to Nicla. He held her gaze for a moment. "Please, continue."

Nicla was thrown off by Piero's reaction, but she resumed her tale. When she told of Luca and Alberto's execution, Piero blurted, "My God! Is Luisa alright?"

"Luisa?" She stared at Piero incredulously. "Luisa hasn't worked at the villa for a long time."

"How long?"

"I don't know for sure... maybe a few months. She left before I was hired."

"Do you know where she is now?"

"No." Nicla was not lying. She didn't know where Luisa was. Something told her not to mention seeing Luisa in the car with the German officer. She needed to know more about this man driving the truck. "How do you know, Luisa?"

Piero kept his eyes on the road. "She's my daughter."

Nicla was astonished. "Your daughter? Why isn't she staying with you?" Immediately, Nicla wished she hadn't said that. "I'm sorry. That's not my business."

"No. You were right to ask. That is an excellent question. I deserve it."

They were rounding a bend that offered a spectacular vista of the ocean below. Piero gazed on it. "Luisa loved the ocean when she was a little girl. I would take her to the reef. She would swim and I would fish." He smiled faintly. "She had a little pink bathing suit. I called her *mia pesciolina* – my little minnow."

He reached forward and pulled a small, crinkled photo from its nook on the dashboard. He handed it to Nicla. A little girl stood on the rocks by the sea with her arms curled trying to show off her muscles. Her skinny body betrayed her.

Nicla was fascinated to see Luisa as a little girl. She saw herself in the picture. Their lives had taken such disparate trajectories. "I want to know about Luisa," she inquired.

Piero thought for a moment. "It's hard for me to talk about what happened with her."

"Please."

"Very well." He took a deep breath. "When Luisa was sixteen, she got pregnant by some boy I never met. If I knew who he was, I would have killed him." Piero made a fist. "So, what did I do? I sent Luisa to live with the nuns. I threw her out." He brought his fist down on the steering wheel. "My own daughter. I threw her out."

Nicla could see tears in Piero's eyes. She considered letting it go at that, but she had to know more. "What about Luisa's mother?"

"Maria? She tried hard to stop me. But I was young and proud... and stupid. I thought honor was everything. I didn't want shame on our family. You know something..." He shook his head. "I never told her that I took Luisa to the nuns." His voice broke slightly. "Maria never forgave me."

"What happened to Luisa?"

"After the baby was born, Luisa ran away from the convent. About a year later she came looking for her mother. But she was dead. The influenza took her." Piero's lip began to tremble. He put his hand over his mouth. He struggled to compose himself, then continued. "When Luisa found out her mother was dead, she blamed me. She said her mother died of a broken heart - that I killed her."

"Oh my God. How awful."

"Yes. It was." Piero took a hand off the wheel to wipe a tear from his eye. "I begged Luisa to stay with me. But she told me I betrayed her, and I wasn't her father anymore. So, she left."

Nicla sat thinking of Luisa's story. Compelling as it was, she couldn't believe it had taken her mind off the nightmare she had just witnessed at the Villa. Still, something else about Luisa's story needed to be settled in her mind.

"Is the stable boy Luisa's son?"

Piero turned to her. "You met him?"

"Just before I saw you. I came from the stable."

Piero looked ahead, far down the road. "Yes. Alessandro is her son."

Nicla was baffled. "How did he end up with you?"

"I was all alone after Maria died. Then the Germans came. I lost my job in the city and moved up to Montenero to become caretaker of that villa. I lost myself in my work, weeding and cutting grass, but I was still alone... with my memories... my guilt. So, I went back to the nuns and found Alessandro. I raised him."

"Didn't Luisa know you had him?"

"No. I don't think so. I didn't see her for years. I didn't know where she was. Then, one day, a few months ago, when I was trimming the bushes near the Contessa's property, I saw her hanging out clothes. I wanted so bad to run to her and beg forgiveness. But I was too ashamed to let her see me. I haven't seen her since."

"You still want to see her, don't you?"

"Of course! I've changed so much. I learned what's important in life. Raising Alessandro taught me that. I have a lot to make up to Luisa." Piero's voice turned mournful. "Now, who knows where she is. It's probably too late."

Nicla was still holding the photo of Luisa. She handed it to Piero. "God gives second chances. I believe you'll see her again."

Chapter 17

The next day, Nicla was on the bus to Montenero. She had to find the two old men on the bench. They were her only connection to the Partisans. Perhaps they could get information on Claudio.

She felt safe enough. The Germans had clearly come to the villa for the artwork. If they had come investigating the sabotage, surely they would have taken Luca for questioning. Alberto and he were just accomplices in concealing the art and therefore dispensable.

When she reached the square on Montenero, the two seniors were at their usual post. A checkerboard lay on the bench between them. They were engrossed in their match.

"King me!" exclaimed the shorter one.

His taller counterpart obliged. "Fine, but it won't help you."

"It's only a matter of time."

Nicla cleared her throat. The two gentlemen looked up. "Ah, *Signorina*," exclaimed the stout one. "What a pleasant surprise. *Boun giorno*"

"*Buon giorno*," Nicla replied flatly.

"Did we miss some instructions from Montanini?" asked the taller one. "We weren't expecting you. Do you have a message for us?"

"No. I have questions. Are you aware of what happened to *la Lucertola* yesterday?"

The men looked at each other, then back at Nicla and shook their heads. Nicla was half-expecting this. She was probably the only Italian besides the Contessa who knew.

"He was shot by the Germans behind the villa. I was there. I saw."

The men were visibly shaken.

"How? What was he doing at the villa?" asked the stout one.

Nicla informed them of the nighttime mission and Luca's return to the villa.

"We will get word about this to the Partisans," assured the lanky gentleman. "In the meantime, we should keep this to ourselves. It will be a blow to the general morale if it became known that *la Lucertola* was killed."

"Can you find out about my boyfriend?" Nicla interjected. "His name is Claudio Frontieri. He fought the sentries on the bridge so Luca could pass on the canal."

"How do you know all these details?" asked the squat fellow.

"I delivered the explosives."

The two pensioners were staggered. Nicla saw the awe in their look. But she had no time for pride. All she cared about was getting news on Claudio.

"We will do our best to find out about Claudio for you," offered the shorter one.

"Yes," concurred his bench-mate emphatically. "Give us a few days."

After two anxious days, Nicla returned to Montenero to seek news on Claudio. As she crossed the square, the two old men caught sight of her. Seeing their expressions turn somber, Nicla was filled with trepidation. They maintained their solemn countenances as she approached.

"I'm sorry, Signorina," consoled the short one, removing his hat.

The square began to spin. The two men stood up and helped Nicla to the bench. The short one sat next to her with his arm around her shoulder. The taller stood holding her hand. Nicla put her other hand to her forehead. She was swaying.

"*Signorina*," the tall one spoke, patting her hand. "Can we get you some water?"

Nicla shook her head.

"Do you need to lie down?" The short one began to rise from the bench.

"No." Nicla continued shaking her head, looking downward, one hand over her eyes and the other still held by the tall man.

Over the next several minutes, the two men made the usual attempts to comfort her. The tall one fanned her with his newspaper. The short one even offered her a whiskey to help calm her nerves.

"*Signorina*." The slender one lifted her chin. "Claudio was a hero. He and two other Partisans lured the guards down a street away from the bridge. That's what allowed *la Lucertola* to pass under the bridge. Then, your boyfriend Claudio stayed behind and engaged the Germans while the other two men escaped."

Nicla opened her eyes for a moment and looked back and forth at both men. They were nodding and smiling.

"The mission was a huge success," boasted the short one. "The ship tried to make it out of the harbor and listed into the channel. No Germans killed. No reprisals on civilians, so far at least."

"Success?" Nicla asked angrily. "Who cares about your missions! Was it worth it? The Americans are coming soon. The Germans are losing. They'll be gone either way. What's the difference?" She looked up to Heaven then back at the men "Claudio and Luca are dead! They're not coming back! For what?"

"The war will end sooner because of them," the shorter one spoke gently as he sat back down next to Nicla. "It's hard to see the larger picture, but everyone has their part in it. You did too." He put his hand on Nicla's arm.

"I wish I never delivered those messages! Or those damned explosives!" Nicla jumped up. "You can all go to hell!" She ran across the square.

Tears were streaming down Nicla's face as she passed the café. A waiter wearing a white jacket looked up from wiping a table. "Can I help you, *signorina*?"

Nicla was oblivious. She didn't know where she was going, but she needed to be alone. Seeing the Sanctuary of the Madonna, she bounded the stone stairs, sobbing as she went.

Inside, Nicla passed through the votive gallery and saw the outfit of the little girl saved from Turkish pirates. Unlike the girl's Blue Prince, Nicla's was not coming back.

Entering the nave of the church, she was crying loudly. An old woman with black lace over her hair turned and glared. Nicla had no handkerchief to put on her head, and she didn't care. She sat down quickly. Before her was the colossal altarpiece of the Madonna. Nicla threw herself to her knees.

Help me, Holy Mother, she prayed. *Ask God to give me strength. I don't know how I can bear this.*

Nicla was beginning to feel anger. She wrestled with it. Still, as distraught as she was, she could not blame God for her losses, nor for so-called unanswered prayers. Before the war, she had seen too much beauty and love in the world for her faith to be completely shaken, however tenuous was her present hold upon it. Her mother and little brother were home waiting. Her older brother, Vivi, was still alive with the Partisans. They had each other. Some families had lost everything. Somewhere inside, Nicla grasped for that thread of faith that, having been laid in a lifetime of prayer and commitment, can be grasped at such a time.

Nicla continued to pray for the better part of an hour. When she had reached a stage of peace, as well as exhaustion, she made the sign of the cross and rose from the pew. Sitting directly behind her were the two old gentlemen from the square.

"How long have you been here?" she whispered in amazement.

They looked at each other and fidgeted with their hands.

"For a little while," answered the shorter one.

"You've been here since I came in, haven't you?"

"It was hot outside," declared the taller one.

Nicla imagined the old men climbing the stone steps to the sanctuary. They must have paused at the top, catching their breaths and wiping their brows with their neatly folded handkerchiefs.

Nicla was deeply touched. "I'm sorry for what I said to you back at the bench."

"Signorina," the shorter one began, "you don't have to be sorry to anyone. It is for us to be sorry for you."

Choking up, Nicla nodded and attempted a smile in gratitude.

"Now. You should go home and hug your mother," the taller one counseled, "there's nothing like mother's love. Go dear."

The men insisted on giving Nicla *filobus* fare to get back to the city and "something extra." They couldn't say for what, but they insisted. Nicla parted, giving each a kiss on the cheek.

Her world was upside down. She wasn't sure how she would get through the coming days, but the compassion shown by the men reassured her that human kindness existed in the world. It was there amidst the evil of war and loss. She knew it was abundant in her home, as the old man had said. Nicla sought to anchor her mind on this bedrock during the sorrowful ride home on the *filobus*.

Chapter 18

The following months were filled with hardships for Nicla and her family. There was little sewing work. Few cars came into Zio Fiore's garage. As a result, there was generally little else than polenta on the table. Fortunately, her little brother Matteo occasionally brought home a fish from the reef. And though meals could often be somber affairs, Zio Fiore could always add some levity.

One night, at *cena*, the evening meal, smaller than the midday *pranzo*, Fiore asked Nicla, "Do you remember the time you got your shoe stuck in the toilet?"

Nicla smiled sheepishly and stirred the polenta on her plate.

"Tell me, Zio!" requested Matteo.

"You be quiet!" Nicla ordered.

"Well," continued Fiore, "She was a little younger than you and about this tall." He held his hand just above the height of the table. "Your mother left her at the garage for the day. Nicla was always interested in cars. Did you know I taught her to drive?" Fiore winked and nodded toward Nicla's mother.

"What?" Silvia's eyes popped wide.

"That's a story for another day." Fiore resumed. "So, Nicla went to use the squat toilet in the garage." Fiore referred to the porcelain fixture which wasn't more than a hole in the floor with foot stands astride it.

"When she was done, our little peanut had to jump up to grab the chain from the water closet up on the wall."

"She came down with her foot in the hole!" Matteo concluded gleefully.

"Right in the hole," confirmed Fiore, tousling Matteo's hair. "I had to stick a coat hanger down there to get her shoe out."

"We're trying to eat, Fiore," Silvia grumbled.

"My new shoe was ruined," Nicla lamented. "But you know what Zio Fiore did? He brought me to the store to buy the exact ones." She turned to her mother. "We never told you, Mamma."

"Fiore." Cooed Silvia.

"I don't remember that part." Fiore turned and winked at Nicla.

"Now," Silvia demanded, spooning a helping of polenta on Fiore's plate, "tell me about the driving lessons."

Day after day passed for Nicla. She tried to occupy herself with chores, as she had while waiting for Claudio's return. Now she was avoiding the pain of his loss.

She often found herself walking from Fiore's garage on the edge of town to the more affluent quarter to pick up what little sewing jobs she could find. Sometimes she would fit women in their apartments and bring the pinned garments home for alterations.

More than once, Nicla had to run for a bomb shelter during an air raid. These attacks were becoming more frequent as the allies were approaching from the south and trying to soften German positions. When Nicla huddled in a shelter, she would close her eyes and dream of being with Claudio. These fantasies were so real that she would be oblivious even to the most earthshaking explosions. It was the quiet after the raid that brought her back to the reality that he was gone.

Sometimes on her errands in the city, Nicla would walk through a small park. Here, a pebbled walkway passed under a canopy of trees. It created an oasis of shade in an otherwise sunbaked city. Black wrought iron benches with wooden slats lined the sides of the path. It was quiet here.

A very old woman dressed in black always sat on one of the benches in this patch of serenity. She was often crocheting but never missed a chance to study a passerby. Nicla had come to know her from simple greetings at first, to occasionally sitting down next to her for a rest. The woman had a deeply wrinkled face with light blue eyes, one of which was clouded over with a milky white haze. Her name was Speranza.

"There is a sadness about you, dear," she spoke to Nicla as they sat together one afternoon.

"Yes. I know."

"You told me before that you lost your father. It's more than that, isn't it?"

"It's my boyfriend, Claudio. The Germans killed him."

"I'm very sorry, my dear." Speranza studied Nicla intently with her good eye. "Your whole world is shattered, isn't it?"

Nicla nodded, looking down at her folded hands.

"And you feel no one can replace him, yes?"

Nicla looked up at her. "He was my Blue Prince. He was supposed to come home and save me."

"From what, child?"

"This." Nicla waived her arm around. "War... hunger... loneliness." She looked earnestly into Speranza's face. "I try to have faith. I pray. But I'm losing hope. It's the same thing, day after day. I don't see any end to it."

Speranza took Nicla's hands. "Listen, child. I've seen a lot of pain in my life. It seems like it will never end. But eventually it does. It fades over time, somehow. And sometimes it changes overnight. It's like God pulls away a cloth that's covering your eyes - right when you don't expect it."

Nicla stood up, her hands still in Speranza's. "Thank you." She appreciated Speranza's words, but talk of some vague, future deliverance did little to assuage her present despair. How long would she have to wait? Besides, she didn't want Claudio diminished in her heart.

"You've been very kind." Nicla began to pull away from Speranza's grasp, but the old woman held her hands tight and gazed hard in her eyes.

"God has other plans for you. Have faith."

That God had other plans for Nicla, or Livorno for that matter, was difficult for Nicla to see in the ensuing months. The city was subjected to more massive bombings by the Americans. They hit their targets in the port, but many of the bombs fell on the rest of the city. The results were devastating. Livorno was turned into a jagged shell of hollowed-out buildings. The loss of life was horrific. Nicla could never have imagined suffering on such a scale before the war. But now, it was the reality all around her. Each time she stood outside Fiore's garage and saw the dark wave of death slide over the city, she imagined the lives being torn apart by the exploding bombs. It caused her to relive the loss of her father over and over.

After each bombing, Nicla would learn of some particularly tragic incident. Bomb shelters took direct hits killing scores of civilians in an instant. In one bombing raid, an orphanage was struck. Forty children and many nuns were killed. Nicla, as the rest of the citizens of Livorno, was sickened in her heart by the thought of the little ones buried in the rubble. It occurred to her that this was the same orphanage where Luisa had left her son Alessandro before running away. Luisa couldn't know that he was safe with her father, Piero. Did she think Alessandro was buried in the rubble as well?

The district from the seaport to the center of the city was declared a "black zone" by the Germans. All inhabitants were ordered to evacuate. From Zio Fiore's garage, Nicla watched as the beleaguered and dispossessed streamed lifelessly out of the city seeking refuge in neighboring towns.

Nicla and her family often went days without food. As much as they were tired of it before, they would be happy to eat polenta again. Hunger gnawed at Nicla's stomach. There were times when she noticed the struggle for survival taking her mind off Claudio. She wondered if this were not a blessing.

One day, Nicla heard unexpected explosions coming from the city. Some were emanating from elsewhere in the countryside. It was unusual, as there were no bomber planes.

"What are those explosions, Zio Fiore?" she asked her uncle.

"It's not the Americans," he replied. "If they were engaging the Germans in battle, it would be a lot worse. I think the Germans are getting ready to leave. They must be destroying the docks so the Americans can't use the port."

The Germans were doing just that. They also scuttled ships in the harbor, blew up the lighthouse and destroyed bridges that led to Livorno from the south. This was done to hinder the approaching Americans.

The next day, Nicla's little brother burst through the door of Fiore's house. "The Germans are gone!"

Nicla could hardly believe it. She turned to her mother. Silvia already had tears in her eyes. They embraced.

"I have to go see this," Nicla declared, turning toward the door. "Matteo, you go tell Zio Fiore in the garage."

Nicla saw few people on the road to town. She expected throngs. News had not spread yet, but even if it had, there was little reason for many residents to return, having left behind homes that were

obliterated. The people she did see were stoic. They marched
determinedly toward the unknown – pushed by a primal need to
return to one's home. The question of whether it was still there,
was another issue.

At one point she was passed by a bicycle carrying three boys.
One was on the handlebars, another on the seat, and the third was
standing while peddling. The one on the seat waved an Italian
flag.

"*Viva Italia!*" he shouted triumphantly as they passed.

Nicla simply waved and forced a smile. She was beyond patrio-
tism at this point. She remembered all the flag waving and nation-
alism that had led them all into this disaster of a war. She thought
how much better off the world would be without demarcations
that pit children of God against each other. This labeling of "us"
and "the other" was the first step toward treating fellow humans
like animals – worse than animals, she believed.

When she reached the city, Nicla was overwhelmed by the extent
of the destruction. She could hardly recognize the city she once
lived in. Few of the buildings escaped the wrath unleashed by the
American bombers. It was a scene of utter devastation.

Here and there, former inhabitants began to appear. Like Nicla,
they were in disbelief at what they laid their eyes upon. They also
felt an uneasiness that the Germans might not be completely gone.
Such was their combination of bewilderment and trepidation.
They drifted among the ruins like wary phantoms.

Nicla continued through town. She saw some people hugging
and crying at finding their home intact. Others were hugging
and crying before debris that was once the place they called home.
She was struck by the arbitrariness of it all. Why had one family
merited salvation and the other been forsaken? She could not
fathom it. She continued moving through the city.

She came upon a large wooden sign in the road. It was painted
black with white letters. The top half was written in German
under the bold warning: "*Achtung!*" and the bottom half was the

Italian translation titled: "*Attenzione!*" Nicla read the bottom portion. It warned that anyone passing beyond that point without documented permission would be shot. This sign marked the frontier of the black zone.

Nicla began seeing more people of all ages appear on the street. Some of the younger men were carrying guns. Older people had their hands to their mouths as if to hold in their souls as they gaped at the destruction.

One of the younger men hoisted a friend upon his shoulder and moved close to the black zone sign. The young man on top was waiving a hammer. This brought cries of "*Buttalo giu!* Bring it down!" from the crowd. He raised the hammer slowly on high. The crowd accompanied him with a choral "ahhhhhhh," rising in pitch until they burst into cheers as he brought the hammer down violently on the hated symbol. Pieces of wood splintered off the sign.

Each swing and cheer drew more people from the surrounding area. The spectacle culminated when the crowd succeeded in tearing down the jagged remnant upon which the despised message was written. There was not enough room on that piece of board for all the feet that wished to stamp upon it.

Nicla moved on, into the former black zone. It was like entering a ghost town. There was an eerie quiet. She could see farther in the city than she could before. The absence of many buildings revealed neighborhoods which were blocks away. She could hardly get her bearings. It was as if she were walking in a dream.

On a spot where Nicla was sure an old synagogue had stood, Nicla found nothing but a pile of blocks. Livorno had a large Jewish population before the war. From the time of the Medici rule, laws protected oppressed Jews who arrived from other parts of Europe and beyond. Nicla thought of the Jewish friends she had known before the rounding up had begun. Where were they taken? Were they alive? She stood before the ruined synagogue and prayed for them.

Arriving at the waterfront, Nicla could not believe her eyes. There were hulks of scuttled ships protruding from the water and cranes toppled over into the harbor. What the allied bombers had not destroyed, the retreating Germans had obliterated. Nicla looked further out at the great breakwater, *Molo Nuovo*, where she and Luca had spent the day. It was still there in its ancient majesty, protecting the harbor, but the lighthouse was gone. The symbol of Livorno's historic maritime fame, that had stood for centuries, was no longer there. A deep tie with her cultural past was cut. With all that had to be rebuilt, Nicla wondered if life could ever be the same.

She turned somberly and began walking back into the city. There were many more people than before. Nicla noticed how gaunt most were. There were some children climbing and playing in the rubble. She thought how resilient and creative little ones could be. If only she could so quickly erase the images of war that haunted her. As she was contemplating this, she became aware of a low rumble. It was far off, but it was increasing in volume.

From around a corner came a young man running and shouting, "*Arrivano gli Americani!*" A clamor arose from the crowd. People turned and hugged one another. Hats were thrown in the air. More residents began to come out of side streets and line the avenue on which Nicla stood filled with anticipation.

The first American soldiers appeared. They were walking single file along the side of the street. Some were carrying rifles in their hands. Others had them strapped over their shoulders. They were all wearing helmets. In the middle of the road, lumbered the tanks which had heralded their arrival with the growl of their engines and metallic grind of their treads.

As they reached the throngs of citizens on the sidewalks, a cheer erupted which did not cease. It sent chills through Nicla's body. Hands were waving high, and a broad grin was on every face. Many had tears rolling down their cheeks. Nicla had never seen unbridled joy on such a scale. It took years of suffering and fulfillment of their desperate hopes to unleash this jubilation.

Boys were riding bicycles alongside the procession of soldiers. Men rushed out of the crowd to trot alongside as well. Nicla saw one man with a bottle of wine in one hand and a glass in the other scamper up to the soldiers. He was pouring and splashing the wine into the glass, holding it up to some soldiers sitting on a tank. More of the wine found its way to the ground than to the Americans.

And all the Americans were happy as well. Nicla could see the exuberance of the crowd reflected in the soldiers' smiling faces. They felt the gratitude of the people who viewed them as saviors. Bouquets of flowers were tossed from the back rows of the crowd. No Roman legion returning from conquest could have been received with such adoration as these foreign troops.

Many young women in the front of the crowd began grabbing soldiers and kissing them on the cheeks. The soldiers' helmets would wobble, and they would readjust them. Some seemed slightly embarrassed and tried to continue marching. Others reciprocated with kisses on the young women's lips. Nicla smiled. She understood they were all caught up in the moment, and perhaps taking small advantage of it. She herself could not participate in the revelry. She still grieved Claudio.

The crowd lifted an old woman so she could reach the men in a jeep that had stopped. She took one soldier's head in her hands and kissed both his cheeks. As she was lifted back away from the jeep, the soldier took her hands and kissed them. Nicla saw how caringly he treated the old woman. It warmed her heart. The soldier looked up and noticed Nicla. It caught her off guard. The jeep began pulling away. With a smile raised slightly higher on one side of his face, he held Nicla's gaze as the jeep disappeared down the street.

It was an odd feeling. Nicla hadn't been admired like that for a long time. Before she could think twice about it, the world around her demanded her attention. An American standing on a tank was

causing a stir by tossing loose cigarettes into the crowd. Like desperate bridesmaids lunging for a bouquet, needy citizens formed a
sea of outstretched hands. Nicla thought it unseemly. She wished
the soldier would stop. Of course, she had never smoked. *The
rocks in the water know not the suffering of the rocks in the sun*, she
thought back to Piero's proverb in the truck.

Next to march down the street was a regiment that stunned
not only Nicla, but all the other Livornese onlookers. The entire
group wore American uniforms, but every soldier was Asian. By
the score they marched past Nicla. And though Livorno was a
worldly seaport, Nicla had only seen Asian persons in schoolbooks. Now, watching them pass by in the flesh, she marveled at
them. They were not caricatures as they had been depicted. They
made a fine appearance. Still, it was strange to see them on Italian
soil. Had they been the first soldiers to march into Livorno, Nicla
would have thought they were invaders.

She did not know that these were the *Nisei* soldiers of the 442nd
Regiment. They were American citizens, but they were segregated
from the other US soldiers. They were known as *Nisei* because
they were descendants of Japanese immigrants. *Nisei* means second generation in Japanese.

Back in the US, a hundred thousand of their fellow Japanese
Americans had been ordered from their homes and into internment camps for fear they may be loyal to Japan. Yet these soldiers had eagerly volunteered to fight for their country. They had
suffered horrific loses fighting the Germans all through Northern
Africa and up the Italian peninsula.

Down the road, something was coming into focus that gave
Nicla great anticipation - an Italian flag. As it approached, she saw
another flag she did not recognize, but she knew whose it must be.
It was the Partisans'.

The men in this brigade were not dressed in any uniform, yet
there was something that set them apart. Each man had some
article that gave them a military look. From the obvious – a rifle

or band of ammunition strapped across their chest, to a kerchief or cap from the Italian army unit they had belonged to before it was disbanded. Above all, they looked battle worn. This worried Nicla. What losses had they suffered? Had Vivi survived?

Nicla began walking swiftly alongside the formation of civilian fighters, looking for her brother. She knew it was not certain that Vivi would be with this brigade. She was full of breathless anticipation as she called out his name, hoping someone would know him.

Finally, one of them, hearing her pleas, responded.

"Vivi? *La dietro* – back there." He flipped his thumb back over his shoulder.

Nicla was giddy. "Vivi! Vivi!" She ran through the marching freedom fighters. They smiled or laughed as she bumped into them, almost knocking them over.

"Nicla!" came a shout from farther back.

"Vivi!"

The remainder of the formation parted. Nicla leapt into her brother's arms. He lifted her off the ground as the crowd cheered. The Partisans, like a parting river, continued marching around them.

"You're home! Finally!" Nicla took him by the arm and pulled him out of the column. "Come, let's go see Mamma."

"I can't."

"What?"

"We have to keep going. The Germans keep retreating north, but then they dig in. We have to push them all the way out."

"You did your part. They're out of Livorno. The Americans will finish this."

"These men are like brothers to me. I can't leave them." Vivi turned toward the ragged but proud group marching past. "Look at them. You can't see the dead tired fatigue in them, can you? Or what they've been through, or how many we lost." He turned back to Nicla. "Look how proud they are in front of these people.

That's what's carrying them. That's who we're fighting for. We can't stop now."

"You don't have time to at least visit your own mother?"

Vivi smiled and lifted Nicla's chin in his hand. "Let me check, *carina*. Wait on the side here." He dashed off toward the front of the formation, spoke a few words with his superior and returned to Nicla.

"Alright, *bellina*. You got your way. The whole brigade will wait for you while you take me home and back."

Nicla tilted her head and scrutinized Vivi with a half-smile.

He broke into a chuckle. "Well, not just for you. They are going to make camp here tonight anyway."

Nicla threw her arms around his neck again.

"But we move on in the morning." Vivi croaked from Nicla's stranglehold.

"Then we better get home." Nicla tugged his arm, and off they set for home.

"How is everyone?" Vivi asked.

"Everyone's fine." It sickened Nicla to lie so. Vivi didn't know about their father. Nicla felt like Judas about to turn Jesus over to the temple guards. She would have to plunge a dagger into Vivi's heart, but she couldn't bring herself to do it. Their demolished former home was on the way to Fiore's garage. They would pass it soon.

She tried to make conversation, asking Vivi to talk about the exploits of his brigade. He asked her about Claudio.

"I've learned to accept it," she stated flatly. "That's what war does. It rips away the people you love."

"You've aged."

Nicla looked at him with surprise.

"I don't mean your looks. You have wisdom that should come with age. This war took away your *gioventù*."

At that moment, the remains of the building where they had lived came into view.

Vivi froze. "My God! No! Was anyone hurt?"

"*Babbo, è morto.* Daddy is dead." Nicla hugged her older brother.

Vivi remained motionless, numbed.

"Mamma and Matteo are fine." Nicla was crying with her head against Vivi's chest. "Forgive me. I couldn't tell you about *Babbo*."

"It's alright, *bella*." He rubbed her back. "You have the best heart. The war couldn't take that away from you. Come on, where is Mamma? Take me to her."

All the way to Fiore's garage, Vivi turned Nicla's thoughts toward happy days. With his arm around her shoulder, he reminisced about their childhood.

"You remember when I taught you to catch *le lucertole*?"

"*Mascalzone*! I had nightmares about it. The tail was wiggling in my hand."

So, they continued, lost in recollections, toward a joyful but bittersweet reunion with their loved ones.

Chapter 19

After the jubilation over the Americans' arrival wore off, life for Nicla returned to a daily struggle to survive. She made trips into town to find sewing work – often without success. On one such trip, when she was downtown, she heard a commotion coming from around a corner. People were scurrying to see what was happening. Nicla cautiously followed.

A crowd had gathered in the street. They formed a circle. In the center sat three women on folding chairs. Two had their heads shaved and one was having her head shaved by a man with clippers. Nicla was horrified.

The two women whose heads were already shaved sat in utter wretchedness, their eyes cast downward in shame. Nicla knew from the vile taunts of the crowd that these were woman who had taken up with German soldiers during the occupation. This was retribution. The Germans were gone, and these women were the objects upon whom the people could unleash their wrath.

The man clipping the last woman's hair was working very methodically. He had a cigarette dangling from his lips. The woman was trying to look downward away from the crowd, but another man was holding her face up by the chin and the back of her head. He flashed an evil grin as he turned her head in different directions for the crowd to see. So abject was the woman's humiliation that Nicla was about to turn away. But then it dawned on her. It was Luisa, the Contessa's former maid.

The man with the clippers brushed off the remaining clumps of hair from the woman's bare scalp. The other man loudly and foully proclaimed that justice was fulfilled, and the abashed three went running through the jeering gauntlet of the crowd.

Nicla watched Luisa disappear down the street. Something compelled Nicla to follow. She thought back to speaking with Piero, Luisa's father, and the photo he showed her. *There goes the little girl in the bathing suit,* she thought. *What path brought her to this?* She wondered what it must have been like to be pregnant and thrown out by her father. Nicla couldn't imagine her own father doing such a thing.

Passing an alley, Nicla heard sobbing. Against the wall, she saw Luisa sitting on the ground, knees drawn to her chest, her face in her hands. Nicla was moved to deep pity by the sight. She went and kneeled beside her, putting her arm around Luisa's shoulders.

Luisa glanced up, then buried her face back in her hands. "Please, leave me alone. Don't look at me."

"It's me, Nicla. Do you remember me?"

Luisa looked up slightly. "You're the girl who came to the villa sometimes." She wiped her nose. "You sewed the Contessa's clothes." She hid her face once more.

"That's right." Nicla smiled. "Where do you live now? I'll walk you home."

"Home?" Luisa turned to Nicla. Her face was red and bathed in tears. "What home? A German officer was keeping me in an apartment. When the Germans left, the landlord threw me out and reported me to those men back there." She waved her arm toward the scene of her humiliation and put her forehead back against her knees. She cried bitterly.

Looking at Luisa, Nicla envisioned the day she came upon her with the German officer in the car. She recalled Luisa's shamed but helpless expression. There was nothing Nicla could do for Luisa back then.

"You're coming home with me." Nicla held out her hand.

Luisa looked up at Nicla in disbelief. "You would be seen with me? Like this?"

"Like what? Come." Nicla helped Luisa to her feet. She wiped the tears from her cheeks and straightened her dress. Taking Luisa by the hand, they began walking out of the alley. Before they reached the end of it, Luisa stopped and threw her arms around Nicla. "Thank you. It's been so long since anyone has been kind to me." She began crying again. "So long."

Nicla looked hard into Luisa's eyes. "It's alright. You are going to be fine. This..." She caressed Luisa's scalp. "This is going to grow back in no time. You can stay with us until it does. Then, you are going to start over. *Tante belle cose.*" Nicla wished her many beautiful things. "*Andiamo.* Let's go." Nicla took Luisa's hand again and they walked out of the alley.

As they walked through the city, they were the subjects of many derisive looks and comments. Nicla squeezed Luisa hand. "*Forza.* Be strong."

Nicla herself was the subject of some of the vilest comments. She reacted by holding her head up and marching more determinately than before, always holding fast to Luisa who was cowering at the avalanche of filth.

Nicla looked to find a route less traveled. Coming around a corner on a quiet backstreet, they came upon two men sitting on some steps. They looked to be in their thirties. Their clothes were worn and grimy. One of them put out his cigarette with his foot and stood up. He moved into the path of the two women.

"*Buon Giorno!*" He bowed mockingly.

"Leave us alone," Nicla commanded. "Move out of our way."

"What's your rush?" asked the other, stepping behind the women to hem them in.

"You're wasting your time. Now move away." Nicla pushed aside the man in front and moved forward, pulling Luisa with her.

"Your friend hasn't spoken yet." The one in the rear tugged Luisa back. "From her hairdo, I would think she enjoys the company of men." He pulled Luisa close. "Don't you, *signorina*? Or should I say, *fraülein*?"

"Enough!" Nicla shoved him with both hands. She charged up against him, chest to chest. He was tall. She looked up with her hands on her hips. "You'll have to get through me first."

"Oh, this is a lively one." The other man grabbed Nicla and spun her around.

She slapped him hard across his face. "I was a staffetta," she proclaimed striking her chest. "You think you're more intimidating than a German soldier with a gun in my face?" She pointed between her eyes. "And if you touch me again, when my brother gets back from the Partisans," she leaned forward and whispered in his ear, "he'll kill both of you."

The would-be assailant turned to his friend. "Let's go." He motioned toward the other end of the street. "*Boun giorno*, ladies." His tone still smacked of condescension, but it was just covering the start Nicla had given him. Putting his arm around his accomplice's shoulder, they sauntered away chuckling.

Luisa stood in awe of Nicla. "Are you really the quiet girl that used to come sew for the Contessa?"

"Feel my hand." Nicla held it out. "See? I'm shaking like a leaf."

"But you were so brave just now."

"I don't know about bravery. I just did what I had to do." Nicla contemplated for a moment. "Lately, I've had to do that more than I ever thought I would."

Nicla saw the admiration in Luisa's eyes. She did not feel worthy of it.

"You would do it too." Nicla took Luisa by the shoulders. "You don't think so now. They broke you down and tried to take your womanhood with those clippers. But it's not in your hair that can be shaved. It's in here." Nicla placed her hand over her own heart and then over Luisa's. "They can't touch that. You still have it in you."

"I don't know. It's been a long time since I felt like I had control over my life."

"You're taking control now. And you have a lot to live for. You have a son."

"My son?" Luisa stepped back. "How do you know I have a son?" Her eyes were wide. She seized Nicla by both arms. "Where is he? Is he alright?"

"He's fine. You should see him! He's beautiful! I'll tell you all about him. But first," she looked around, "we need to get out of downtown in one piece. Hold your head up and ignore whatever they say to us."

Walking through town, they continued to face a barrage of vicious remarks. Nicla tapped her hand under her own chin and lifted it high to remind Luisa to do likewise. Mercifully, Luisa was lost in thoughts of her son. She imagined what he might look like. What type of person had he become? More importantly, would he want to see her?

Nicla sought the more heavily bombed areas of the city. There were less people from whom they would have to endure taunts - or worse. On one particularly devastated street, the two women saw men working clearing rubble from the road. The men were being watched by American soldiers with rifles. They were German prisoners of war.

As the women passed on the other side of the road, Nicla saw something familiar in one of the men. It was the German sergeant who had taken her sewing machine.

He looked much less like a soldier now. There was no cap on his head, and his shirt, the top three buttons of which were undone, was blotched with sweat. He was carrying a stone block from the road.

"It's a lot heavier than my sewing machine, isn't it!" she called out to him.

The man glanced at Nicla and kept working. Clearly, he didn't recognize her. And barbs from passersby were nothing new to him.

"What sewing machine?" Luisa asked.

"He came in our house and stole my sewing machine. And his friend slapped me!" Nicla glared at him, but he continued toiling in the sun unaware. "Let's go. He doesn't recognize me. I'm wasting our time on him." She turned away.

"Wait!" Luisa pulled her back. To Nicla's amazement, Luisa began shouting at the prisoner in German. The man stopped and put down the block he was carrying. He wiped his brow with his shirtsleeve. Looking at Nicla he tipped his head slightly in recognition but showed no emotion. Then he turned to Luisa. Ogling her bald head with a lecherous smile, he pronounced something scornful upon her in German.

Loosing a squeal of rage, Luisa bolted toward him. Nicla lunged, but it was too late to hold her back. Halfway across the street, Luisa ran up against the chest of an American soldier. Reaching around him, she flailed her arms at the target of her fury, who stood sneering. Nicla could not understand the German slurs he returned at Luisa, but she did make out an Italian word *troia* - slut.

The American soldier, with the help of Nicla, was finally able to move Luisa along. She was still agitated and breathing heavily as the pair walked arm in arm.

Nicla spoke. "I couldn't understand the German, but I know you were standing up for me. Thank you."

"I guess the few German words I picked up were useful for something. If only to use on that pig. I was glad to stick up for you."

Nicla smiled. "You were like a tigress back there." She patted Luisa's back. "You're strong. You're going to make it just fine."

"I suppose so. But surviving hasn't been my problem." She looked off in the distance. "If I could just find a little happiness for a change." She turned back to Nicla. "Please. Tell me about my son."

Nicla put her arm through Luisa's. As they walked, Nicla began by recounting how she met Luisa's father, Piero, behind the Contessa's villa. She left out that she had just witnessed Luca and Alberto's execution.

At the mention of her father's name, Luisa became troubled. "I can't believe he lived behind the Contessa's villa. You say he saw me once?"

"Yes."

"He didn't have the nerve to show his face. Not after what he did to me."

"He's really very sorry." Nicla was surprised to find herself defending Piero, but it was more for Luisa's good. "I would say he's miserable."

"Good. He should be."

"He keeps a picture of you in his truck. He showed it to me."

"He does? What picture?"

"You were a little girl, and you were standing on the reef."

"In my bathing suit? Like this?" Luisa curled her arms, flexing imaginary muscles. She smiled momentarily as her mind took her back. Then her countenance darkened. "How could he betray me like that. I loved him so much." Tears welled in her eyes. "I thought he loved me."

"He does. He wants you back."

"No. No, he doesn't. He told me he was ashamed of me when he threw me out. Imagine if he saw me like this?" Luisa waved her hand over her shaved head.

"Luisa, if you saw the regret I saw in him, you would believe me."

Luisa shook her head. "Enough about him. Tell me about my son. He still goes by, Alessandro, yes?"

"Yes."

"What does he look like?"

"Like you. He has your eyes, exactly."

Luisa put her hand over her mouth. "My God."

Nicla grabbed her by the shoulders. "You can see him! He's living right there with Piero! I can take you."

"No!" Luisa bent over with both hands covering her shaven head. "He can't see me in this condition." She put her head against Nicla's chest.

Nicla pulled Luisa close. "You come home with me. Your beautiful hair will grow back." She stroked Luisa's scalp. "Then, I'll take you to see your son."

Nicla and Luisa arrived at Zio Fiore's house and stood before the door.

Luisa stepped back. "I'm afraid to go in."

"I'll go in first. It will be alright." Nicla opened the door and stepped in. Luisa stayed back, hiding behind the door frame.

Nicla's mother was at the stove finishing her preparation of the midday *pranzo*. Nicla's little brother, Matteo, was flicking his linen napkin at a very nimble fly. Coming out of the bedroom was her older brother, Vivi, with his arm in a sling. They all turned to see Nicla at the door.

"Vivi! Are you alright?" Nicla rushed toward him. "What's wrong with your arm?" She reached for it but stopped short of touching it.

"I was shot in the shoulder. Not long after I saw you in the parade. We caught up with the Germans. They're dug in just north of Pisa." He rubbed his shoulder. "I have to give them credit. They're putting up a hell of a fight."

Matteo ran up and put his arms around his big brother's waist. "But Vivi killed about a hundred of them himself! Didn't you!"

"Matteo!" Nicla scolded. "Those are young men with mothers and sisters and little brothers, like you. Don't take joy in their deaths."

"Your sister's right," Vivi concurred, ruffling Matteo's hair. "You do what you have to do in war, but it's a terrible business and there's no joy in it." He turned to Nicla. "And when did you become a philosopher?"

At that moment, Vivi saw Luisa in the doorway. "What the hell is she doing here?" he demanded, knowing well the meaning of her shaved head.

"This is Luisa."

"I don't care what her name is. She's a traitor. Get her out of here!"

Luisa turned and ran from the doorway.

"You know nothing of her, Vivi." Nicla turned and ran after Luisa. She saw Luisa run behind Fiore's garage. As Nicla pursued her, Fiore came out of the garage. He saw Luisa disappear around the back.

"What's going on? Who was that girl with her head shaved?"

"I can't talk now." Nicla was out of breath. "Do you have a car I can use to go to Montenero?"

"Yes. I just finished one. Is everything alright?"

"Yes. May I take it?"

"Of course. The keys are in it. The owner is coming later. Don't be long."

"Thank you, *Zio*." She kissed his cheek. "Go eat. I think pranzo is ready." Nicla turned and headed for the back of the garage.

Luisa was standing with her arms folded and back against the wall. Her head was tilted back, and her eyes closed.

"Listen," Nicla began calmly, "I'm taking you to your father *now*. He will take you back. You must trust me."

"Why not?" Luisa chuckled wryly. "I don't care anymore. At least I can tell him what I think of him."

"Come here." Nicla took Luisa and embraced her. "It's going to be alright." She lifted Luisa's chin. "You and Piero and your son are going to start a new life together. You are going to find forgiveness and love. Come on now. *Coraggio*."

"If you say so." Luisa shrugged her shoulders.

"You'll see. Now, I'm going to the house to get us something to eat. Wait here."

After they had eaten behind Fiore's garage, Nicla and Luisa departed for Montenero in a small Fiat.

"I can't believe you can drive," Luisa marveled.

"It's not hard." Nicla shifted gears. "I'll show you sometime."

"Maybe when my hair grows back. I want it to blow in the wind like yours." Luisa reached over and flipped the ends of Nicla's hair that were dancing on the breeze.

"Sure it will. Just like this." Nicla tossed back her head, causing more locks to join the dance.

After they had driven a bit, Nicla turned to Luisa and became serious. "I want to ask you something."

"Go ahead."

"Why did you leave the Contessa's?"

Luisa gave several, understanding nods. "I had it good there, didn't I?"

"I'm sorry. I can't help thinking that."

"I've spent many nights thinking that myself." Luisa looked out the window at the Tuscan countryside. "At first, I didn't have any intention of leaving."

"How did it happen?"

"I think it was just loneliness. You would think I had everything I needed at the Contessa's, but I was lonely. I spent 14 years at the villa. I got there when I was a teenager, right after I ran away from the nuns. Alberto found me going through the garbage. The Contessa felt sorry for me and took me in."

"You were at the villa all that time?"

"Yes. And all that time, I never had a life of my own. No boyfriends... no friends. Luca was little when I got there. Even after he grew, he didn't show any interest in me. It was like I was still with the nuns.

One day, I was in town on an errand, and I was walking past café Allegra. This German officer grabbed me by the arm and sat me down at a table. I was petrified. I didn't know anything about those soldiers. I didn't know about anything outside of the villa. I should have run right then and there."

"I'm sorry, Luisa, but you didn't look scared when I saw you in the car with him."

Luisa looked down at her hands and shook her head. "No. I didn't look scared at that point, did I? It's funny how you fool yourself. At first I wanted to get away, but I was afraid to try. I was sure he would find me and hurt me. Later, I would use that as an excuse. Somewhere inside, I was liking the clothes, the apartment... the attention." Luisa turned to Nicla. "It just felt good to get some attention." She hung her head. "But that's no excuse."

"You're only human. You were vulnerable and he took advantage of you. You have to believe you are worthy of much more."

"I can't feel that now. Not after what I did."

"You will feel it when you see the beautiful son you created." Nicla smiled. "Let me tell you about him."

So, Nicla described, and Luisa dreamed, as the little car made its way up the winding roads to Montenero.

Arriving at Piero's cottage, they found no one there. "He must be next door." Nicla moved toward the hedges. "Maybe Alessandro is there too." She took Luisa by the hand and led her toward the space in the bushes through which Nicla had first come to Piero's cottage. It brought back memories of the terrible day when Luca and Alberto were killed. She chased the thoughts from her mind and focused on Luisa.

"This is the stable where I met Alessandro. Maybe he's inside." They looked into the open door of the stable. It was empty.

"He must be helping his grandfather by the villa." Nicla led Luisa around the corner of the stable. They came upon a little girl carrying a doll. She appeared to be about four years old. Her hair was extremely short, almost shaved. Nicla and Luisa stopped in their tracks.

The girl took Luisa's hand. "Do you know where my mother is?" She looked up at Luisa with her tiny features.

Luisa and Nicla looked at each other baffled. Luisa knelt to the girl and caressed the side of her face. "No, *carina*. I don't know your mother." She looked over the girl's shoulder. "Who is watching you?"

At that moment, a tall, gaunt man came around the corner of the stable. He appeared to be in his thirties. His clothes were too large for him. His hair was extremely short.

"Hello," he addressed Luisa. "Can I help you?"

"We are looking for Piero," she replied. "I'm sorry. We didn't mean to trespass. Do you live here?"

"Yes, this is our home." He looked intently at Luisa from head to toe. Then he turned and bent down to his daughter. "You run along now, Miriam." He patted her on the head. The little girl skipped away stroking the hair on her doll.

Standing up, the man continued with Luisa. "Were you at Fossoli? Did you know my wife?"

"I'm sorry. I don't understand."

"You were somewhere else? Have the Americans liberated more camps?"

"Camps?" Luisa was becoming uncomfortable.

"Your hair. You weren't in the concentration camp?"

Luisa was horrified. She shook her head.

Nicla intervened and took Luisa by the hand. "We won't disturb you any longer *signore*." She pulled at Luisa.

"You are a collaborator, aren't you?" The man set his jaw. His face darkened. "You have a lot of nerve coming here," he growled. "My wife died in Fossoli. They starved us and treated us worse than animals."

He stepped closer to Luisa. "I saw thousands of innocent people shipped out of there in freight cars packed like cattle. They took them to death camps in Poland." The man leaned close to Luisa. "And you slept with one of those NAZI devils?" His face flared with rage. "Get out!"

Luisa stumbled backward. "I'm sorry... I didn't..."

"Get out!"

Nicla grabbed Luisa and pulled her toward the hedges. "We are so sorry!" she called over her shoulder. The inadequacy of this gesture was sickeningly apparent, but it was all she could muster. "We're so sorry," she repeated futilely as they disappeared into the bushes.

When they emerged into Piero's yard, Luisa fell to her knees. She was gasping deep, heaving sobs. "Oh God," she repeated between breaths, "I'm so ashamed."

Nicla could find no words to comfort Luisa. The man had spoken the horrible truth and Luisa had to hear it. How Luisa would live with it, Nicla could not imagine.

"What's going on?" Boomed a voice from the driveway. It was Piero emerging from his truck. Luisa, still on her knees, lifted her head as he approached. Her face was crimson and covered with tears.

Piero bent down to her. Their eyes met. "Luisa?"

Luisa hung her head. "No. Don't look at me."

"Luisa... it's you." He held her face in his hands and beheld her shaved head. "Luisa. My God. What have I done to you?"

Luisa looked up in astonishment. "What *you* did?"

"Yes Luisa, *me*." He held out his hands over Luisa's head, grieving at the sight, "Whatever has happened to you - this is all my fault. I abandoned you when you needed me. You were so young."

"You don't know what I've done, Father. I joined myself with evil! I did it of my own free will. Do you understand? Oh God! I can't stand myself." She dropped her head and sobbed violently.

"I don't know what you're talking about. But I know that I set you down that path. You were so young." He shook his head. "God forgive me. Luisa, *you* forgive me. Come. Stay here with me. We will find forgiveness together." He lifted her chin. "You are still my little *pesciolina*. You remember, my little minnow?"

Luisa looked into her father's eyes. She saw the man she knew as a child. "*Babbo!*" she cried as she threw her arms around Piero.

Nicla wiped a tear from her own eye. She saw Luisa's son Alessandro walking up behind the kneeling pair. "*Nonno,* who is this?"

Piero looked up and took Alessandro's hand. He placed it in Luisa's.

"Alessandro, this is your mother, the one I've been telling you about, the one we've been looking for all these years."

Luisa gazed, wide-eyed at her son in wonder but also in trepidation, unsure how he might react to her in this condition.

Alessandro looked her over intently. Even for Nicla looking on, it seemed an eternity. Finally, he spoke softly, "Mamma. I knew I would see you someday."

"Alessandro!" Luisa burst into joyous tears. "My son!" Pulling him down into her arms, she lavished fourteen years of motherly kisses on his cheeks and forehead as the three embraced on their knees.

Nicla no longer attempting to wipe the tears from her own cheeks, turned and slipped quietly away, unnoticed by the rejoicing trio.

On her way home in the Fiat, Nicla pondered the miracle she had witnessed – unconditional love and forgiveness. The war had produced so much pain and suffering for so many. Yet here in this little yard by a cottage on a hill, she thought, God was at work, healing two souls. There were countless more who needed healing. The scope of it boggled her mind. She couldn't question it or reconcile it, but she could take some hope in it. Perhaps healing would come to her.

Chapter 20

Weeks passed. There were days when Nicla looked back upon all she had lost. Those days were dark. It was on one of those days that Nicla found herself walking into town.

She was carrying empty bags for shopping. She would not be filling them with much. Her family barely scraped out a living from some sewing or an occasional car repair for Zio Fiore. After the initial euphoria, the arrival of the Americans had not changed much economically.

As she walked along the road, Nicla took note of the beautiful countryside. She was just outside the city, and the devastation found therein had not been visited upon this stretch of road. There was an occasional crater from an errant bomb. It fascinated and disturbed Nicla just how far from their intended targets the destroyers could sail.

Nicla rounded a corner formed by a tall stone wall. It was a remnant of the fortifications that had surrounded the city in medieval times. She looked down the long stretch of road to the city in the distance. She had ridden down this road on bicycles with Claudio, leaving the city behind, en route to secret hillsides of their own. Her laughter and squeals had pierced the quiet morning as

Claudio rode his bike close to hers trying to steal a kiss. Now, for Nicla, there was quiet and solitude.

Suddenly, from behind the corner of the old wall, an American jeep rounded at high speed. Nicla sidestepped, but a handle to the rear of the jeep struck her hip as it sped by. She spun and fell. She was disoriented from the swiftness with which she had been whirled and thrown to the ground. Instinctively, she stood up.

The jeep stopped about fifty yards down the road. Two American soldiers in the front seat turned to look back at Nicla. The driver of the jeep began to shift the vehicle into reverse. The move was met with a shove from his passenger. Nicla could see they were arguing about something. After another shove from his passenger, the driver turned back to look at Nicla standing in the road. He held her gaze for several seconds before putting the jeep back in gear. It lurched forward and the two drove off.

Nicla, shaken and dazed, turned her attention to her bags which had been hurled to the other side of the road. As she stepped toward them, a searing pain shot through her hip. She fell to the ground. Attempting to rise, she was met again with a knife-like sensation in her hip. She collapsed and lay prostrate with her head on her hands.

Lying in the empty road, a feeling of total forsakenness overtook her. She had fought so long, treading water on the unending tide of grief the war had brought her. It was futile. She was sinking, succumbing. It felt good to lie still - not feel the pain in her hip or soul. Her body relaxed. Blessed oblivion. She began to drift in and out of consciousness.

In Nicla's dreamlike state, the sanctuary of the Madonna of Montenero came into focus. She found herself walking in one of the halls. On a wall, she saw the ornate Turkish outfit of the kidnapped girl. She began to imagine the Blue Prince in distant lands searching for the girl. The hero valiantly battled the girl's captors. The scene receded as Nicla felt her own body becoming weightless. She rose through the vaulted ceiling of the sanctuary.

She found herself gliding high above an ocean. Clouds began to gather below and obscure the wide expanse of water. As she flew onward, the clouds darkened. Nicla could see lightning rippling through them. She imagined the maelstrom on the sea below the veil of the tempest. She was safe far above it, impervious to the giant waves roiling beneath.

As Nicla soared onward, the angry storm clouds gave way to lighter, softer types. These became sparse, and she could see the ocean once more. In the distance was a shoreline.

To her wonder, Nicla saw a tiny craft approaching. It was dwarfed by the immensity of the sea. As she drew nearer, it appeared to be a small, wooden boat. Someone was rowing it. Their back was turned to Nicla as they churned the oars.

Nicla keenly wished to see who it was, but suddenly her flight accelerated. She ascended high above the solitary voyager.

"No!" she called down, trying to turn and look back. But her ascent was dizzyingly swift - the dream was fading. A voice was calling from beyond the wall of sleep.

"*Signorina*." She felt a touch on her shoulder. "*Signorina*. What happened to you?"

Nicla opened her eyes. Floating above her was the face of an American soldier. He was on one knee. "Are you all right?"

Nicla thought she might still be dreaming. He was speaking Italian.

"You're American?" She touched her hip and grimaced. "One of your military cars hit me."

"A jeep?" The soldier looked up the road. "They didn't stop?"

"Yes, but they drove away."

The soldier shook his head in disgust. "Can you get up?"

"I don't know." She tried to roll onto one side but winced. "I can't. My hip is injured."

"I'll take you to the hospital." Reaching to put his arms under her, he paused. "May I?"

Nicla nodded.

The soldier slipped his hands under Nicla and lifted. The deftness with which he swung Nicla up into his arms made her lightheaded. She put her head against his chest and closed her eyes.

"I'm sorry. I'll slow down." He carried Nicla over to the jeep and gently placed her in the passenger seat.

"Aiya!" Nicla could not sit from the pain in her hip.

The soldier picked her up once more and laid her, curled on her side, on the rear bench seat. He took a small haversack from the front seat and placed it beneath her head. "Is that better?"

"Yes. Thank you." Nicla rested her head, but suddenly lifted it. "My bags!" She pointed across the road.

The soldier trotted over and picked up the crocheted sacks, dusting them off as he did. Returning, he placed them on the rear floor. He gave Nicla a smile that was raised slightly on one side.

Nicla's eyes widened. "It's you!"

The soldier was perplexed.

"When the Americans marched into the city! You were in the little military car. The old lady kissed you and you held her hand. You were so sweet with her."

He smiled slightly more on the same side, but he quickly became more serious. "You better rest and let me get you to the hospital." He bounded into the front seat of the jeep.

"The hospital? Wait! Maybe I can-" but speaking was useless. The grinding of the jeep's gears and the winding of the motor drowned out her words as the little vehicle turned in a wide arc. For Nicla, looking skyward, the clouds seemed to rotate on a grand turntable. The jeep had made a U-turn and was heading away from the city.

That she would be checked by a doctor gave Nicla a feeling of security. Relaxing, she allowed her head to sink back onto the military bag. The clouds, which had previously wheeled about the heavens, were fixed now, and seemed to be following her.

Nicla turned from her celestial escort to look at the soldier. She could only glimpse him from behind. His jet-black hair was short on the sides and slightly longer on top, where it waved in the wind. Nicla wondered how he spoke such fluent Italian. She thought it was such an odd coincidence to see this man again – bordering on ridiculous, given that being hit by a jeep had brought it about. But there was something providential about it. She felt it. She looked back to the clouds as the jeep rumbled onward. A faint smile slipped across her face as she drifted off to sleep. Nicla did not know that in the front seat, for a moment, the soldier smiled as well.

Nicla woke to the hum of the jeep's engine. Lifting her head, she could see they were traveling along the coastal highway. To one side, lay the ocean. On the other, a forest of low, brushy pines. Nicla felt the vehicle slowing. She lifted herself and looked out again. A wooden sign bore the inscription: "33rd Gen Hosp," painted in block letters. She lay back and felt the vehicle turn off the road. It ground to a halt.

The soldier hopped out and stood beside the jeep. "Come," he reached out his arms, "they'll take care of you here." He lifted her out of the jeep.

Nicla saw she was being carried toward a palatial, white building. She immediately recognized it as the Fascist youth center. Long ago, she had seen boys in their black shirts, and grey-green shorts marching about the grounds like stormtroopers, singing songs of glorious empire while their friends on break played soccer on the beach.

The speed with which the Americans had turned this place of corruption into one of healing was dizzying. It was now a full-blown hospital with all the amenities commensurate thereto.

As the soldier pushed the glass doors open with his back, Nicla looked over his shoulder to see surprise on the face of the nurse stationed at the desk. "Where are you going with that civilian?"

"Where's Major Osgood?" the soldier replied with his back to the nurse. He continued down a hallway.

Nicla watched the flustered nurse pursuing them. Her white cap, swept back like dove's wings, was pretty to Nicla, as was the nurse's white, fitted dress and stockings. The Italian nurses Nicla had seen looked more like nuns with kerchiefs and aprons.

The soldier paused before an opening to a large room. It was full of men either on tables or in chairs receiving physical therapy from nurses. The soldier glanced into the room and turned to find himself cut off by the nurse who had followed him. "Look soldier. I don't know what you think you're doing, but-"

At that moment an officer emerged from an office across the hall. He had on a khaki summer uniform like the soldier, but Nicla noticed epaulets which the soldier did not have. He was fortyish and tall, with thinning hair, combed straight back. He wore round, metal glasses. "Is there a problem?" he demanded.

The nurse pointed. "Sir, this soldier-"

"Amici," the officer addressed the soldier, "you can't bring her in here."

"Major, one of our jeeps hit her."

The officer started. He looked at Nicla then back at the soldier. "Nurse, go get a wheelchair and meet us in this exam room. Amici, bring her in here." He led them into a nearby room.

"Put her on that stretcher." The officer pointed to an army-green stretcher supported on both ends by some chests.

The soldier placed Nicla gently on the makeshift examination table. "This doctor is the best," he reassured her in Italian. "You'll be fine." Turning to the officer he added, "It's her hip, Sir."

"Tell her to point to where it hurts," the officer commanded, leaning over Nicla. After the translation, Nicla complied.

The officer put one hand around Nicla's ankle and the other under her knee. He bent her leg and lifted. Nicla felt uneasy. She gathered her dress to the inside of her leg out of modesty. The officer manipulated the leg and observed Nicla intently. Retaining his focus on Nicla, almost out of the side of his mouth, he addressed the soldier. "By the way, Amici. Are you trying to undo all my handywork carrying this girl around?"

"No, Sir." The soldier swung his arm in an arc. "The shoulder still feels great."

"Keep that to yourself, Amici." The officer began pressing Nicla's stomach and abdomen. "I can't sign off on that arm yet. The colonel wants me to keep you around." All the while, the officer's eyes never left Nicla's, as he watched for a reaction.

"Yes, Sir," the soldier replied dutifully.

Nicla understood none of the conversation, but the officer's confident tone kept her anxiety somewhat in check.

"Tell her to take a breath and hold it," the officer instructed. The Italian was spoken, Nicla held her breath, and the officer completed his examination with some heavier pressing to Nicla's middle.

"Internally she's fine, and I don't think anything is broken. Let's get some x rays to be sure." He turned toward the door. "Nurse, bring that wheelchair in here."

On cue, the nurse, who had been waiting just outside, opened the door and entered with the wheelchair. She helped Nicla into it.

"I want x-rays on her right hip."

"Yes, Sir." The nurse turned and began wheeling Nicla out."

Nicla turned and reached back toward the soldier. "*Aspetta!* Wait! Where are they taking me?"

The nurse paused with the wheelchair.

"Can I go with her, sir?" the soldier asked.

"Sure, Amici." He smiled. "You know, there are easier ways of meeting girls."

"I wasn't looking, sir. I think she just fell from the sky."

"How so?"

"She was just sleeping in the road when I found her."

"Must have landed on her side." The officer rubbed his chin. "That explains the hip." He looked at Nicla. "I guess it's not far from Heaven, though. She's in good shape." He turned back to the soldier. "Get going, Amici."

As the soldier turned to accompany Nicla, the nurse gave him a condescending look before pushing the chair out of the room. They proceeded down the long, wide hallway.

"Where are they taking me?" Nicla asked the soldier.

"Just for some x-rays."

"What were you talking about with the doctor?"

"We were talking about how lucky I was to find you."

Nicla's face lit up.

"I mean... you could have been lying there a long time before someone else came down the road."

"Oh." Nicla's bright expression dissolved.

Another nurse was passing in the opposite direction. The wheelchair stopped. Nicla's nurse addressed the other. "Get Sergeant Conrad for an x-ray."

"You want to deal with Conrad?" the nurse replied warily.

"I can handle it. Go get him."

As the two nurses spoke, Nicla noticed there was a guard posted outside an open room. Within, were half a dozen men in beds.

"Who are they?" she asked her Italian speaking escort.

"They're German prisoners."

Nicla thought it strange that men should be killing each other one moment and curing in another. Would the guard shoot them if they tried to escape? The nurse began pushing the wheelchair down the hall once more.

Nicla looked up at the soldier. "I heard the officer call you Amici."

"Yes. Anthony Amici. They all call me Tony."

"*Piacere*. Pleased to meet you, Tony. My name is Nicla. I haven't thanked you for what you've done."

"It's nothing – a ride in a jeep. Besides, my days around here are pretty boring. I should thank you for the distraction."

The wheelchair stopped. The nurse opened a door. "You wait out here," she addressed Tony, then wheeled Nicla inside.

In the middle of the room, stood a mobile x-ray unit. To Nicla, it was something from a Frankenstein movie. Its lower portion consisted of a metal skeleton fashioned out of tubular rails. A mechanical arm arched up and over a stretcher laid on this frame. A conical horn, like a megaphone pointed down on the stretcher. A tangle of hoses led to a cart next to the monstrous device.

Nicla envisioned crackling bolts of lightning arcing down from the horn, electrifying some unfortunate subject extended upon Frankenstein's table.

"Right this way, private," announced a sergeant barging in with Tony in tow. He stopped abruptly at the sight of Nicla. "Hello. Who is this?"

"Stick to your job sergeant," the nurse ordered. "Major Osgood wants X-rays of the right hip.

"But Nurse Hightower, I am forlorn." He held his hands over his heart. "Can you not see that your rebuffs are driving me into the arms of another?" He gestured toward Nicla.

"Save it for the young nurses, Conrad. And this one," she nodded toward Nicla, "doesn't speak English.."

"Pity," the sergeant pursed his lips. "Oh well." He shrugged his shoulders and turned to Tony. "Grab the end of that stretcher."

Tony complied and Nicla was helped into it.

"It's the rack for this lovely prisoner." The sergeant motioned with his head toward the contraption.

Nicla felt herself lifted by the two soldiers.

As they passed the nurse, the sergeant continued, "The course of true love never did run smooth."

"Sorry golden tongue." She turned to Tony. "He was an English teacher in the States."

"*Ho paura!* - I'm scared," Nicla blurted as they placed her beneath the alien camera, "What are they talking about?"

Tony moved quickly to her side and took her hand. "It's all right. I was on this thing a few weeks ago. It looks scary, but it's just a camera. Romeo over there is just romancing the nurse."

"She *is* pretty," Nicla acknowledged absently, gazing up at Tony. She searched his face wondering what made her feel so safe at that moment.

The sergeant began to speak from behind the control cart. "I heard the name Romeo pronounced in his native tongue. I hope, soldier, you were kind to me in your translation." He adjusted some knobs on the control panel. "Now, seeing as you speak the vernacular, you'll have to remain and tell the young lady how to position herself."

The sergeant donned a long, black apron and shiny black gloves up to his elbows. Nicla thought he looked like a sinister butcher.

"There's another apron on the hook over there," he addressed Tony. "And to you, dear nurse Hightower, I must speak words which heretofore I could not imagine passing my lips-"

"I know. I know... Get out," concluded the nurse. "I'm leaving."

"Alas, yes," the sergeant lamented holding out a plaintive hand. "Out, out, brief candle of love!" His voice rose as the nurse closed the door heavily behind her.

The x-rays were taken, Nicla was placed back in the wheelchair, and she was being wheeled down the hall with Tony as her pilot.

Passing the room with the German prisoners, the guard at the door addressed Tony. "Hey Mack." His face was stoic, his mouth a line curving down at the corners. "There's a Kraut in there who made a fuss the first time you walked by. He's starting up again."

Nicla could hear someone speaking faintly in German from the other end of the room. She leaned forward to look in. It was the German sergeant who had taken her sewing machine.

"You two know him?" asked the guard, barely moving his lips.

Tony turned to Nicla. "*Lo conosci?*"

Nicla nodded.

"Doc says you can talk to him," the guard stated blandly.

Tony wheeled Nicla into the room. It was spacious, with a high ceiling. Beds lined the walls on both sides. The men in the beds were in varying states of convalescence – from the heavily bandaged to those whose ailment was not apparent.

The prisoner at the end of the room, who beckoned her weakly with his hand, fell on the latter end of this spectrum. While Nicla could not discern a visible injury, she sensed he was not well at all. But for his head, he was completely covered with a blanket. An intravenous bottle hung on a pole next to his bed. His face was ashen.

"He says he has something to tell the girl," announced the doctor standing at the prisoner's bedside. "I don't speak a lot of German, but that's what I gathered."

"What's wrong with him?" asked Tony.

"He was on a work detail moving debris and a wall fell on him – pinned him up to the chest." The doctor leaned toward Tony and whispered, "He's on morphine. We did all we could do for him."

"*Ich weiss, ich sterbe,*" came a raspy voice from the bed.

The doctor winced. "He says he knows he's dying."

The man in the bed turned his glare from the doctor and fixed it upon Nicla. "*Signorina,*" he managed in Italian.

Nicla could see pain in his expression. Gone was the haughty sneer he had flashed while pointing a gun at her in her own home.

He attempted to speak, but his voice was feeble. With trembling hands, he began sewing with an imaginary needle and thread.

"*Mia macchina?*" Nicla intuited. "My sewing machine?"

"*Ja. Ja. Nähmaschine.*" The man in the bed nodded and began coughing. When he regained enough breath, he added, "*Via Oleandri.*"

Nicla recognized the street name. It was behind the Contessa's estate.

The man then held up a finger on one hand and two fingers on the other. "*Einundzwanzig.*"

"That's twenty-one," the doctor interjected. He looked at Tony, who returned the doctor's puzzlement at what the German could possibly be conveying to Nicla.

The dying man motioned Nicla closer. Tony wheeled her over to the prisoner's bed. The man grasped her wrist.

Nicla was taken by his eyes. They were exceedingly tired, but remarkably clear and blue for someone in his condition.

He squeezed her wrist and leaned forward. "*Entschuldigung.*"

Nicla looked to the doctor.

"Forgive me."

Nicla was taken aback. He had been so callous. She remembered vividly the trauma he had caused pointing a gun at her. She gazed upon him now – broken and alone. She could not begrudge the dying man. She nodded. "*Sì. Ti perdono.*"

"*Danke schön.*" He seemed greatly relieved. "*Perdono,*" he repeated weakly. He began speaking German again, pausing between phrases, taking labored breaths. At each pause, the doctor translated into English and Tony into Italian.

"Tell your friend... the one with the shaved head... we all did things we regret... she has time to make up for her mistakes... I do not."

Nicla thought his offenses were more than mere mistakes. But she could feel his genuine need to repent, so she nodded once more. The man put his head back on the pillow and closed his eyes. He continued whispering, "*Perdono.*"

"Oh, there you are," came a voice from the hall." Tony turned Nicla around. It was Major Osgood. "The X rays are negative. She'll be fine – just a deep bruise. I'll give her something for the pain and you can get going. She might get a little groggy." He looked at Tony sheepishly. "Unlike Sergeant 'Romeo,' I can trust you to be a gentleman. Right, Amici?"

"Yes, sir." Tony smiled.

Tony carried Nicla past the nurse at the front desk and out the door of the hospital. "What is this army coming to?" she groaned.

As they approached the jeep, Nicla spoke. "I think I can sit in the front seat now."

"Good. I can use the company." Tony leaned over and set Nicla lightly on the front passenger seat. She flinched slightly.

"Are you alright?"

Nicla shifted slightly and found a comfortable position. "Yes."

Tony scampered around the front of the jeep and hopped into the driver's seat. "I'm going to drive slowly. There'll be less bumps." He started the jeep.

"Is that the only reason you want to drive slowly?" Nicla gave a sideways glance.

"I guess whatever the doctor gave you worked. You seem to be feeling a lot better."

Tony eased the jeep onto the road. He set out at a leisurely pace down the coastal highway toward Livorno.

"You don't seem to belong at that hospital – not as your duty," Nicla noted. "I would've taken you for a combat soldier."

"You have a good eye."

"So, you were wounded weren't you?"

"Would you like to tell me where?" Tony waved his hand over his body.

"Your shoulder."

"What?" Tony nearly lifted from his seat. "Now you're scaring me." He looked her over. "You're too pretty to be a witch."

Nicla laughed. "Don't worry. I'm no *strega*. I saw you swing your arm around for the doctor when he was examining me."

"Ah, very good. It's true. I took some shrapnel in my shoulder, north of here, on the Gothic line. Doctor Osgood fixed me up."

Just then, a jeep approached from the opposite direction. It was occupied by two American soldiers, with an Italian girl on each arm. All were laughing. The women were holding bottles of wine. They beeped their horn and waved. Tony and Nicla reciprocated. It reminded Nicla of passing other couples on the funicular to Montenero with Claudio.

"What are you thinking about?" asked Tony.

"Oh. Those girls that just went by. They reminded me of someone." Nicla turned back to Tony. "Why are you still at the hospital? You look like you've recovered from your wounds."

"You don't miss a thing, do you? If you must know, the answer is *gnocchi alla carbonara.*"

Nicla was intrigued. "The reason you're still at the hospital is *gnocchi alla carbonara*?"

"That... and some other dishes." Tony smirked.

"You mean they feed you so well that you won't leave? No. Wait! You reinjure yourself to stay. That's why you insisted on carrying me."

"No." He drove on, whistling nonchalantly. "So, you give up?" Nicla glowered at him.

"Alright," Tony relented, "I cook for the officers."

"You cook?"

"Yes. Back in New Haven, I worked in a restaurant. I started as a teenager twirling pizzas, but they had a great cook. I learned a lot from him. While I was recuperating here in the hospital, they put me to work in the officer's mess, peeling potatoes and washing pans. Good therapy for my shoulder." Tony feigned scrubbing the steering wheel.

"So, while I was in the kitchen, I gave the cook suggestions on dishes for the officers. The next thing I know, he has me cooking special meals for the Colonel. Now, the Colonel likes my *gnocchi alla carbonara* so much, he won't let the doctors sign off on my release."

Nicla gazed at Tony in disbelief. Then she threw her head back and laughed. "The warrior chef! He swings his sword on the battlefield and chops zucchini in the kitchen." She waived an imaginary scimitar.

"I don't know about the warrior part, but you should taste my *cappelletti con brodo*."

Nicla scrutinized him. "You are an interesting one, Tony Amici."

"Not really. I'm a simple guy. But there's a mystery about *you* I'd like to know about."

"Go ahead."

"Back in the hospital. The German in the bed. What was all that about a sewing machine and the address?"

"That German and his friend came in our house and stole my sewing machine. He even pointed a gun at my mother and me."

"He pulled a gun on you? And your mother? And you were kind to him back there in the hospital? You let him hold your hand."

"It was my wrist. But yes, and I was surprised at my reaction." Nicla paused to think for a moment. "I don't know. He was a different person in bed. He was just a person."

"Well, you're a bigger person than me. Let's forget about *why* he took your machine. That's weird enough. I suppose the address he gave you is where it's at now."

"That's what I'm hoping."

"Alright then." Tony slapped the steering wheel. "Let's go get it."

"You'll do that for me?"

"Of course. My mother sews. I know how important that machine is to her. When I was a kid, I tried to sew my popped football with it. The needle bent and she chased me around the yard with *il mestolo*." Tony waived the imaginary cooking spoon above his head. "I didn't know she could move like that."

Nicla laughed, but suddenly felt woozy. Tony brought the jeep to a stop.

"The doc said the medication would make you sleepy. You want me to put you in the back, so you can lie down?"

"No. I want to stay in front with you."

"Well," Tony pointed to the empty space where a door would be on a car. "That belt isn't going to save you if you keel over." Nicla turned and saw a thin strap hanging across the opening. It was strung very low. She envisioned toppling over it.

"If you want to stay in the front, you should lean against me." Tony tapped his shoulder. "You can take a nap while I drive you to your sewing machine."

Intuitively, Nicla trusted him. But for decorum's sake, she gave him a wary look, and held up a finger. "Don't get the wrong idea." She put her head against Tony's shoulder.

He put his arm around her shoulder. "Are you comfortable?" Nicla nodded.

"There's only one problem," he continued.

Nicla lifted her head.

"I have to shift to get going."

Nicla sat up. Tony removed his arm and shifted through the gears as they got on their way. They reassumed their positions.

"I have one more question before you fall asleep," Tony declared.

"Hmm?"

"What was that address again?"

Chapter 21

N icla opened her eyes to find herself still in the jeep. Tony was sitting patiently beside her.

"I didn't want to wake you. You looked so peaceful."

Nicla whirled to look around. "I knew it! This is the address, isn't it?"

"Yes. Via Oleandri, twelve."

"It had to be!" Nicla unhooked the strap on the side of the jeep and began to step out. She grimaced.

"Wait. I'll help you." Tony came around to her side. "Are you sure you can walk?"

"Yes. Take my arm just in case. We need to start at that cottage on the other side of those hedges." They took a few steps. "Look," Nicla waived her arm across the estate before them. "You see this villa? It's beautiful isn't it? The Germans took it from the Jewish family that lived here. They're back now... except for their mother."

As they approached the cottage, an older man came around from the back. "Nicla!"

"Piero!" Nicla broke from Tony's grasp. Piero dropped his pruning shears and ran to her. They embraced.

"Nicla." The caretaker held both her hands. "I haven't seen you since you brought my Luisa back. How much I've longed to thank you. But you're limping. What happened? And who is this?"

"This is Tony. He helped me more than I can say."

"*Piacere.*" Tony held out his hand. "She's exaggerating. I just gave her a ride."

"He speaks Italian!" Piero marveled.

"Yes. He has surprising talents." Nicla smirked at Tony. "So, Piero. How is Luisa?"

"*Vieni.* I'll show you." Piero led Nicla, arm in arm to the space in the bushes from which Nicla and Luisa had run shamefaced from the outraged concentration camp survivor.

Peering between the bushes, Nicla saw perhaps a dozen children playing. Some boys were chasing a ball and the girls were dancing in a circle. None was dressed very well. All had very short hair.

On a stone patio next to the house, a woman with short hair and an apron sat on a stool. She was reading a book to a little girl on her lap.

"It's Luisa!" Nicla gasped, putting her hand to her chest. "But how? I thought..."

"Go speak to her." Piero directed, putting his hand on Nicla's back. He motioned with his head to Tony. "Bring her over there."

Luisa looked up just as Nicla stood over her. "Nicla!" Luisa turned back to the little girl on her lap. "One moment my darling." She helped the girl down and threw her arms around Nicla.

Tight in Luisa's embrace, Nicla glanced down at the little girl. She recognized her. It was the girl whose mother died in the concentration camp.

"I don't understand, Luisa. How can you be here... with this girl? Her father! He was so angry."

"I know. It's a miracle, isn't it?" Luisa spoke with tears in her eyes. "I wanted so badly to do something for them." She caressed the little girl's face. "So, Piero took me to see her father. It's only because of Piero's friendship that he would even speak to me. I groveled. I begged. I got him to let me clean toilets and scrub floors. After these other children started arriving, he let me cook for them. In between cooking and cleaning, I look after them."

"Who are they?" Nicla looked around.

Luisa bent to the little girl. "Run along and play with the others."

The little girl hugged Luisa and skipped off.

"They're children who came back from the camps. Their parents haven't been located yet." Luisa gazed around. "I'm afraid some of them never will be. The little girl's father, Signore Bianchi, he offered to let the kids stay here until relatives can be found."

"You're at peace, aren't you, Luisa?"

"All I know is I'll work the rest of my life to help this family. I have my father and my son back." She looked out at Alessandro leading a horse, atop which sat a little boy. "Yes, I am at peace." Luisa turned her eyes toward Tony. "Who is your handsome escort? And what brings you here?"

After introductions and an explanation of their mission, Luisa led Tony and Nicla into the villa to meet Signore Bianchi. The four of them stood before the sewing machine in a small room overlooking the yard. Signore Bianchi's attitude toward Nicla was decidedly different from their first encounter.

"I was hard on you," he conceded. "You can understand. I'm sure."

"Certainly. You had... you *have*, every right." Nicla affirmed.

"I spoke to Piero, Luisa's father," Bianchi continued. "She was vulnerable. She was taken advantage of." He turned to glance at Luisa. Her eyes were downcast.

Bianchi continued, "She has shown great remorse, and she has worked hard to make amends. How she helps the children is remarkable." He looked out the window at the little ones playing.

A photo of Bianchi with his wife and child sat framed on a nearby desk. He held it up and gazed longingly at it. "There is much that can never be forgiven." He nodded pensively, returning the picture gently to its place. "But as for Luisa's past... I'm willing to leave it in the past. I only see *this* Luisa now."

Luisa did not lift her downcast eyes. "Thank you, Signore. Your forgiveness..." she began to choke up, "It has helped me... find myself." Throwing a hand over her mouth, Luisa hurried out of the room.

"Well." Finzi made a gesture toward the desk. "This sewing machine certainly doesn't belong to our family." He looked to Tony. "Why don't you carry it, and I will help this young lady." He put his arm through Nicla's.

Nicla thanked Bianchi while Tony lifted the machine. Fashioned from black iron, it resembled a slender bird pecking at the ground. In ornate gold letters, "NECCHI" was emblazoned on its body.

"This thing is heavier than it looks," Tony grunted. "Those NAZIs are strong bastards. I'll give them that."

Nicla's head rested on Tony's shoulder. "Wake up, sleeping beauty." He gently touched her cheek.

Nicla woke to find herself in the front seat of the jeep. She spun her head and saw Fiore's garage. She could barely remember getting into the jeep at the Bianchi villa or explaining to Tony where she lived.

"This is it, isn't it?" Tony asked, "I couldn't miss the garage."

"Yes." Nicla was still a bit dazed from the medication and all that had happened. She looked in the rear and saw the sewing machine. "I can't believe this is not all a dream." She gazed back at Tony. "You've been so kind."

Tony smiled warmly, slightly higher on one side of his mouth than the other. To Nicla, it was an understanding smile.

Suddenly, from around the corner of the garage came shouts. Nicla's little brother and several of his friends came dashing around the corner. Each was wearing some tattered piece of military regalia – an oversized shirt, a canteen, or cap. They carried various sticks and poles for guns.

Climbing onto the spare tire at the rear of the jeep, Nicla's brother shouted, "Our evacuation has arrived! Hurry men! The Germans are closing fast!"

The others started hopping onto the rear bed. Tony's smile broadened. One boy, wearing an authentic Italian helmet, flopping on his small head, pointed to the sewing machine. "What's this doing in here?"

"That's a machine gun, soldier," Tony barked. "You two lay down cover fire, and you two carry the machine gun into that house."

The boys' mouths hung open, not only at Tony's complicity in their antics, but that this American soldier spoke to them in their own language.

"If we set up a machine gun nest facing out one of those windows to the south, we can hold off the Germans till reinforcements arrive," Tony continued, to their wide-eyed delight. "I'll bring up the rear with this wounded nurse." He pulled Nicla close by the shoulder. "Now get going!"

With much clamor and alacrity, the boys set to their task. Nicla watched with mixed emotions. It reminded her of Luca and Matteo cavorting around the Isotta in mock battle.

Tony came around to Nicla's side of the jeep. "What's wrong?" He held out his hand.

"Nothing." Nicla took his hand and cautiously stepped out. "You remind me of someone."

"Someone good, I hope." Tony took Nicla's arm and placed it over his shoulder. They began to walk toward the house.

"Yes. He was very good."

"Was?"

"He was killed by the Germans."

"I'm sorry."

After a few more steps, Nicla turned and looked Tony in the eye. "Why do boys love war?"

"Because they haven't been in it."

"You sound like you have."

"Yes," Tony pronounced solemnly. "I have."

Instantly, a vision flashed in Nicla's mind. It was the look on Luca's face just before the volley of the firing squad. She imagined Claudio overwhelmed by the Germans at the bridge. The specter of another loss fell like a heavy blanket on the nascent feelings she had for this kind man. She had to distance herself immediately.

"Nicla!" Her mother called, bursting from the front door. "Are you alright?"

"I'm fine. I just bumped my hip."

Silvia looked at Tony, then back at her daughter. "Bumped your hip? I don't understand."

"I'll explain inside." Nicla reached for her mother's shoulder. "This is Tony. He helped me more than I can say. Thank him, Mamma, and help me in the house."

Silvia marveled at the baffling but handsome soldier, wondering what heroic deed she should thank him for. "The sewing machine! You helped her find it, didn't you? But how did she get hurt?"

Before Silvia could formulate another thought, a throng of young voices came from inside the house.

"*Commandante*! Come in! The German's are advancing!"

"Excuse me, Signora." Tony turned toward the boys. "Hold that position, men! I'm going for reinforcements!" He turned back to Silvia and Nicla. "I should be going."

"No! You must come in," insisted Silvia. "I have to thank you for-"

"I'm sure Tony has to get back to his soldier duties," Nicla interrupted.

"Yes, she's right." Tony agreed. "I've got to start some salsa Bolognese." He grinned playfully at Nicla who fought back a smirk.

"I still don't understand," Silvia lamented.

"I'll tell you the whole story, inside." Nicla turned to Tony and became very serious. "Tony, I am so indebted to you – for picking me up off the road, for the medical attention, for my sewing machine. I can never thank you enough."

"Don't mention it." He whirled and jumped back in the jeep. "It was a pleasure to assist you, *Signorina*." He started the jeep and put it in gear. "*Signora*," he tipped his head to Silvia, "Thank you for your invitation. It would have been nice, I'm sure."

"*Ciao*, Tony," Nicla pronounced somberly.

"*Arrivederci*, Nicla."

They held each other's gaze until the jeep backed out and turned around. As Tony drove away, a thought, perhaps a hope, forced its way into Nicla's mind. Could Tony have meant his salutation literally? *Arrivederci* – until we meet again.

Chapter 22

It took Nicla several days to get back on her feet. She walked, but gingerly. She was able to accomplish much at the helm of her sewing machine and it took a burden off her mother. Yet as Nicla toiled, she often pictured Tony.

Had she been too hasty in dismissing a man who could have been her Blue Prince? What more did he have to do? He had literally swept her up in his arms and carried her to safety. But he was a soldier. That alone made his prospects for survival questionable.

Worse, he was the heroic type – selfless and ready to sacrifice. And that made him as likely to survive as Claudio or Luca.

So, as the sewing machine hummed, she kept her eye on the needle as it dove between the tiny, metal foot sledding across the fabric. When a thought of Tony arose, she sped up the darting needle and focused more intently. Thus, she kept her mind occupied until one day, the trill of the stitching was broken by a sound she immediately recognized.

She rushed to the window to see a jeep pull to a stop with Tony at the wheel. In her haste, she hadn't noticed that her hip was still quite sore. Adopting a more measured gait, she made for the front door. Still, it was all Nicla could do to keep from bounding out.

Zio Fiore, thinking the soldier had stopped for gas, approached the vehicle. Tony hopped out. They shook hands.

"This young man is here to see you," announced Fiore as Nicla hobbled up.

"*Ciao*, Nicla," Tony greeted.

Nicla was about to speak but was interrupted by Fiore. "He's the one who brought you home the other day, isn't he?"

Nicla's lips were left parted - her greeting for Tony still on her tongue. Regrouping, she addressed her uncle. "Yes, *Zio*. But I don't think he's here for gas." She turned to Tony. "Are you?"

"No. I was just passing by and wanted to check on your recovery. I'm sure Major Osgood, the doctor, would like to know how you're doing."

"Yes. I'm sure he would." Nicla gave Tony a sidelong glance. Turning to her uncle, she put her hand on her hip. "You were working on a car, *Zio*?"

Fiore, captivated by the unspoken language between the young people, was startled. "Oh, yes. The car." He glanced at the garage then back at Nicla, rubbing his chin. "Are you sure I can't help you with anything?"

"Nothing," interjected Nicla.

"Well seeing as Nicla has everything under control here... as usual..." Fiore winked at Nicla, "I'll get back to work. *Buon giorno*."

As Fiore walked away, Nicla put her hand on the jeep. "So. You were just passing by?"

"Yes. But first, how are you?"

"Much better. I'm just a little sore."

"You were limping when you came from the house."

"It gets less each day." Nicla glanced in the back of the jeep. "Looks like you went to market."

"I picked up some things for the officers' meal tonight."

"This is not on the way back to the hospital. I thought you were just passing by."

Tony reached in the back and opened a sack of potatoes. He took a few out and placed them in a smaller bag. "I realized I had more than I needed for the meal, so..." He handed the small bag to Nicla and grabbed two others from the jeep. "Come on. We have some cooking to do."

Nicla stood astonished.

"Are you coming?" Tony was waiting, two steps ahead.

Nicla looked askance at him but followed. Outwardly, she held her look of suspicion. Inside, she was delightfully intrigued.

Silvia was already at the door. "Tony!"

"The warrior chef," announced Nicla.

"What? I don't understand."

"I don't either, Mamma, but let's just go along with him."

"*Buon giorno, Signora*," Tony bowed slightly, but quickly rose to prevent his bags from spilling. "I thought you must have been busy caring for Nicla. If I may, I'd like to cook something for you."

"Well... I was just going to make some sauce for pranzo. There's some polenta in the cabinet."

"Do you like *gnocchi alla carbonara*?" Tony put his bags on the table.

"Carbonara? What kind of gnocchi are those?"

"It's popular in Rome. The officers picked up a taste for it when we were stationed there. It's gnocchi with guanciale, eggs, and Pecorino Romano."

"It sounds like pasta *alla gricia*," noted Silvia.

"Exactly!" Tony exclaimed, "My mother used to make that. When the Colonel described the carbonara he had in Rome, I knew I could make it."

Tony pulled out a chair at the table. "I'd like to make it for you, now. Please, Signora." He gestured for Silvia to sit.

"Go ahead, Mamma," Nicla instructed. "There's no use arguing with him. After all, the Americans are the occupiers."

"Liberators," corrected Silvia, "And *your* savior the other day. Well," she turned to Tony. "I'm not used to a man cooking for me, but I'd like to see how the dish is made." She sat down at the table. "Go ahead."

Nicla joined Tony washing and putting potatoes to boil. They cleared and washed the kitchen table leaving only a small bag of flour, an egg, and a fork.

"The potatoes are done." Tony announced pushing a fork through one of the boiling spuds. "Where is your *schiacciap-atate*?"

The potato masher, resembling an immense nutcracker attached to a cylindrical basket, was brought to the table. Tony pulled the plunger up from the basket and placed a peeled potato inside. Squeezing the handles together, he unleashed a shower of riced potatoes, like strings of confetti, down on the table. After repeating the process for each potato, the downy tangle of starch was allowed to cool.

"You grew up in America?" Silvia inquired, still marveling at Tony's almost fluent Italian.

"Yes, in a small town called Hamden. It's in Connecticut, about an hour from New York City.

"New York?" exclaimed Nicla. "Have you been there?" She imagined the glamorous place she had seen in American movies.

"Once, for a boxing match."

"That's why you went to New York? Boxing?"

"Maybe you won't understand. It was our hometown hero getting a shot at the heavyweight champion, Joe Louis.

At that moment, Zio Fiore came in. He was untying a kerchief around his neck. "What about Joe Louis?" Fiore wiped his brow with the cloth as he walked over to the sink. He began washing his face.

"Nathan Mann from my hometown fought him for the title."

Fiore lifted his head from the sink. "Fought Joe Louis?" Pulling a towel from the hook on the wall, he hurriedly dried his face and sat next to Tony. "What's his name again?"

"Nathan Mann."

"Never heard of him." Fiore paused to contemplate. "Still, he got the chance to fight Joe Louis?" Fiore held up his fists, feigned a combination of punches and bobbed his head, slipping jabs from an imaginary opponent. He sat back musing. "I bet it was a big deal for your town."

"It was. My father, my brothers, me... all the Italians in Hamden went. There were thousands of us. They had to find extra trains to take us all to New York."

"Why the Italians?" Nicla interrupted. "What do they care about someone called *Nayton Mahn*?"

"Nathan Mann." Tony chuckled. "His real name is Natalino Manchetti."

Nicla was mystified at this reverence for what she considered a barbaric sport. "And what about you, Zio? How do you know about this other American... the great Joe *Lewees*?" she added derisively.

"He's just the greatest champion ever." Fiore declared as he and Tony grinned knowingly at each other.

"My, how violence gains one notoriety." Nicla noted.

"Maybe boxing is cruel sport," Fiore admitted, "But you know what Joe Louis did? Here is a black man, who dismantled Mussolini's champ, Primo Carnera, and then destroyed the German, Max Schmeling. How's that for Hitler's racial superiority?"

"Good," Nicla conceded. "I suppose it's better for two men to pummel one another in a ring than the whole world going up in flames. Maybe that's the best we can hope for from the male species."

"You see," Fiore counseled Tony, "She's a sharp one – always was." Fiore rose, kissed the top of Nicla's head, and made for the door. "I'll see you for pranzo. In the meantime, Tony... try to keep up with her."

"*Zio!*" Nicla huffed as Fiore exited.

"Well," Silvia declared, "I think these potatoes are cool now... even if Nicla is a little warmer."

"*Mamma!*"

"Alright. I'm sorry." Silvia touched Nicla on the hand, then turned to beam impishly at Tony. "That strainer on the wall over by the sink, Tony. Would you bring it here?"

"Sure. But I can't get my uniform shirt dirty." He doffed it. "This is how I usually work in the kitchen." He stood in his undershirt.

"So, you *are* a cook," bubbled Silvia.

"Not exactly. You see..." Tony struggled for a quick explanation.

"It's a long story, Mamma. Let the man cook."

Tony received the gesture to proceed from Silvia. With his fingers, he hollowed out a well in the center of the curly mass of potatoes on the table. Cracking an egg, he poured it into the well and began to scramble. The golden yolk yielded to the fork and whirled within the little volcano. Flour was then sifted over it until it resembled some Icelandic fissure waiting to erupt.

After some salt was applied, Tony dug in and began to knead. Nicla watched him nimbly roll and flatten the dough. His forearms, powdered with white flour, were strong, and his hands dexterous. A tattoo on his forearm caught Nicla's attention. It was slightly obscured by flour. It appeared to be a stone cross with some flowers at its base.

"What's inscribed on your tattoo?" she asked.

"In memory of my father." Tony continued kneading. "He died when I was fourteen."

"I'm sorry." Nicla searched Tony's face for some reaction, but he did not look up from his labor.

"Nicla lost her father, too," Silvia revealed. "Not long ago."

Tony paused and looked up at Nicla. "I'm sorry." His gaze remained on Nicla for a moment before turning to Silvia. "My condolences, Signora."

"Thank you, Tony," Silvia replied. "It hasn't been easy on Nicla, as I'm sure it wasn't for you."

Nicla and Tony looked at each other contemplating the deep wound they had in common.

"Well." Silvia interjected. "It looks like that dough is ready. Let's make some gnocchi."

"Yes." Tony broke from Nicla's gaze and probed the dough. "You're right. Perfect consistency." He took pieces of the golden dough and rolled them into logs, like long bread sticks. From these, he cut each *gnocco*. Nicla and Silvia tapped the gnocchi with forks to create the ridges meant to cradle any sauce they should be tossed in.

After setting the gnocchi to boil, Tony produced from his bag the ingredients for the carbonara. "I picked up this guanciale at the market." He proudly held up the cured pork cheek. "I even found pecorino Romano." Tony cupped the wedge of hard cheese in both hands.

"Pecorino Romano? Why? Pecorino *Toscano* not good enough?" Nicla jested. "You betray your Tuscan heritage."

"How did you know my family is from Tuscany?"

"Your accent. The way you pronounce some of your Cs. Instead of *piacere*, you say *piashere*."

"I didn't know that was Tuscan. I'm just speaking like my mother spoke to me since I was little." Tony began dicing the guanciale.

"What town are your parents from?" asked Silvia.

"Siena."

"I was there!" Nicla brightened. "Zio Fiore took me to see the Palio when I was little." Nicla was referring to the annual horse race full of medieval history and pageantry. Neighborhood versus neighborhood, their jockey proxies hurtle bareback with reckless abandon around the town square.

"He put me on his shoulders so I could see over the crowd. I never saw so many people... and they were going crazy!" Nicla sat up slightly as if, even now, she needed to peer over the cheering mass of humanity. "I remember the colorful costumes of the jockeys. And when the horses passed by, the ground rumbled."

"That's how I remember it too," replied Tony scrambling some egg yolks in a dish. "We moved to America when I was five, but I remember it. Hey, maybe we saw each other there when we were little." He grated the Pecorino onto another dish.

"Maybe..." Nicla drew out the word. "But I don't think you could have been more compelling than the race."

"Nicla!" Silvia scolded.

"No," Tony acknowledged. "I'm sure we didn't see each other." He gazed at Nicla for a moment. "If we did, you'd remember me." Tony smiled and turned quickly to toss the diced guanciale in a pan on the stove. "Clean and set the table for your mother while I finish this," Tony announced over his shoulder.

Nicla looked at Silvia with raised brows, then complied with a smirk. The guanciale sizzled.

"Zero hour!" Tony announced. Removing the gnocchi from the water with a slotted spoon, he tossed them into the pan with the crisped guanciale. "A little juice..." he splashed some pasta water in, "and the Carbonara..." he folded in the egg yolks and cheese, "is *pronto*."

He dashed to the sink. A quick clean up and he was back in his uniform shirt. He straightened his sleeves in crisp strokes and lifted his chin to affect the severity of a waiter. Nicla was quite entertained.

"Your Carbonara, signora... and yours, signorina," he announced setting the dishes before the women with an elegant flourish.

"Bravo!" Silvia clapped enthusiastically.

Nicla scrutinized this soldier who, not far removed from the conflagration of battle, had swept her off her feet, recovered her sewing machine, prepared a gourmet dish, and now served her obsequiously.

"Signorina? The meal not to your liking?" Tony inquired standing at attention.

"Oh." Nicla started. She lifted her fork and sampled. In her mind, she searched for some teasing remark, but her taste buds trumped the inclination. "They're wonderful.".

"Good." Tony broke from his waiter character. "Then I have to get going."

"You're not eating with us?" Silvia exclaimed.

Nicla could not hide her disappointment, either. She did not speak it, but her eyes betrayed her.

"I'm sorry. I have to get back and make this for the officers. Good day, ladies." Tony walked toward the door.

Silvia looked incredulously at Nicla. She gestured with her head for Nicla to stop him. Nicla shook her head.

Silvia grasped for some reason to detain the man. "The rest of the cheese? And the Guanciale? Don't you need them?"

Tony paused in the doorway. "No. I have more in the jeep. That's for you, *Signora*." He gave Nicla a last look and a gentle smile. "I'll tell your uncle that *pranzo* is ready. *Arrivederci*." He closed the door.

Chapter 23

Silvia chided Nicla for not showing more gratitude towards Tony. And in the next two days, Nicla wrestled with why she hadn't. Then, Tony appeared to make good on his "*Arrivederci*."

"May I take Nicla for a ride?" he asked Silvia.

Soon Nicla was riding next to him with her light brown hair dancing in the breeze.

"You'll like this place," Tony assured as the jeep hummed along a stretch of road that cleaved a wide expanse of Tuscan farmland in two. "There's something special about it."

"How does a *soldier* know about special places?"

Tony became serious. "I'm a man first."

Nicla sensed something earnest, almost plaintive, in his tone. "I'm sorry, I'm sure it's a beautiful place."

Tony's spirit lightened. "Well... when you see it, you let me know what you think."

Shortly they came upon what looked like a small oasis off in a field. There were several trees surrounding what Nicla could barely make out as a pond, but it was mostly obscured by high grass and bushes. Tony pulled the jeep over.

"On our way up to the Gothic Line, my Lieutenant sent a squad of us through here. He wanted to make sure no Germans were going to ambush the column." Tony jumped out and helped Nicla out of the jeep. He took his haversack from the back of the jeep and threw it over his shoulder. An olive-drab military blanket he placed under his arm. He held out his hand to Nicla.

They made their way through a field of grain and squeezed between some bushes. Nicla was overwhelmed by the beauty. Golds and greens of tall grasses and wild shrubs reflected on a placid pond that had somehow appropriated a piece of the sky to shine on its surface.

"What do you think?" Tony stretched out his hand.

Nicla was almost at a loss for words. "It's beautiful."

"I thought you might like it." Tony spread the blanket on the ground. He sat and reached up to Nicla. "Sit with me."

Nicla sat on one hip, leaning on one hand. Tony could not help noticing how this posture flattered her figure. Sitting low on the blanket, Nicla felt enveloped by the flora. She was in another world. The destruction of war lay far beyond these ramparts of nature. It was a sanctuary.

She felt an easing. Her mind floated, like the lily pads on the water, back to a time before the war. She felt light and unburdened. It had been so long. She had forgotten this feeling. And here was this man she was sharing it with. But he was not Claudio, the boy with whom she associated such sweet memories. Nor was this Luca who had brought her to Molo Nuovo and let her drive the Isotta. She wondered if Tony was trespassing on their legacies. Perhaps it was too soon.

Nicla's eye caught a falcon on the branch of a nearby tree. It reminded her of the falcon she had seen while driving in the hills with Luca.

"What are you looking at?" asked Tony, leaning closer to adopt Nicla's point of view. Their cheeks almost touched.

"A falcon." She pointed to the tree but leaned away from Tony. "You see?"

"Oh, yes." Tony tried to act unfazed by Nicla's recoil. "He's a fine specimen."

"*She*," corrected Nicla. "It's a female."

"How do you know that?"

"Her colors are more muted than a male. She needs to be less conspicuous, so she can hunt for her family. The males on the other hand, like humans..." she pulled at the insignia on Tony's uniform shirt, "can wear fancy uniforms to intimidate other males - kill for territory - you know, what men are good at."

"Yes..." Tony conceded, looking down and straightening out the blanket. "From what I've seen of war... I agree with you."

Nicla's pride in Tony's capitulation was short-lived. What *had* he seen of war?

"Tony, how do you feel about being a soldier?"

"What can I say? I do my duty." He shrugged. "That's all." He reached over and plucked a clover flower at the edge of the blanket and tossed it into the pond. They watched the ripples spread.

"I see." Something told Nicla to leave it at that.

"Say," Tony brightened, "where did you learn about falcons, anyway?"

"My *Zio* taught me. He was giving me a driving lesson out in the country, and we stopped to watch two falcons nesting."

Tony's eyebrows raised. "You drive?"

"Yes."

"You sew, you take care of your family, you drive... What *can't* you do?"

"Actually, you'd be surprised at what I've *had* to do." Nicla couldn't begin to tell him about being a *staffetta*. She could hardly believe it herself. She looked to the falcon again. "You know what I like about that bird? She doesn't need anyone to take care of her."

"Neither do you." Tony smiled. "It's what I admire about you."

Nicla scrutinized Tony's face. She wondered if this was just flattery or if he truly understood her.

"But as strong as you are," Tony continued, "we all need some-one...sometime... don't you think? Take me, for instance. Right now, here, this peace I feel. You are saving me."

That her presence should have any salvific effect on someone as confident and resourceful as Tony surprised Nicla. After all, he was the one who had rescued *her* on the road. "What would *you* need saving from?"

Tony looked down in thought. "Back at the hospital, it can be overwhelming."

"How?" Nicla put her hand on his shoulder. Tony seemed to struggle for words.

"It's a lot of pressure to make sure the pasta is al dente."

"Oh!" Nicla pushed him hard. Tony fell over dramatically. She grabbed his arm and righted him. "Now. Stop hiding." She looked earnestly into his eyes. "You said I was saving you. How?"

"It's hard to explain. It's like you're bringing me back to life."

"Go on."

"I don't like to talk about it." He looked away at the tall grass. "What I saw in those battles - it took something from me. I don't know what. It was so bad. My mind couldn't take it. I became numb. Afterward, something was dead in me."

"*I* brought you back to life? *Me?* Come on. There are so many pretty nurses at the hospital."

"Everything in that hospital reminded me of war. As good as everyone was to me, I was still in a bad dream. It's sad because they were all trying to help me. But when I picked you up in the road, you needed me. That's when something inside me woke up." Tony pushed a lock of Nicla's hair from her face.

"I feel bad for you, Tony. I've seen what war did to the people of my town...what it did to some resistance fighters I knew. That's what I wanted to talk to you about."

"You had a boyfriend, didn't you?"

"It shows?"

"He was killed, wasn't he?"

Nicla nodded.

"You don't want to get involved with another soldier, do you?"

"That's right." Nicla wiped her eyes.

"I understand." Tony touched Nicla's hand. "I want you to be happy. Let's just relax, have something to eat, and enjoy this place. We don't even have to talk. At least not for a little while. Just enjoy." He began taking food from his bag.

Nicla immediately began to regret what she had said. She watched Tony carving some cheese and placing it on a linen napkin. He showed no sign of resentment. He only cared about her well-being. *Look at him,* she thought. *He's perfect.* She could now add patience and understanding to his list of attributes - not the least of which were his looks. She was remarkably attracted to him. But she knew how things worked. He could get ordered to the front at any time. And he would go. He was loyal - a man of duty.

She lay back as Tony continued his preparations. Birds were chirping. The sun had dipped low behind an Italian cypress. An imperceptible breeze barely rustled its branches. From between each backlit needle, the sun shone like a million sparkling diamonds as the branches swayed.

For Nicla, this miracle of nature was like other mysteries of life that remain hidden and unnoticed. They were always there, behind the exigencies of daily life, part of a plan waiting to be discovered. They burst forth in fleeting moments of clarity, like the light from behind the tree. It made Nicla think of how she found herself there with Tony. God had brought them together through such a series of unlikely circumstances. It must have been more than chance. If a future with Tony was part of a grand plan, it was not something for Nicla to reason away with doubts.

She sat up. Tony was focused on carving some bread with a small knife. Laying her hands on both sides of his face, Nicla turned his head and kissed him. Tony, still clutching bread and knife, dropped them and pulled Nicla close.

For Nicla, it was wonderful not only to be held in Tony's arms but to lose herself. For so long she had been living for others – her family, her country. The trials she endured had left part of her soul empty and barren. Now it was reawakening, like a flower starting to bloom. Their kissing and embracing continued unabated, knowing nothing of time.

Later, after eating, they sat and shared stories of their childhood.

"That tall grass reminds me of the marsh near my house." Tony pointed to some high reeds at one end of the pond. "When we were kids, we'd jump off a train trestle that passed over it. I don't think my brothers or me wore shoes all summer in those days." He shook his head. "Mostly because we couldn't afford them."

"Come on."

"Really. It was the Depression and my father had died. Things were tight." Tony looked across the pond at the reeds sparking his memory. "From the trestle, the train tracks ran through my backyard. Every morning, I'd go out when I heard the freight train coming. Do you know why?

"You wanted to be an engineer, didn't you?" Nicla pinched Tony's cheek.

"No." Tony lightly brushed her hand away. "The freight train moved slow. When the coalman saw me, he'd dump a shovelful or two of coal on the track. It must have been my clothes. He figured we could use it, I'm sure."

"Coal? Really?"

"Yes. After a while, I started laying out this burlap sack that I ripped open. The coalman got so good at hitting it, all I had to do was pick up the corners of the burlap." Tony demonstrated. "Not a lump wasted. Then I'd bring it home for our furnace. That's how hard up we were."

Nicla eyed him warily. "I believe you were poor. We all were during the Depression. But that sounds like a story. The coalman with the good aim?"

"Look." Tony pulled his collar down to reveal the back of his neck. "You see that?"

Nicla saw a birthmark in the form of a light brown stripe.

"That's the mark from carrying that coal bag over my back."

"Pfft!" Nicla slapped the back of Tony's neck. "How many brothers do you have?"

"Two. One's on a ship somewhere in the Atlantic, in the navy. The other is home."

"He's not in the war?"

"No. He has an exemption because my mother is a widow and he's her only support."

"How old were you when your father died?"

"Fourteen."

"How did it happen?"

"You really want to know that, too?"

Nicla nodded solemnly.

"It started out a nice day. I was helping him fix the rabbit hutches. We went to find some wood scraps at the junkyard. While we were walking back home, he just collapsed. They say it was a heart attack."

"How awful. You were all alone. What did you do?"

"I went in a house across the street. The lady called the police, and I called my uncle. He had a friend with a car. When we got home, my mother was upstairs in the bedroom cleaning. They sent me up to get her.

"You had to tell your *mamma*?"

"I couldn't. I couldn't stick that knife in her heart like that. I told the worst lie of my life. I said Dad was sick and she should go in the kitchen and check on him."

"Oh, no."

"I'll never forget the look on her face when she saw my uncles at the kitchen table. She knew it was bad. Then one of them said, 'Elio closed his eyes.' I never heard such a wail. I saw what twenty-five years torn away looks like."

Nicla was moved. "I saw that in my mother too, in the street, in front of our house. My father was inside when the bomb hit."

Tony shook his head and thought for a bit. "As bad as it was, we should all hope to find a love like that. Even if we know it has to end. Don't you think?"

"It doesn't end."

"No. It doesn't."

Once more time ran away, into the blue sky, into the clouds.

Chapter 24

The next day, Tony returned to Zio Fiore's home. "I have a job for you," he told Nicla after they embraced next to the jeep.

"A job?"

"Yes, *lavoro* at the hospital. They hire local girls for cleaning. Maybe you can get some sewing jobs too."

"I don't know. My mother, the house, the sewing. She needs me."

"You don't have to work that many hours. The best part is I get to drive you both ways." He pulled Nicla close. "It's an excuse to spend time together."

"That sounds nice. But I don't know." Nicla looked back at her house.

"Alright. Think about it today while we go swimming."

The jeep pulled into the hospital parking lot. Nicla was incredulous. "Who ever heard of a beach for soldiers... much less at a hospital?"

"Once the engineers cleared the German mines, the doctors figured it would be good therapy for the wounded. Wait till you see it. They took beach chairs and umbrellas from the villa down the road. It's a regular resort, now."

Nicla smiled as Tony took her hand. She had on a light summer dress over her bathing suit. Tony was more than cognizant of how the silky dress accentuated her shape.

After strolling through some brush and over a low dune, they came upon a scene that shocked Nicla. A large section of the beach was fenced off on both sides with barbed wire. There were signs that Nicla assumed to be warnings not to venture beyond the wire. She needed no translation, having seen similar signs from the Germans and the Americans

But between these ugly reminders of war, there was a veritable paradise. Oiled bodies lounged in seaside furniture. Beach balls danced in the air. Rafts floated under paddling seafarers. Presiding over the oceanside retreat was a lifeguard in his wooden tower.

"Some of the rehabbing soldiers swim and relax here," Tony mentioned as they descended from the dune, "The hospital personnel have a lot of fun here, too." He pointed to a volleyball match. "On their free time of course."

"I see." Nicla looked about in disbelief.

"Hey Tony!" a bronzed volleyballer called out. "We need someone to take Ribelli's place."

Tony rotated his arm above his head as if to check its functioning.

"Come on!" shouted the tan fellow. "Your arm's all better. We all know why you're still here. What's for dinner tonight?"

"Porchetta with Rosemary. But if it's all right with you Lieutenant, right now I'd like to go swimming with my friend, here." Tony nodded toward Nicla.

"Ah," the Lieutenant grinned, admiring Nicla. "Well, I could *order* you to play... But that would be a crime against true love... and a poor way to show appreciation for how you've been feeding us. Look how fat I'm getting." He let his chiseled stomach distend slightly. "OK, Amici. You two lovebirds go find a nest." He turned back to the game. "Let's go, knucklehead! Serve that thing! And try to keep it on this side of the barbed wire!"

"What did he say to you?" Nicla asked as they walked toward the ocean.

"He said you are very beautiful."

"No, he didn't. I know that word in English. And it's a good thing I know about your cooking, otherwise I would ask why you used the word porchetta. I saw him look at me. What did he say?"

"He said we should go find our *nido di amore.*"

"He did? Well, Falcons don't nest on the beach." Nicla held her chin up. "He's mistaking us for some other birds."

Tony recalled the falcon at the pond. He was surprised that Nicla's affinity with the bird ran this deep.

He led Nicla over to some unoccupied beach chairs by a striped umbrella and laid down a blanket. They removed their street clothes from over their bathing suits. As Nicla laid her dress over a chair, Tony grabbed her arm.

"*Vieni!*" he shouted, pulling Nicla with him as he ran for the water.

"*Aspetta!* Wait!" Nicla cried as they splashed into the foaming sea. Tony lifted her up in his arms and swung her around. It was dizzying but exhilarating. Closing her eyes, Nicla felt she was flying. Suddenly she was back in the Contessa's basement being whirled in Claudio's arms.

"Stop!" She pushed away.

"What's wrong?"

"I'm sorry." She forced a smile. "I just got dizzy."

"I'll take you for a ride, then. Grab hold of my shoulders." Tony turned, took one of Nicla's hands, and placed it on his shoulder. Nicla spontaneously latched onto the other shoulder. Tony began to breaststroke toward deeper, calmer water, with Nicla stretched out in tow,

"I can swim you know," Nicla called over his back. From under her hand, Nicla could see the scar from Tony's wound stretching across his shoulder. It was still fresh and bright. She did not notice a large wave lifting before them.

"Submerging! Hang on!" Tony dove under the wave. Nicla clung to him. Beneath the water, Tony turned and enfolded Nicla in his arms. They sank downward. For Nicla, time stood still. She wanted to remain, suspended in silence, no past or future, just being with Tony. Eventually, they came to the surface and so did Nicla's doubts. She was struggling to focus on Tony's smiling countenance and remain in the present, but another wave hit like a sobering slap. It reminded her of the harshness with which reality could crash down upon the most fervent hopes and dreams.

"You're distracted." Tony's voice broke through.

Nicla did not want to spoil Tony's happy moment. "I was thinking of how I can beat you to shore." She turned and began digging great, arcing strokes with her arms. Tony threw himself into the chase. It wasn't till they reached the shore that he finally pulled even. They stumbled, breathless, out of the water, and fell on the beach.

They sat shoulder to shoulder looking out at the sea. Nicla watched as each wave crashed, and spread across the sandy floor, gently caressing her feet before being drawn back by its successor. With each undulation, her feet sank deeper in the sand. Pulling one foot out, Nicla noticed how quickly the sea erased her imprint. She turned to Tony. "They'll send you back to fight."

"That's right. I'm not going to lie to you. I play along with this cooking thing because my shoulder isn't a hundred percent yet. But when it is, I'm going to demand to be sent back to my unit. But you're going to make that very hard to do."

"Why would you want to go back? It's terrible, isn't it?"

"It is. But it's my duty. And the men I fought with are like my brothers now." Tony turned toward the rest of the beach. "Look around. Look at the wounded."

Nicla followed Tony's eyes and saw a man hobbling through the sand toward the water. He had a large scar running over his knee and down his shin.

"There are men who truly belong here," Tony continued. "Soon I won't belong here - if I don't already."

Nicla pondered what Tony had said. She looked at the clouds and followed them down to the horizon. Tony's future held far more peril and uncertainty than hers. He had saved her, and she would save him, for now, for however long she could.

"Is this the arm?" Nicla took hold of Tony's wrist in both hands. "I'll fix it so you can't leave." Playfully, but carefully, she lifted it up over Tony's head causing him to tip sideways. With his other arm, Tony pulled Nicla as he rolled onto his back. Nicla pinned his shoulders down.

"I am at your mercy," he conceded.

"Too easy." Nicla leaned down and kissed him. "You'll have to work for another." She stood and ran for the water. Tony gave chase. In this way they spent the morning enjoying each other, playing in the waves and along the beach.

Later, as they placed their things back in the jeep, Nicla spied a large billboard across the street from the hospital. The massive image of a baseball player swinging a bat was painted on it, along with words "Victory Field: Home of the Ramblers and Dodgers." The ballplayer's pose reminded Nicla of a medieval warrior holding a club. She envisioned him as the *fante,* or infantryman, in a deck of *scopa* cards used in the traditional Italian game.

"Is he supposed to inspire you to fight harder?" she asked pointing to the sign.

Tony laughed. "No. He plays baseball."

"It's a game? They dress like *that*? Like at the *Palio*?"

Tony smiled, realizing the blousy uniform *was* reminiscent of the medieval costumes of the *Palio*. "You want to see them play? Come on. I'll show you."

Tony took Nicla by the hand, and they crossed the wide road. Trees and bushes obscured what lay beyond the sign. As they approached, Nicla heard shouts. Passing the sign and the bushes, she beheld a wonderous sight. An immense field was populated with people playing a game she had never seen. A ball, like a small grapefruit, was sailing through the air. It was being thrown and batted and caught. And the most amazing thing to Nicla was that the players performing these feats were women.

"It's the nurses. They play softball," Tony explained. "The men play baseball down that end." He pointed far across the field at a larger diamond.

Nicla did not hear Tony's last comment. She was completely engrossed in watching the women play. They were not wearing the white skirts and stockings Nicla had seen in the hospital. Instead, they sported military shirts and khaki pants rolled up at the ankles. Nicla liked the outfits. The women looked strong and feminine in a way she had never seen. She wished she could try on their clothes. The closest she had ever come was donning a pair of Zio Fiore's overalls – much to her mother's consternation.

A stout woman holding a clipboard approached Tony. "What can I do for you, soldier?"

Nicla thought she was telling them to leave.

"Hello, Nurse Harding. I heard you were hiring civilian women for the cleaning crew. I have a recruit for you." Tony nodded toward Nicla.

The nurse glanced at Nicla then back at Tony. "Being pretty isn't the only qualification, you know."

"Oh, I know, Nurse Harding. She's quite a girl. She takes care of her whole family on her own."

Nurse Harding's attention was drawn away towards the women on the field. "You gotta back her up on that play! Come on! Like I drew it up for you!"

"She can even drive a car!" Tony blurted.

Nurse Harding turned back to Nicla and studied her with pursed lips. "Hmm. Drives a car, eh? Bring her to see Corporal Thomas in the quartermaster's office. Tell him I sent you." She turned suddenly toward the field. "Keep your glove *down*, Bukowski!"

"Can she have an at-bat, Nurse Harding?" Tony asked.

"What? In that dress?"

Tony formed praying hands. Nicla couldn't imagine why.

"Alright," Nurse Harding grumbled, "but make it fast. I gotta get these women ready for a game against the 16th in Pistoia. We ain't the nurses' league champs for nothin' you know."

Tony took Nicla under one arm. "Come on. They're going to let you try."

"What! I don't know how to play this game!"

"Don't worry. I'll show you." He pulled Nicla toward home plate.

Nurse Harding called out to the nurses on the diamond. "It's alright! Give her an at-bat!"

The nurse at home plate handed Nicla a bat and stepped away. Tony positioned Nicla next to the plate. "You saw them hitting the ball. You can do it."

"No! I never did this."

"You *can*. Watch." Getting behind her, Tony reached around Nicla and helped her take some practice swings. "There. Like beating a rug on a line."

Nicla's mind was whirling. To a small degree, she enjoyed Tony's arms around her, but she was more afraid of looking foolish trying to hit the strange ball. Fortunately, she could not understand the chatter in the field. "I'm next, Tarzan!" one nurse called to Tony. This brought more than a few laughs from the others.

Sensing they were mocking her, a feeling of determination rose in Nicla. She pushed her shoulders back to shed Tony. "I can do this myself," she snarled.

Tony stepped back in awe. The pitcher underhanded a soft toss. Nicla swung with all her might. To her shock, Nicla's bat made contact and sent the ball sailing over the pitcher's head. It bounced into centerfield. Nicla spun around and faced Tony with wide eyes. "I did it!"

"Run!" Tony shouted.

"Where?"

"Toward that bag!" He pointed to first base.

Nicla ran as fast as her sandals permitted. Her delay in commencing however, gave the centerfielder time to make a fine throw to first. It arrived before Nicla.

"You're out!" cried the first base coach.

Nicla remained on the bag. "Now what?" she called to Tony who was jogging up the line.

"Wow! That was fantastic!" He took Nicla by both hands and led her off the bag.

"Did I score any points?" Nicla was ecstatic but breathless.

"Forget about points! You really showed them something. You showed me too."

Nicla beamed.

Nurse Harding nodded with her arms folded. "*Brava. Tu lavori per me*? She had a heavy American accent, but Nicla understood she had been asked to work for her.

Nicla nodded back. "Yes," she accepted in English.

As Tony and Nicla left the park, Nurse Harding called to them. "If I had the time, I could turn her into a heck of a player!"

Tony explained in the jeep while driving Nicla home.

Each morning, in the days that followed, Tony arrived in the jeep to take Mirada to the hospital. There, she cleaned and fetched supplies for the nurses. She quickly learned the meaning of a few short commands in English: "get blankets, bandages," etc.

More than once a day, she would be ambushed by Tony around some hidden corner. He would pull her close and steal kisses over Nicla's halfhearted protests. Sometimes she would abandon caution and push Tony against the wall in passionate reciprocation.

Later in the day, Tony would drive Nicla home. Never was the route direct. On one occasion, they stopped to walk hand in hand by the canal in the city. The low sun shone bright on the canal's stone walls and the sounds of small motors purred as boats came back to their moorings for the day. Looking down at the emerald water, Nicla saw one boat heading out toward the sea. It carried a young couple. Memories of Luca bringing her to Molo Nuovo took shape. Nicla looked for a diversion.

"Have you ever had *ricci di mare?*" she asked Tony.

"What?"

Nicla grabbed Tony's hand and led him across the street to a vendor's cart. It did not surprise Tony that upon the cart rested a flat box of ice, but its other contents truly asonished him – black spiny orbs, the size of baseballs.

"What the hell are they?"

"*Ricci.*" Nicla didn't know the word for sea urchins in English.

"What do you do with them? Throw them at your enemies?"

"No," Nicla giggled. "You eat them."

Tony's eyes widened and he stepped back slightly. "Not me."

"Come on. Where's my brave soldier now?" Nicla turned to the vendor and held up a finger.

The man behind the cart picked up one of the prickly creatures in his gloved hand and turned it over. With artistry, he cut a circle in the bottom of it, removed the "lid" he'd created, and pulled out what looked like several segments of an orange. Placing them on some paper, he handed them to Nicla.

Nicla picked one up with her fingers and placed it, with great flourish, in her mouth. She closed her eyes as she chewed. "*Buono!*" She held out the paper with the remaining urchin innards.

Tony looked closer. They did not have the slimy exterior he anticipated. Instead, their surface looked like terry cloth. He leaned in further. The fresh smell of the ocean met his senses and gave him a modicum of courage. Nicla watched intently as Tony placed the urchin roe in his mouth. He took two faltering chews. The clean, briny taste of the sea and the creamy texture were delightful. He smiled.

"Delicious, right?" Nicla effused. "I told you they were good!"

"How could something so scary taste this good?" Tony ate some more.

"See. You must trust me."

"I do," Tony replied, "and you're going to have to trust me, too."

"About what?"

Tony gave Nicla that smile that was slightly higher on one side of his mouth – the smile with which she had been enamored since they first met. It was a confident smile, but it was also a smile that said, "I know something. You'll see."

They finished the delicacy from the ocean floor, paid the vendor, and continued their stroll along the canal.

"So, warrior, you conquered ricci. What will be your next triumph?"

"You really are *la spiritosa*," Tony observed, using the Italian word for someone who is lively and facetious.

"You noticed? It's a Livornese trait. We can be pretty sarcastic."

"Oh really? I didn't notice."

"Yes. I'll give you an example. A Livornese sees Jesus walking on the water in the canal. You know what the Livornese says? Look, he doesn't know how to swim."

Tony shook his head. They continued their stroll.

There were many other detours on their rides back from the hospital. Once they stopped by the public beach. Since she had tried softball, Nicla wanted Tony to try an Italian game. The young men there were playing soccer inside *il gabbione* or "the big cage." It was a large concrete court, entirely closed-in by a metal fence which also formed its roof. At each end, a goal was formed by a box of the same metal fencing projecting outward.

The young men playing in the *gabbione* immediately took a liking to Tony. Especially since he readily obliged them with a lesson in English expletives.

Nicla was quite amused at how Tony ran up and down the court in his t-shirt, long army trousers and boots, while the others wore shorts and tank tops. He was not very adept at the game either - also to Nicla's merriment. But the young men kept passing him the ball and cheering him on. Each time he kicked the ball wildly, he would turn to Nicla and shrug his shoulders or make a funny face. She returned looks of mortification and embarrassment.

At one point, being in the right place at the right time, the ball crossed Tony's path as he ran toward the goal. With little conscious effort, and simply continuing in his stride, he kicked it. Miraculously, it sailed into the upper corner of the goal. A cheer erupted from the young men, including the opposing team. Tony was lifted on their shoulders and paraded around the cage to the chant of "*Viva l'americano!*"

When Nicla saw the joy in Tony's face as he received the accolades of his newfound friends, she was filled with happiness for him. Whatever he had experienced on the battlefield was behind him at that moment. She also thought of how Tony had relieved her own troubling memories.

But these young men carrying him around, celebrating victory, reminded her of the nature of man. There was a primitive need to rally around the "us," be it teammates, tribe, or countrymen, and vanquish the opposing "them." *Wars will never end*, she thought. And Tony would be returning to his comrades with whom he had celebrated victory and endured loss. She wondered how she could reconcile this with what was also becoming evident. She was falling in love with him.

Chapter 25

After coming home from a detour to the pond with Tony, Nicla walked in the door of Zio Fiore's house. She was surprised to find Vivi at the table. Although he had been home from the war for some time, he always left early for work and was never home before her.

"Who is that soldier that dropped you off?"

"Tony. He gives me a ride home from work."

"More than a ride."

Nicla furled her brow. "What are you talking about?"

"I saw you kiss him before you got out of the jeep."

"Alright. We've been seeing each other. Where's Mamma?"

"She's dropping off some clothes to a customer. But let's stick to the subject."

"Fine." Nicla sat across from Vivi. "What do you want to know?"

"I want to know what you think you're doing running around with a soldier?"

"What do you mean running around?" Nicla's voice rose.

"I know soldiers. They have their fun and move on. That's how it is."

Nicla studied her brother. "You've had your fun too, haven't you?"

"I'm a man."

"So, it's different for you?"

"You know it is!" Vivi paused and composed himself. "Look. Without *Babbo* here, I have to look out for you."

"I can look out for myself. You have no idea what I did when you were gone."

"Yes. I'm sure you and mamma had to work hard to make ends meet."

"No..." Nicla shook her head. "No...You don't know..." She was tempted to tell Vivi about her life as a *staffetta*. But it was a badge she had paid for dearly and she would share it on her own terms, at her own time - not having it drawn out under duress. Moreover, she felt it her right as a woman to see any man she wished without Vivi's imprimatur. Something like righteous anger began to well-up in her. "I *will* see him, and you better get used to it."

Vivi was flabbergasted. Never had his sister spoken to him so. It hardened something within him, and it fell like an ax between them. He stood and turned away. Looking out of the window, he spoke deliberately. "I won't have you running around like..." he hesitated.

"Go ahead. Say it. Like my friend Luisa? Or worse?"

"No. You're nothing like that whore for the Germans."

"Just a whore for the Americans."

"No! My God!" He took Nicla by her forearms and helped her out of her chair. "You have to understand," he spoke gently. "It looks bad for the family. And you're going to get hurt. He's going to leave you and go home... maybe leave you in a bad condition."

"You think I'm going to get pregnant? How could you talk to me like that? Like I'm a stupid child!" She pulled away. "I've grown a lot since you were gone. If you only knew. And let me tell you something else." She gathered herself. "I love him! And I'm going to keep seeing him no matter what you say." Bursting into tears, she flung open the bedroom door and rushed out of the room.

Vivi followed, putting his hands against the closed door. "You think so?" he shouted through the door. "If I catch him around here again, watch what I do to him! You watch!" He pushed away from the door and stormed out of the house.

Nicla lay on the bed, tears streaming down her face as she stared at the ceiling. She could hardly believe what had just transpired. She had known nothing but kind words from her brother. And though she knew he had her best interest in mind, it pained her terribly that he should use such an ugly tone with her. Worse, now she feared for Tony's safety. Surely Vivi didn't mean what he said. But she could not rule out his becoming violent with Tony. She fought to block the images it conjured. And then something more profound took hold of her thoughts. It was something she hadn't been able to admit even to herself. She had professed her love for Tony.

The following day at the hospital, Nicla was clearing a wash pan on a table next to a bed. In the bed lay a soldier whose eyes were bandaged.

"Hey babe, what's your rush?" he asked.

She did not understand. "*Non parlo inglese.* I no speak English."

"Ah! *Sei Italiana!* So am I! *Anch'io!*"

His Italian wasn't very good, but Nicla understood him perfectly. She looked him over. In addition to his bandaged eyes, his face was crimson red. Nicla wondered if he had been burned. Perhaps he needed something. "What did you ask me before?" she inquired in Italian.

"To keep me company." He flashed an impish smile.

"How did you know I wasn't a male orderly?"

"By how soft you moved things. The men bang and clank stuff."

Nicla smiled. He reminded her of Tony with his Italian and his sense of humor.

From the corner of her eye, Nicla saw her boss, Nurse Harding, enter the ward. "I need to go."

"Oh, stay for a little." With a lunge, he found Nicla's wrist and pulled her closer. She put the wash pan down with her free hand.

"Do you have a boyfriend?" he asked.

Before Nicla could respond, Nurse Harding was making a bee line for her. "What are you doing with that soldier? Get to work!"

Nurse Harding's tone left no need for translation. Nicla began to pull away from the soldier's grasp.

"Aw come on, Nurse Harding. She's just teaching me some Italian."

"I'll bet she is."

"Just another minute. I have to learn how to say, 'Will you marry me?'" He pulled Nicla back by the waist this time.

"You already speak Italian." The brawny nurse stood with arms akimbo. "And if you think you'll get any sympathy from me, forget it. Sunburn on your eyes from laying out in a boat all day with one of my nurses won't get you a purple heart. In fact, it's gonna get you a kick in the ass from me tomorrow when those bandages come off."

"Please!" He held a finger to his lips. "I can still get some sympathy from *her*." He nodded toward Nicla.

"You'd like to get a lot more than that from her, wouldn't you?" Nurse Harding looked about the ward. "Hey!" she shouted across the room at a very young nurse, "Get over there. You call that a dressing!" She turned back to the soldier in bed. "See. I've got bigger fish to fry, lover boy. And wipe that smile off your face." She pivoted to Nicla. "And *you*. Go!" Motioning for Nicla to do just that, she walked briskly away.

Nicla tried to pull away from the soldier's grasp, but he drew her by the sleeve closer to his face and whispered in Italian, "I'm going to teach you a word for Nurse Harding." He leaned closer, almost bumping into Nicla's nose. Holding a hand beside his mouth, in English he whispered, "Asshole."

Nicla could tell by his grin that the word was not meant to flatter Nurse Harding. "*Grazzie.*" She pulled free from him. Picking up the wash basin, she hurried away. The soldier fell back on his pillow chuckling.

As she walked down the hall, Nicla thought of how the soldier reminded her of Tony – an American boy speaking Italian. She had not understood the sunburn story. She still thought he had been blinded by some battlefield misfortune. This disturbed her. It could have been Tony in that bed.

Once again, reason cast over her heart the specter of losing another man to this war. And again, she fought to push it out of her mind. The tasks at hand helped. But there was something else. It was a thought that swept her up in fantasy and carried her through the rest of the day. That night, Tony was taking her to a dance.

Walking into the ballroom on Tony's arm, Nicla was overwhelmed at the sight. This had been the rehabilitation ward of the hospital, where nurses carefully helped men move limbs stiffened by wounds and surgery. Now, music blared as couples danced with joyous abandon. Streamers crossed the ceiling above tables covered with festive cloths.

"What do you think?" Tony leaned toward Nicla's ear to speak over the music.

"I've never seen anything like it." She continued looking about the room. "Maybe at a wedding. But not with music like this... and not this dancing."

"It's called swing."

The music and tempo were so foreign to Nicla. She was transfixed by the frenetic movements of the couples. Feet and legs darted and zigzagged in rhythm with the syncopated drums. Torsos bobbed and hips swung as the pairs whirled about the dance floor at arm's length.

"Come on. Let's try it!" Tony shouted over the raucous scene, towing a very reluctant Nicla with him. On the floor, he pulled Nicla close with one hand around her waist. With the other, he lifted Nicla's hand in ballroom dancing position. He started swaying with the upbeat tempo of the music. His feet moved quickly and deftly. Nicla giggled and matched him step for step.

"You've done this before?" Tony asked.

"No." Nicla looked around. "But these other couples are making us look like old folks!"

"OK then!" Tony pushed Nicla away grabbing both her hands. He swung her around at arm's length, alternating from pulling her close and letting her swing at the end of their tether. Nicla laughed and threw her head back. She was dizzy but exhilarated. When Tony held her close again, she could feel her heart beating with the pounding drums.

Suddenly he dipped her. Before she could react, he pulled her upright. Her hair fell across her face, and she tossed her head back to clear it. Tony's face moved closer to hers.

When their noses just about touched, he swung her around, letting go of one hand. Nicla uncoiled like a yoyo until she reached the end of her string. By sheer momentum, and instinct, she let her free hand fly into the air. Then, like a snap of the string, Tony pulled her back, closer than before.

So, they danced, song after song. Their movements became less conscious and more spontaneous. When the slow dance commenced, Nicla put her head on Tony's shoulder. This was where she wanted it to stay. It was becoming clear to her. But here was that uniform under her cheek. Where would it lead him? And where would it lead her should she follow?

"Let's get a drink," Tony suggested as the song ended. They found a table. There were many empty glasses around the table and one lonesome soldier nursing a drink. Tony pulled out a chair. Nicla sat.

"Hey, bud. Keep an eye on my girl, would you?" Tony asked.

"Sure." The soldier raised his glass and took a swig.

Tony leaned and whispered in Nicla's ear, "I'm going to get us some drinks. Try not to let this guy fall in love with you." He stepped away.

Nicla looked at the soldier. He was very young and very slight. He held her gaze for a moment, then nodded and looked away at the dance floor. Nicla continued to study him. There was something familiar about him.

"Here we are." Tony appeared placing a drink before Nicla. "So how did you hit it off with our friend here?"

"I know him from somewhere."

"You probably saw him working around the hospital."

At that moment, a beefy soldier came up behind the seated one and slapped him on the back. "Hey! Stop drowning your sorrows. You got dumped. Get over it!" He pulled his friend to his feet. "Come on. I met two of those Italian girls they bussed in. They wanna dance with us." He turned to Tony. "I see you found one yourself, buddy."

"We're already going out, but she did come on the bus."

Suddenly, Nicla squeezed Tony's hand beneath the table and leaned toward him. "He is the one that hit me with the jeep!" she whispered.

"Hey babe," the hefty soldier bellowed at Nicla, "maybe you can translate for us with the Italian girls."

Tony stood up and marched determinedly toward him.

"What?" The beefy soldier shrugged his shoulders and held up his arms. "Did I say something wrong?"

Tony stepped in, chest to chest with him. "You think it's all right to run a person over and leave them lying in the street like a dog?"

"What the hell are you talking about?" He held up his arms.

"I knew it!" interrupted his friend. "She's the girl in the road. I told you we hit her." He looked at Tony. "I'm very sorry. Can you tell her that? I tried to go back."

"What are you sorry for?" exclaimed the brawny one. "Are we supposed to stop for every guinea skirt faking something for a buck?"

"I'll give you about three seconds to apologize to this lady," Tony simmered.

Nicla understood none of this, but she could tell by Tony's inflection, and more so by his clenched fist, that she had to act immediately. Grabbing a glass from the table, she rose and tossed its contents over Tony's shoulder, squarely in the face of the ogre. He winced. Then his eyes grew round with rage.

Nicla stood tall. She raised her chin and pronounced judgement upon him in his own vernacular. "Asshole!"

The brute was taken aback by the epithet delivered so artfully by the Italian girl. A smirk spread across his face. Calmly reaching down, he took a napkin from the table, and dried himself. Wagging his head, he began to snicker. "Well, I'll be damned. You taught her some good English."

"No. You just brought it out of her. But if the shoe fits..."

"Oh yeh?" The gorilla leaned into Tony, who, although well built himself, was significantly outweighed. Tony leaned forward, nonetheless. Nicla's mind spun thinking of a way to diffuse the situation. She was not beyond grabbing a chair to defend Tony.

Just then, two Italian girls came up behind the boorish soldier. "*Vieni a ballare!*" they exclaimed almost in unison. They tugged at the large soldier.

"They want you to dance," Tony noted coldly, maintaining an icy stare.

"Yeh, I figured that," the large one replied without breaking their mutual gaze.

The young soldier stepped over to his friend. "Come on, Gus. Let's go dance with these girls." He gently shook his friend by the shoulder. It broke him from his primal state.

"Well..." Gus turned to look at the girls then back at Tony. He took a step back, "You got lucky, buddy. I ain't got time to waste on no knight in shining armor tryin' to act like a tough guy." Then he turned and took both Italian girls by the arm. "*Andiamo!*" he ordered with a heavy American accent and began walking away with them.

"You forgot to apologize," Tony announced.

Gus turned and walked slowly back toward Tony.

Nicla looked for another projectile on the table.

Gus put his finger in Tony's chest. "You know something? You got guts." He pursed his lips and tipped his head to one side. "And you know what else? So does your girlfriend. I gotta respect that." He turned to face Nicla. Placing his hand over his heart, he bowed slightly. "*Scuzi.*" His tone bordered on actual sincerity.

Tony looked at Nicla. She nodded.

"Good!" Gus gave his hands a conclusory clap. "That's settled. Everybody's happy. You two sweethearts have a wonderful evening!" He turned and sauntered away with the Italian girls.

The young soldier stayed behind. "I really did try to turn the jeep around."

"I'm sure you did, kid," reassured Tony. "Here's some advice. Find another friend."

The young soldier nodded sadly, turned, and hurried away.

Tony looked to Nicla. "That was unbelievable! That big *cavone* said you have a lot of guts, and he was right. You *do!*" He picked Nicla up and twirled her around. "But where did you get that word from?" He repeated the expletive.

Nicla shook her head. "I was just so mad, it came out."

"Yes, but how did you know it?"

"I know a lot more English than you think." She tipped her head back. "I know a lot more about a lot of things."

"I know you do. Tell me. In your great wisdom, how did you figure I needed help with that guy?"

Nicla could see Tony's pride showing. "No you didn't," she assured. "It was just anger. I surprised myself even. Listen, it meant a lot that you should stand up for me like that."

"How else should I act for the woman I love?"

Nicla's heart welled up. "Love?"

Tony nodded. "Yes."

Nicla put her head against Tony's chest. He embraced her. They began to sway to a slow number that was playing. They remained so, barely moving, through the next several songs, oblivious to the surging tempo of the music and the looks of revelers who came spilling past them like falling stars from the spinning galaxy of the dance floor.

The rest of the night was filled with more dancing. Nicla caught on quickly and the swing dancing became ever more daring and exciting. The slow dances became slower and more intense. They moved as one.

In the end, Tony obtained permission from his superiors to drive Nicla home - Fiore's garage being too far from the bus route for Nicla to walk.

As they drove, Nicla's mind whirled with happiness. She threw all doubts to the wind that rushed through her hair as the jeep drove through the cool night. They did not speak much. The glances they exchanged affirmed what they felt.

Before getting in the jeep, Nicla had told Tony that there could be no "detour" that night. It was late enough, and she had to get home. Her mother was not particularly happy about Nicla going out at night with Tony. As for her brother Vivi, Nicla had serious concerns. He thought she was working at the dance - cleaning and serving. Nicla hoped her story would hold up.

"Pull in slowly to Zio Fiore's," Nicla cautioned, "I don't want to wake anyone." They stopped out by the gas pumps. Tony grabbed Nicla and began kissing her.

"Stop," she giggled, pushing him away. "Didn't you get enough kisses at the dance?"

"No." Tony pulled her near again.

"Listen," Nicla managed, "I've got to get inside now. If my brother sees you, there'll be trouble."

"Your brother will like me. I'm Italian. Besides, I want to meet him."

"No. You don't understand. There's a lot we have to... Oh no!"

From around the side of the garage, Vivi approached at a quick pace. He had a wrench in his hand. Nicla got out of the jeep to intercept him. Vivi pushed past her.

"Wait! Vivi!" she cried.

Tony had come around the jeep. He walked toward Vivi holding out his hand in greeting. Vivi raised the wrench. Tony's outstretched hand rose quickly to restrain it. With his free hand, Vivi grasped Tony's neck and leaned him backward over the jeep. Nicla saw the silver wrench flash in the moonlight as the two struggled.

"*Aspetta!* Wait!" Tony blurted. "*Sono italiano!*" This startled Vivi and allowed Tony to rise from the jeep. "Please. I love your sister," he continued in Italian.

"Like hell you do!" Vivi raised the wrench and swung.

Nicla screamed.

Tony dove to the ground, dodging the cudgel. It clanked on the jeep's hood. Vivi swung again. Tony, on his back, caught it an inch from his head. Vivi grabbed the other end of the wrench and with both hands pressed down toward Tony's neck. Tony pushed back with both hands.

"You think you can take advantage of my sister, talking about love?" Vivi grunted and pushed the wrench closer.

"No!" Tony pushed back. "I want to marry her!"

"Marry?" Vivi fell back.

"Marry?" Nicla uttered in shock.

Tony sprang up and rushed to Nicla. "Yes. Marry." He took Nicla by both hands. "I'm sorry you had to hear it this way. I was going to ask you tomorrow at the pond. Now it's ruined."

"No. No, it's not. I-"

"Stop!" Tony interrupted. "Don't answer here. Not like this."

"Alright." She squeezed Tony's hands. "I understand. We'll pretend this never happened. Yes. You come get me tomorrow. Take me to the pond. You can ask me at the pond... if you still want to." She turned and cast a stern look at her bother.

"Of course, I want to. It's just-"

"Please!" Nicla implored. "No more talk. Quick. Get in the jeep."

Tony, head cast downward, climbed in.

"I'll see you tomorrow," Nicla whispered into his ear. She kissed his cheek and stepped back. "Tomorrow."

Tony managed a half smile and drove away. Nicla turned and glared at her brother.

"I'm sorry," Vivi murmured. "Maybe he's alright." He looked down the road at the receding jeep. "Maybe not." He walked past Nicla. "We'll see if he shows up tomorrow."

That night, Nicla did not sleep. Her mind whirled. There was no question she loved Tony. It had been a relatively short time, but they had grown close in a way that went beyond romantic infatuation. It was as if she had known him many years. They had shared so much, especially in their times by the pond, which had been intimate on so many levels. Childhood memories, hopes, the importance of family – these were the bedrock upon which their relationship had become unshakable. Their physical bond was as passionate and strong as their spiritual one. But it was only part of something more profound and lasting. Nicla knew she wanted to spend the rest of her life with Tony.

She thought back on Claudio. Their romance had been intense – as youthful romances are. She would always cherish his memory. Even Luca floated across her mind's wanderings that night.

That she could love again was Tony's gift. Her love for him was so strong that it gave her the courage to put fond memories away in a special place in her heart. There, they could be visited and treasured, but they would not cast a shadow over her future joy.

"You're awake," whispered her mother, who had been sleeping next to Nicla. "What's on your mind?"

Nicla could tell by Silvia's tone that nothing short of a direct reply would suffice. Her mother had a way of seeing through her. Besides, Nicla wanted to unburden herself of something still holding her back with Tony.

"Tony is going to ask me to marry him tomorrow."

"Marry?" Silvia sat up slightly. "How do you know he's going to ask you?"

"It's a long story. But he's going to."

"Oh," Silvia pronounced solemnly, putting her head back on the pillow.

"You see? You know what that means. I would have to leave you and go to America with him."

"Yes. I know." Silvia's eyes remained fixed on the ceiling.

"I can't do that to you – leave you without *Babbo* or me. I won't."

Silvia sat up. She took Nicla by the shoulders and raised her up. "Do you want to marry Tony?"

Nicla held her eyes closed tightly. She grimaced.

"Do you?" Silvia squeezed Nicla's shoulders.

Nicla nodded, her eyes downcast.

"How much?" Silvia lifted Nicla's chin. "Look at Mamma. How much do you want to marry him?"

Nicla looked into her mother's eyes. Here was the woman to whom she owed everything and whom she loved beyond measure. How could she abandon her to follow her own romantic dream?

But Nicla could not lie to her, and she could not hold it in any longer.

"With all my heart!" Nicla burst into tears. "I want to marry him, with all my heart."

Her mother gazed fondly on her. She smiled and stroked Nicla's cheek. "It's alright. I already knew. I've known for a long time. I see that hint of a smile when you're sewing, and I know you're thinking of him. I see how you jump when he drives up in his jeep. After all you've been through, I finally see you happy again. That's what brings me joy." Silvia took her daughter's face in both hands. "If it's what your heart tells you, you marry him."

"Oh, Mamma!" Nicla hugged her mother. "You're so good. I know you'll do anything for me. But I'm still scared. A new country, so far away from you."

"I'm not going to push you one way or the other. It's a big decision and you must make it for yourself. I know how smart you are. You've always done the right thing. And I know how brave you are. So don't let fear cloud your judgement now. Come on." Silvia laid back and took her daughter's head to her chest. "Pray to Mary. She will ask God to show you the way. Then, while you're asleep, God will help you work things out in your mind. You'll see." Silvia began to caress Nicla's hair. "There, close your eyes."

Nicla obeyed. And with her head nestled in the crook of her mother's shoulder, she prayed. Silvia, as she had done when Nicla was a little girl, hummed lullabies as Nicla drifted off to sleep.

The next morning, Nicla woke to find an empty place next to her in bed. She feared she had slept late, and Tony might come before she was ready. Lightly splashing water on her face from a basin on a dresser, she patted her fair skin dry with a linen. As she brushed her hair in the mirror above the dresser, she studied her face. She became aware of herself as the woman Tony wanted to marry. Her hair was still youthful and silky; her eyes still hazel-green. But she could see the anxiety in them. As much as she wanted to spend a lifetime with Tony, she wasn't sure she could bring herself to say yes to him.

Entering the kitchen, she saw her mother was gone. Vivi sat at the table. "You didn't leave for work yet?" she asked.

"No. I wanted to see you before I left." Vivi looked serious.

"Please don't talk to me about Tony. I heard all you had to say."

"No," Vivi shook his head. "I want to talk about *you*. Come, sit." He patted the seat of the chair next to him.

Nicla moved cautiously over to the seat. Looking in Vivi's eyes, she could not divine his intent.

"I talked to Mamma this morning," he began. "I wanted to tell her how foolish I thought you were behaving. I figured maybe she could talk some sense into you."

"Listen, Vivi. I told you-"

"Wait." He held up his hand. "Mamma told me about you being a staffetta."

"What?"

"Why didn't you tell me?" Vivi took Nicla's hands. "You always told me things. You know, important things."

Nicla could see the hurt in her brother's eyes. "I'm sorry. It's hard to talk about. It brings back memories of how Claudio and Luca were killed." She looked down.

"Yes. I can see that now. And there's something else I can see." He put his hand on Nicla's cheek. "You're not that little girl that I had to look out for all these years. Not anymore. You're a brave and smart woman."

Nicla's eyes glistened as she leaned her cheek against Vivi's palm. She put her own hand over his.

"So," Vivi took Nicla's hand in his and held it up. "If you have judged Tony worthy to take *this* hand in marriage, then he must be exceptional." Vivi took Nicla's hand to his lips and kissed it. "And I will defend your decision to the end."

Nicla threw her arms around her brother's neck. "Oh Vivi! You don't know how much that means to me." She squeezed him tightly.

At that moment, through the open window came the sound of Tony's jeep pulling to a stop.

Vivi grasped Nicla by her shoulders. "Go. Don't think of anything else but what makes you happy. That's what we all want. Go do what's right for *you*."

Nicla gave Vivi one last hug and rushed for the door.

"Remember! I can still boss you around if I want to!" Vivi called. "I'm still your older brother."

Nicla turned at the door. "You always will be." She smiled fondly at the brother she loved so dearly, before turning to race for Tony's jeep.

Chapter 26

Tony and Nicla arrived at their favorite detour, the pond in the countryside. They had not spoken much on the ride there. There was some small talk. Tony asked about Vivi, and Nicla simply said not to worry; things had been smoothed out with him.

Most of the drive, Nicla was deep in thought. As much as Vivi's encouragement empowered her, it reminded her how deeply she was tied to her family. To break that bond with a simple yes to Tony seemed more than she could manage. But looking at him driving next to her, returning her gaze with his familiar smile, she felt the depth of their love.

At the pond, they set a blanket close to the water's edge where the pond was deep and still. Nicla looked down at the smooth surface. It was like a black mirror. The blue sky and the white cotton clouds floated on it. To Nicla, it was like looking down from Heaven. *Is this what God sees?* she wondered. If only she could see like God – penetrate the clouds, look into the future. She remembered the little girl from the painting in the basement of the Contessa's villa. Like her, she was crossing a mountain. She couldn't be sure what lay beyond the crest, beyond the clouds.

"I was a staffetta, you know."

"A staffetta? One of those women in the Resistance?"

"Yes. I ran messages for the Partisans. People's lives depended on me." Nicla paused. She could see the wonder in Tony's face. She waited for a further reaction.

"It makes sense now. The way you fight for your family. Or how you stood up to that guy who hit you with the jeep. You're brave and you have a mind of your own. That's what I love about you."

Nicla's eyes filled with pride. "Thank you. I love you for saying that." She put her hand to her heart. "I do. But I didn't bring up being a *staffetta* to impress you. The point is, as terrifying as that was, it wasn't half as hard as what you're going to ask me to do now.

"I understand. I'm asking you to leave your family, your responsibilities, your homeland. It goes against who you are. I know. I wish it were easier. And now I'm going to make it harder for you."

"Harder?"

"I requested to be put back into combat duty. Doctor Osgood signed off on it. I'm leaving by the end of the week."

"No! Why now?"

"I couldn't stay here and play injured - make fancy meals for the officers while my brothers were risking their lives. I'm sorry. I thought you knew that's how I felt."

"Yes. I knew it. That's who you are. Loyal." Nicla sroked Tony's cheek. "I can see that I have to accept it. When you joined the army, it brought you to me. This is all part of the same picture somehow. Why should I question what put us together?"

Tony held up a finger. "*Un momento*." From his bag, he produced a plate wrapped in wax paper. Carefully, he unfolded it to reveal several golden segments of sea urchin roe arrayed in a sunburst pattern on the white plate.

Nicla's face lit up. "Where did you get those?"

"From the guy with the cart. You remember, near the canal?"

"Of course. You were so afraid to try them." Nicla tilted her head. "For me you did. Didn't you?"

"Yes. For you I did. I had to have faith in you." Tony reached and took Nicla's hand. "What I'm going to ask you is much bigger, but it still comes down to the same thing – faith." He took Nicla's other hand as well. "Do you have faith that I'll make you happy for the rest of your life?"

Nicla's eyes filled with tears. "Yes."

"Will you marry me?"

Nicla was nodding and crying. "Yes!" She threw her arms around Tony's neck. "Yes!"

And with that simple affirmation, a new and very uncertain journey was about to begin for Nicla.

It was a blur of a week leading up to Nicla's wedding. She was busy with work at the American base. The wedding would be a very modest affair; little planning was needed. There was no time, or resources, for a gown. Nicla's thoughts were occupied with what came after the wedding. Tony would be leaving the day after. She wondered when her new life in America would begin. But so much depended on how the war went. One thought was off limits - Tony's part in the fighting and the dangers he surely faced.

It was late afternoon on the day before her wedding when Tony brought Nicla home from a day of work at the base. As she came in the door of Zio Fiore's home, she found her mother at the kitchen table. A mass of shimmery white material lay on the table. It was a wedding gown.

"Nicla. I was waiting," Silvia spoke. "You're just the right size. You would make a good model for this."

Immediately, the spark of hope that this might be her gown was dashed. It was for a customer. Nicla wondered how her mother could be so insensitive.

"Here, before anyone comes home." Silvia lifted Nicla's dress off and dropped the wedding gown in its place. The silky garment slid on easily. Before Nicla knew it, her mother was gathering material here and there, fastening it with the pins sticking from her mouth.

"Looks like I estimated pretty well. It's so close already," she mumbled with half her mouth cinched around the pins.

"Lucky girl." Nicla commented. "When is her wedding?"

Silvia was kneeling working on the hem. "Tomorrow." She pinned some material.

"Tomorrow! But that's my..."

Silvia looked up, beaming. "Yes. And she's the most beautiful and wonderful daughter in the whole world."

"Mamma! This is for me?"

Silvia nodded, gazing lovingly at the joy in her daughter's eyes. Nicla helped her mother up off her knees and embraced her. They swung back and forth several times before Nicla stepped back. She held the side of the dress out in one hand and spun around, watching the silk flutter and shimmer. "It's beautiful! But how? Where did you get the material – or the time?"

"You can thank your brother Vivi for the material. It's parachute silk from an American pilot. The Partisans hid him in the mountains till the Germans left. As for how quickly I made the dress... I had a little help." Silvia turned toward the bedroom door. "Come out, my little helper!"

"Luisa!" exclaimed Nicla as her friend emerged. Luisa stood smiling, enjoying Nicla's surprise. Nicla rushed to her and squeezed her tightly.

"Easy! You'll crush me. We're not finished with the dress!"

"Look at you." Nicla held Luisa at arm's length, spinning her fully round and back again. "Your hair. It's grown back." Nicla touched her hair. It was wavy and just covered her ears. "You look like a movie star from the Twenties."

"You think so?" Luisa took a strand of spaghetti from the counter and held it like a cigarette holder. She threw her head back and blew an imaginary puff of smoke toward the ceiling. "Who am I?"

"Gloria Swanson!" Silvia exclaimed.

"Mary Pickford!" Nicla declared.

"Well," Luisa put her cigarette holder down, "they're nice for now." She fluffed up her hair at the sides. "But in a few months it will be Greta Garbo, because my hair is going to look like this." She stroked Nicla's shoulder length hair. They looked at each other fondly.

"It will be, in no time," Nicla assured. "But wait. How did you work on the dress?"

"She came here every day," interjected Silvia, "while you were at work, and she left before you got home. Piero drove her."

"Your mother came one day with your Zio Fiore to invite me to the wedding," Luisa explained, "and she *happened* to mention she was making the dress."

Silvia chuckled. "A mother does what she has to do. Besides, Luisa is just your size. So, I got a model and a seamstress for the price of one."

"What was the price?" Nicla asked.

"I had to feed her every day! And you should see her eat. If the dress took longer to make, she would have gone up a size." Silvia pulled the front of Luisa's dress out to create a bulge. "Then the dress would fit a girl in a hurry to get married for another reason. Say," she looked at Nicla, "You're not..."

"Mamma!"

"Come now," Silvia announced, "Let's finish this. Here's the veil." Taking it from the table, she placed it on Nicla's head. It was sheer and long. The material was gathered at the crown like a tiara. A delicate sprig of tiny silk flowers danced like a diadem across the front.

"One more thing..." Silvia fetched the last item on the table - a pair of long, white gloves. She handed one to Louisa and they pulled them up Nicla's arms. "There." Silvia stood back with her hands on her hips.

They led Nicla to the bedroom to look in a long mirror behind the door. Nicla was overwhelmed. Never had she suspected this. It was so beautiful. She had harbored some sadness for not having a proper gown for her wedding. But now she was the bride she had dreamed of being. She couldn't wait for tomorrow to come. Little did she know the turn of events that awaited her.

Chapter 27

Nicla stood dressed in her wedding gown. Silvia and Louisa tugged and fluffed it here and there. Zio Fiore straightened his tie while Nicla's little brother, also in a tie, sat in a chair bouncing a soccer ball between his feet.

"Go outside with that." Silvia admonished absently as she primped Nicla. "Fiore, take him outside, please."

"*Vieni.*" Fiore put his hand on Matteo's shoulder and led him out.

Nicla heard a familiar voice. In the doorway was a tall, slender man with a neatly groomed mustache.

"Signore Montanini!"

"Nicla," Montanini spoke with affection. "You look beautiful."

"*Grazzie*, but what are you doing here? I mean, I'm so glad, but …"

"I was given some leave to find my grandparents in Grosseto. I thought I'd stop here on my way. I got into town a few days ago.

"Why didn't I see you sooner?"

"I stopped to contact my sources, and I heard you were getting married."

"Sources? Who told you I was getting married?"

"Remember the two old men on the bench?"

"No! Those two!" Nicla put a hand to her head. "How did they know I was getting married?"

"Let's just say, as a former staffetta, they have a particular interest in your wellbeing. And..." Montanini leaned forward with a hand cupped beside his mouth, "I think they're in love with you."

Nicla grinned shaking her head.

"Who could blame them?" Montanini waived his hand from Nicla's head to her toes.

"Signore Montanini, you're too kind."

"Excuse me," interjected Silvia. "Nicla, where are your manners?"

"Oh, I'm sorry. Mamma and Louisa, this is Signore Montanini. He is..." Nicla caught herself before giving away Montanini's OSS credentials. "He is a good friend of the Contessa."

"*Piacere.*" Montanini bowed. Turning to Nicla, he extracted from his jacket a telegram. "This is from the Contessa." He handed it to Nicla. She looked at him bewildered.

"Go ahead." He nodded toward the paper. "Read it."

Hesitantly, Nicla looked down and began to read.

My dearest Nicla,

I'm so happy for you on your marriage. If only I could be there, but I'm living in Switzerland now. I can never go back to the villa. It would bring back memories of that terrible day. But you are young, and you have begun to make a life for yourself, as you should. It was my fondest wish that Luca had a place in that life, but that was not to be.

I have arranged a little surprise for your wedding day. Do not look upon it in a melancholy way. I believe Luca would want it for you. And you deserve it.

I WANT YOU TO BE FREE OF ANY CONCERNS
AS YOU WED. THEREFORE, I HAVE INSTRUCTED
MONTANINI TO OPEN AN ACCOUNT IN A LOCAL
BANK FOR YOUR MOTHER. I WILL WIRE FUNDS
THERE FROM TIME TO TIME. I'M SORRY, IT WON'T
BE A GRAND SUM. MOST OF MY ASSETS WERE
CONFISCATED. BUT YOU WON'T HAVE TO WORRY
FOR YOUR MOTHER.

AS A WEDDING PRESENT FROM ME, MONTANINI
WILL ALSO FUND AN ACCOUNT IN THE STATES
FOR YOU. I HOPE THIS WILL HELP SECURE A HAP-
PY HOME FOR YOU NEWLYWEDS. MONTANINI
WILL GIVE YOU ALL THE DETAILS. (RESOURCEFUL
ISN'T HE?)

NOW, MY DEAR, BASK IN THE GLORY OF YOUR
DAY AND THE SURPRISE WE HAVE ARRANGED FOR
YOU. THINK ONLY FOND THOUGHTS WHEN IT IS
REVEALED TO YOU. I WISH YOU ALL THE HAPPI-
NESS IN THE WORLD.

WITH ALL MY LOVE,
CONTESSA FREDERICA CASTELLANI

"Oh my. This is all so much," Nicla remarked blankly, still looking over the telegram as if it were not real. She turned to her mother. "Do you know about this?"

Silvia nodded, her lips tight. She wiped a tear from her eye.

Nicla looked to Montanini and held up the telegram. "What does she mean about a surprise?"

"Come." Montanini put Nicla's arm through his and led her out the door. There, before her, gleaming in the sun, was the Isotta. Standing by the driver's door was the tall gentleman from the bench on Montenero. He was wearing a chauffeur's uniform.

By the rear passenger door, holding it open, was his shorter bench-mate.

Nicla gasped and covered her mouth. So flooded with emotion, her power of speech was gone.

"*Principessa?*" the short gentleman offered his arm with a slight bow. "May I escort you to your coach?" As he led her to the car, Nicla turned to look back at Montanini.

"Happy thoughts," he urged. "Remember what the Contessa wrote." He smiled and waved. "You deserve to ride like a princess today."

As she stepped inside the car, the short gentleman helped Nicla with her gown. She looked about the luxurious interior. It made her think of Luca. She pictured him in front pretending to be her chauffeur.

Before she allowed herself to become saddened, she remembered the Contessa's words: *Luca would want this for you.* She was right. He was noble not only by blood, but in spirit. Nicla could easily imagine him offering her the car and wishing her well.

Her thoughts were interrupted by the short man, now in the front seat. "We took the car from the garage right after the German's left with the artwork. We knew they'd come back for anything valuable. We hid it in a barn for the Contessa. Then we got word from Montanini that she wanted us to chauffeur *la Principessa.*"

"I found this uniform in Alberto's closet," added the driver looking at Nicla from the mirror. "Poor Alberto, God bless his soul." Both men made the sign of the cross.

As they drove along, Nicla reminisced about Alberto as well. Suddenly, she jolted upright. "We're not going towards the church!"

"Yes we are," the little man announced with glee.

"But it's back that way." Nicla pointed.

"Not the church we're going to," stated the chauffeur. He smiled at his counterpart.

"What church *are* we going to?" Nicla was becoming anxious. The men looked at each other, then proclaimed in unison: "*Il Santuario della Madonna.*"

As the Isotta made its way slowly through the cobblestone streets of Montenero, curious onlookers gawked at the site of the veiled bride in the back seat of the magnificent vehicle. The chauffeur pulled in front of the stone steps leading up to the square of the sanctuary complex. The other gentleman opened the door and helped Nicla out.

At the top of the stairs stood Zio Fiore smiling down upon her. As Nicla ascended, she thought about climbing these steps on her knees as a schoolgirl, or later, when coming to pray for Claudio. *God had other plans for me*, she concluded.

Zio Fiore stretched out his hand and took Nicla's as she reached the top.

"I can't believe it," she whispered.

"I can't believe we got away with keeping it all secret." Fiore chuckled. Becoming solemn, he fixed Nicla's veil. "You were always like a daughter to me." His voice choked. "Now I get to walk you down the aisle."

Nicla looked lovingly upon her uncle. "When I was thirteen, I could drive a car and change a tire. You taught me I could do anything. When I grew up, I drove that Isotta ninety kilometers an hour, had guns stuck in my face and ran German checkpoints. I was able to do it all because of you." Nicla brushed her uncle's cheek. "I'm the woman I am because you didn't see me as just a girl."

Fiore's eyes glistened. "Come." He took Nicla's arm. "You're supposed to be getting married. Mustn't keep your Blue Prince waiting." He grinned slyly. "But I think you would dawdle just to keep him dangling a bit, wouldn't you?"

Nicla beamed. Not only did Fiore understand her, but he had called Tony her Blue Prince. It reminded her of the little girl saved from the Turkish pirates – the one whose slippers were in the sanctuary she was entering. That girl's Blue Prince had come to her rescue. Now, Nicla's childhood dream of a gallant hero was coming true.

As they walked across the elevated square, Nicla and her uncle were bathed in sunlight. Her gown gleamed so white, it could have been a truant cloud descended from the heavens. She felt as if she might float away.

Ahead, Nicla could see several dozen men emerge from around the side of the church. She knew from their kerchiefs and berets that they were members of the Partisans. A line was formed along Nicla's path to the church doors. They stood at attention with rifles at their side. From the far end of the line, one soldier, without a weapon, stepped out. It was her brother, Vivi.

Nicla was astonished. As she approached the line, Vivi barked a command at the men: "Citizen soldiers! For our staffetta... salute!" The men all stamped one foot and crisply raised a hand aside their heads. Nicla, escorted by Fiore, passed before the line like a queen in review of her soldiers.

At the end of the line, Vivi held out both hands for Nicla to take. He kissed her on the cheek. "You look beautiful."

"I'm overwhelmed." She was fighting back tears.

"You deserve this. *Babbo* would be proud of you." Vivi looked beyond Nicla to see the two old gentlemen making their way to the church along the periphery of the square. "You know those two old fellows?" He nodded in their direction. "They arranged everything...You'll see inside." Vivi smiled. "Now I've got to go take my place next to your groom. He's a good man. I'm honored to stand for him." Vivi kissed Nicla again and trotted off.

The church bells began to ring. Nicla looked at Fiore.

"It's all for you." He spoke tenderly. "Are you ready?" He offered his arm.

As they stepped up to the open doors, a little girl dressed in white met them. She was carrying a basket of rose petals. To Nicla, it was like looking at herself as a child. Not long ago, Nicla was her age. But she had lived a lifetime of travails in that short time. Still, her journey was far from over.

She began to sense something extraordinary further inside the church, beyond the vestibule. It was a hum, like soft voices. Nicla looked at Fiore with some trepidation. He smiled reassuringly and nodded to the little girl to lead on. As the inner doors opened and Nicla traversed the portal, her eyes beheld an astonishing sight. The chapel was filled with scores of people, all standing and turned, facing her. They became silent at her appearance.

Fiore leaned to Nicla's ear. "Those two old goats have a lot of connections," he whispered. "And apparently, the Partisans have big families."

Nicla barely heard what her uncle was saying. None of it seemed real. They had planned a simple ceremony at a tiny church, attended by close family, without a true wedding gown to grace the occasion. Here she stood, in glorious white, before throngs in the sanctuary of the Madonna.

A lone voice somewhere in the crowd broke the silence. "*Viva la staffetta!*" Other cries rang out of "*Viva la staffetta!*" and "*Dio vi benedica!*" followed by clapping that spread through the crowd and grew to thunderous applause.

The pipe organ hit a deep, bellowing chord. When the last of its awesome reverberation was absorbed into the vaulted ceiling, the church fell silent again. Softly, the heavenly prelude to Ave Maria began to play. As the verse began, Fiore motioned gently for the little girl to commence the procession. They began the march down the aisle.

The grandeur of the baroque chapel gave Nicla the sense of being a princess at her coronation or perhaps a royal marriage. Immense marble columns and arches rose in splendor to the ornate ceiling. Partisan soldiers, like royal guardsman, stood at attention before each pew. Sunlight from the round window high above the altar shined down the aisle like a spotlight, illuminating Nicla's gown so that it became brilliant like burning phosphorous.

As she marched radiantly through the majestic surroundings, Nicla began to recognize faces among the admirers. Many were those of Partisan citizens to whom she had made "deliveries."

Eugenio! She almost blurted. It was the old fisherman. From his house she had picked up the pants with the message in the hem. His daughter, who had doubted Nicla's fortitude before that first mission, stood next to him. The two nodded solemnly. Nicla could feel their respect and admiration.

She was approaching Tony. He stood before the altar, Vivi by his side. On Tony's face was that smile, raised on one side, that had enchanted her when he leaned from the jeep in the parade. How their paths had crossed again after that day was a miracle.

It took being hit by a jeep, Nicla thought. How inscrutable were God's ways. She looked up at the painting of the Virgin above the altar, then back at Tony. Nicla knew this was where she was meant to be. She turned to Zio Fiore. He kissed her cheek and put Nicla's hand in Tony's. The betrotheds turned toward the priest. The ceremony began.

As the priest spoke, Nicla began to think back on all she had been through to arrive at this moment. Looking up, she saw the magnificent complexity of the altarpiece. It was a fitting metaphor for the opus God had wrought in fashioning the arc of her life. But her story was not complete.

Pray for him, Mother of God, Nicla supplicated; her eyes fixed on the painting of the Virgin behind the altar. *Hold him in your arms and bring him back to me. Mother Mary, you know what loss is. Pray that God should end this terrible war and bring all the boys back.*

Nicla's contemplation was interrupted by the words of the priest. "Antonio Amici, do you take this woman…"

As they affirmed the vows offered by the priest, they were in a singular place - two persons absorbed in each other's love, they became one with the last "I do." After that, it seemed only a formality to Nicla that the priest should have to pronounce them man and wife.

In these final moments of the ceremony, so sublimely happy was she, that Nicla was able to avoid the thought lurking just below her joyful consciousness: that she had now assumed the station of so many wives and mothers – those whose husbands and sons took up arms and went off to war – women who faced no physical peril but suffered the moment to moment anxiety that the worst could befall their loved ones. This was to be Nicla's condition soon. But for now, such thoughts were held at bay. For as she looked in Tony's eyes, and heard the cheers of the well-wishers, there was such love and joy in Nicla's heart as to leave room for nothing else.

Chapter 28

Nicla sat on the reef looking out at the ocean. The waves crashed on the rocks and the breeze tousled her hair. In her hand she held Tony's letter. It had been almost a year since he left. There hadn't been time for a honeymoon. He had reported back to base the night of the wedding and left the next day.

In the interminable weeks and months that had passed, Nicla received not a letter or a word, as to Tony's fate. V.E. day had come and gone. All had celebrated the demise of the devil, Hitler. Nicla had felt relief but no great joy – not until receiving this letter. Then she had uttered a shriek of jubilation so great that Fiore came running into the house from his garage.

Now Nicla sat on the rocks with the wrinkled correspondence which she had unfolded and folded so many times. She kept it with her always. So there on the reef, she opened it again and read.

Dear Nicla,

I can't believe how long I've gone without being able to write to you. Even on the front, the other soldiers could write a V-mail back home, but I couldn't write to you in Italy. I can't imagine what went through your mind. But I know how strong you are, and you wouldn't give up on me.

We fought our way through France and into Germany. It was pretty bad going. That's all I'll say. I just want to forget about it and get you home with me.

I've only been in Germany a few days, but I'm going home tomorrow because the army gave me a lot of points for time served, being wounded, and having dependents (you and my mother). I'm lucky. Some guys don't know when they'll get home.

There are going to be ships taking war brides to America. I'm sure you'll hear from the war department.

I can't tell you how much I thought about you all this time, especially when things were scary. I thought about walking by the canal and you feeding me see urchins. I still can't believe I ate those things. I thought about our times by the pond. I even thought about you throwing your drink at that ape who ran you over.

Don't worry. I won't ever make you that mad. In fact, I'm going to devote the rest of my life to making you happy. You'll see.

I have to finish this letter and mail it now. Like I said, tomorrow I'm heading home. Hold on just a little bit more. We have a whole new life waiting for us in America. That's what I'm living for. We'll be together soon. I'll write to you when I get home.

Love,
Your husband,
Tony

Nicla folded the letter and tucked it inside her dress near her heart. She looked out across the ocean. The clouds were like white tufts of cotton, their bottoms flattened and dark. Sparse near her, they bunched closer together as they receded toward the horizon. It seemed they were leading her on, over the edge of the world. What awaited her in that strange new land? It had been more than two weeks since she received this letter. *He had time to get home and write,* she thought. Perhaps it was the Italian mail system. There was much disruption after the war. There were so many "what ifs" wedging their way into her thoughts. She wondered if Tony was right about her strength and perseverance. How much uncertainty could she bear?

Chapter 29

Tony Amici sat in the back seat of a 1937 Pontiac. He had disembarked in the port of New York with thousands of other returning servicemen. The train ride to New Haven had been crowded. He was forced to stand much of the way. Now, two of his friends were driving him home to Hamden. It was dark.

Tony was looking at a photo Nicla had given him. It was the one Claudio had taken of her at the beach. She didn't have any others. Tony was not jealous of Claudio's memory. Giving him the picture was proof enough that Nicla had let go.

Gazing at the photo of Nicla in happier days before the war, Tony thought of how much sadness he had seen in her. He was going to bring the smile from that photo back to Nicla's face.

Tony also thought of how much he had gone through to come to this point - surviving the landing at Anzio, fighting house to house in that French town. He had seen so much death. How was it that he had escaped? What did God have planned? He thought of how miraculous it had been to find Nicla in the road. *It was meant to be,* he thought, studying the photo.

"You're pretty quiet back there," noted Tony's friend in the front passenger seat.

"Just tired," Tony muttered absently, without looking up from Nicla's photo.

The two friends in the front looked at each other, concerned for their buddy. No one in the car saw the truck drift head-on into their lane.

Chapter 30

"I'll take your bag out to the car," Fiore announced going out the front door of the house. Nicla stood looking at her family. They were sitting at the kitchen table. She wondered when she would see them again. It was time for her to depart on her journey to America.

"*Vieni qui* – come here," she called her little brother over with a motion of her hand.

"Are you going to meet Jawn Wahyeen?" he asked looking up at her.

Nicla chuckled, "John Wayne? Maybe."

"Tell him I want to fight him." Matteo held up hands formed into six-shooters. "Pow pow!"

"Alright. I'll tell him." She leaned down and took his face in both hands. *He's so young*, she thought. She hoped his childish resilience would save him from the emotional scars of war. His clear, hopeful eyes reassured her. "I'll send for you when I have the duel with Mr. Wayne lined up. For now, use those guns to take care of Mamma." She kissed his cheek.

"Don't worry. Vivi and me will protect her. Pow pow!" He shot at some invisible intruders.

Vivi rose from the table. "Yes. Time for target practice." He put his hand on Matteo's back. "Run along out back. I'll join you shortly." Matteo bolted out the door, guns blazing.

Vivi went to his sister and placed his hands on her shoulders. "Someday, I'm coming. I'll bring Mamma and Matteo."

"I know you will." A tear rolled down Nicla's cheek. They threw themselves into a tight embrace.

"Come on now," Vivi encouraged. "Everything is going to be wonderful. You'll see. And we'll be together soon. *A Dio.*" He kissed Nicla's cheek and turned away quickly. Nicla did not see his lip trembling as he walked out the door.

Silvia was already standing before Nicla. She took her daughter's hands. They gazed at each other silently. Silvia reached into the pocket of her apron and produced a tiny gold object. Gently pulling Nicla's fingers open, she placed the object in her palm. It was a tiny medal bearing the image of the Madonna of Montenero and child. Nicla was familiar with it. Her mother always wore it, attached discreetly to her bra with the tiniest safety pin.

Nicla looked down upon it. The pin was still attached. She studied the raised figure of the Madonna holding the infant Jesus and thought of Mary's heart pierced by the loss of her son. Nicla looked upon her own mother and wondered how the dagger of parting must pain her. "Mamma, I can't-"

Silvia pulled Nicla close and hugged her tightly. "Yes, you can," she whispered in her daughter's ear. Then, she held Nicla out at arm's length. "You wear that. Remember. Mary is with you, and so am I. Always."

Nicla sat in one of Fiore's vehicles as they drove through the city. Tears from parting with her mother bathed her cheeks. Fiore offered words of encouragement. In a way, Nicla welcomed the distraction of having to respond. For between Fiore's well-intentioned offerings, the silence was worse. It was in the quietude that Nicla was tormented by the image of her mother standing alone crying. That was what she had glimpsed by turning back, in disobedience of Silvia's injunction, to look one last time at her mother.

They drove through many scenes of half-razed buildings and other forms of destruction visited upon the city during the bombings. Sculpted gods had not escaped the mortal instruments of destruction that had maimed their bodies. Nicla was taken by a bronze frieze of a recumbent goddess breastfeeding an infant. Her skin, dark, aged bronze, bore bright golden craters where bomb fragments had exposed fresh metal. Nicla pondered how even these garish wounds could not deter a mother from her maternal duty.

The car turned down a street that was surprisingly untouched by the mayhem that had befallen other thoroughfares. Fiore pulled to a stop in front of a massive edifice that occupied most of the block. It was the De Larderel Palace - four stories of ornate windows topped with a triangular pediment, within which a coat of arms proclaimed its noble lineage.

Nicla and Fiore stood outside the main entrance. Posted on the side of the door was a sign: American Red Cross. Nicla was familiar with the name. She had seen it on several buildings which the organization had commandeered for clubs to entertain American servicemen.

Fiore put his hand tenderly on Nicla's cheek. "Alright, *bella*. This is where I must let you go."

Nicla looked upon her uncle who had been so much like a father to her. "Zio, in a hundred years, I couldn't thank you enough."

"You already have. I'm so proud of you."

At that moment, two American soldiers emerged from the entrance. One was lighting a cigarette. The other nudged him and gestured with his head toward Nicla. "Check out that one."

His companion blew a puff of smoke in the air and looked admiringly at Nicla as they passed. "Nice..." he drew the word out. "She beats the ones inside."

Fiore glared at the two, assuming they had said something disrespectful.

"No, Zio. It's nothing. Just a compliment." But she had no idea.

"Maybe I should go in with you." Fiore continued to stare at the soldiers as they walked away. He turned back to Nicla. "What am I saying? I'm sorry. You don't need me. If anyone can handle themselves, it's you."

Fiore had to raise his voice as a large van rumbled up. From the rear door hopped a woman in army-green overalls. Nicla noticed the red cross in a white circular emblem on her shoulder. She carried a stack of empty trays that had previously been filled with donuts. The van was the Red Cross "club mobile." Women volunteers traveled in it bringing coffee and donuts to soldiers posted too far from the city to enjoy the clubs.

Another like-uniformed young lady popped out of the van. Nicla noticed how spry she was and how her curls bounced when she landed on the sidewalk. She was met by a little girl in tattered clothes.

"Hello sweety," she said to the child. "Just a second." She held up a finger and hopped back in the van. Nicla and Fiore were captivated. The "donut dolly," as the women were often called by soldiers, was back in front of the girl in an instant, this time holding a donut.

"I thought you'd be here again today, so I saved you one." She bent to the bedraggled child, who reached up, wide-eyed, with both hands. Neither Nicla nor Fiore knew what the young woman had said, but they were transfixed by the gesture.

"Oh." The young woman turned to Nicla. "Are you one of the war brides?"

Nicla was confused. Was she offering a donut? Reaching down for her bag, Nicla pulled out the letter from the war department. "I go in America." She handed the letter over. "*Mio Marito.*" She couldn't say husband in English.

"Sure." The young woman tilted her head and smiled. "You come with me."

Nicla studied her face. It reminded her of the typical American girl she had seen in magazine ads - not the movie stars, but the girl next door type. She had a small, turned-up nose and freckles on her full cheeks.

"I'll take care of her," the girl said to Fiore placing a hand over her heart.

Fiore understood her gesture if not her words. He turned to Nicla. Pulling her close, he kissed her cheek. "Do they know what they're getting in America? I'd like to see one of those girls drive an Isotta."

Nicla's face began to twist with grief.

"Don't cry." Fiore admonished. "You want them to think you're not tough?" He lifted her chin. "Go, *bella*." He gave Nicla's hand to the uniformed girl. "Look out for her," he said in Italian. Taking a few steps back, he gazed lovingly upon Nicla, blew a kiss, and walked briskly to his car.

The uniformed girl acted quickly. "Come on." She pulled lightly on Nicla's arm. "I'll take you in." She picked up Nicla's bag and gave her an encouraging smile.

Passing through the tall doorway, Nicla was astonished at the grandeur of the foyer. High arched ceilings were adorned with frescoes depicting legends of antiquity. Niches recessed in the marble walls housed statues of long deceased patricians. Wide stairs hugged both sides of the entrance hall and ascended to a gallery. Nicla could not believe the Americans had commandeered such a palatial setting.

"Who do we have here?" asked a woman looking over her reading glass and sitting at a desk no less ornate than its surroundings.

"This is..." began the uniformed girl. She turned to Nicla. "*Nome?*"

"Nicla."

The older woman behind the desk held out her hand somewhat impatiently. "Papers."

Nicla handed her the official letter.

"Take her to the ballroom." The bespectacled woman spoke without looking up from her leger. "They're getting some lessons. She can get settled in later."

"Yes Ma'am." The uniformed girl led Nicla up the grand stairs. "It looks a little intimidating," she waved her arm around, "but everyone is nice here." She glanced down at the woman behind the desk. "Almost everyone." She smiled impishly. Nicla assumed whatever she had said was worthy of a polite grin and nod.

Each room they passed along the second-floor gallery was more opulent than the next. Nicla's head was turned by the Gold Room, as it was called by the staff. Walls of elaborately carved wood were covered in gold leaf. Repeating geometric designs gave Nicla the impression she was looking into a Sultan's palace. But there was no little girl captured by Turkish pirates. Instead, she saw two older secretaries sitting around an elegant table, clacking away at typewriters. A soldier stood before them with a large sack slung across his shoulder.

"Hey, Toots!" he turned to greet Nicla's guide.

"Good morning, Corporal. Any mail for me in that bag?"

"You don't have a boyfriend back home do you?"

"Not at the moment."

"Good." He held up a flat, square box. "You know what film's in here? *To Have and Have Not*, with Humphry Bogart and Lauren Bacall. I'm bringing it over to the Paramount. I'll take you to see it Friday night. How about it?"

"I don't know..."

"Come on. It's got romance and action."

"You'll see action alright," interjected one of the typists without looking up. "He took Mary, the nurse, to a movie last week and she ended up stuck on Montenero. Engine trouble, he told her."

"I heard *his* engine was working just fine." Added the other secretary.

"Come on, ladies. Give a guy a break."

"I'll let you know, Corporal." Nicla's guide flashed a smile. She took Nicla by the hand. "Let's go, honey."

"Hey!" called the soldier leaning out of the Gold Room, "Next month, the USO's bringing in Sinatra. I can get us in the front row!"

"Maybe," the girl replied twirling around and back again, barely breaking stride.

"Maybe?"

The girl spun again, stopping this time, her hands folded behind her back. "Let's see how the movie goes, first. See you Friday night." She smiled, took Nicla's arm, and continued down the hall.

The banter amused Nicla. She didn't understand a word of it, but she was impressed with the girl's confidence. It was as if Nicla were looking at her American self.

They arrived at the tall doors to the ballroom. Nicla looked up at a fresco in the arch above the doors. Several female nudes reclined or stood in modest but sultry poses. Each was paired with a male barely covered by some cloth to avoid indecency.

Nicla, however, did not approve of the domineering stances of the males. "I bet you would have those men eating out of your hand," she spoke in Italian to the uniformed girl, gesturing at the painting.

The girl looked up and back at Nicla. "*Non capisco,* sweetheart. But the art around here doesn't do much for me either, if that's what you mean."

She opened one of the massive doors. There before them sprawled an expanse of white and gold splendor to flutter the heart of a princess. Glimmering chandeliers hung from a coffered ceiling. Golden, fluted columns formed a colonnade around the ballroom floor. Amidst this luxury, two dozen Italian woman sat in high-backed chairs.

"Good morning, Mother-in-law," they spoke in heavily accented unison.

"Again," encouraged a proper sounding woman at the front of the group. She raised her hand.

"*Gude morrneeng, mawther een law*," the women replied.

Nicla's guide brought her to an empty seat at the back of the assembly. "Here you go. I'm sure this young lady can help you." She tapped the girl sitting next to Nicla and walked away.

The girl was small and timid looking. She gazed at Nicla. "You're pretty."

"Thank you."

"They're teaching us English."

"I see."

The proper woman continued. "How are you, mother-in-law?" She raised her hand and the group repeated. This was followed by translations for, "Can I make you breakfast?" and "Where are the potatoes?"

"Are they sending us to be servants?" Nicla whispered.

The shy girl covered her mouth and giggled.

The group continued parroting the domestic lexicon. Nicla daydreamed about what life might be like away from her family. At least her new family would speak Italian. Tony was kind and protective. What should she worry about? But it had been weeks since she heard from him. Had something happened to him? Did he change his mind? She didn't know which possibility was more disturbing. Better to lose herself in the lesson.

"*Ora preparo cena*," announced the proper lady, "I'll prepare dinner, now." Nicla joined in the recitation.

⦗⦘ · ◆ · ⦗⦘

The following days included lessons in the kitchen on how to make hamburgers, pot roast, and other American dishes. Nicla had no contact with her Italian family. She became friends with the mousy girl. Her name was Tina. She was a seamstress like Nicla. Her husband was a big Irish fellow. Nicla wondered how Tina would fit in with his family.

Tina's English was more advanced than Nicla's. Her Irish soldier had taught her some during their time together. Nicla on the other hand had not heard much English from Tony. Now, she endeavored to learn all she could. As much as she loved Tony, she wanted to be independent in America. She pictured herself shopping and haggling with the merchants. She didn't know that open-air markets were already fading into America's past.

"How do you say, 'fifty cents?'" Nicla asked her new friend. "What about, 'For that price, you can take the cabbage home to your mother!'"

Tina giggled shyly. She admired Nicla's confidence. Nicla loved Tina's innocence. For the rest of their stay at the Red Cross palace, Nicla and Tina practiced their English together. As they did, Nicla gave Tina several more occasions to giggle.

Chapter 31

The day arrived when they were to embark on their transatlantic journey. From the Red Cross building, several groups were to be taken to the port. Nicla and Tina were among a dozen women standing before a US army truck. Two were mothers holding their babies. The vehicle reminded Nicla of the German truck in which she survived her ordeal as a *staffetta*. She pictured the kind German soldier retrieving the pants that had been thrown from the truck.

"OK, ladies. Watch your step," a friendly soldier cautioned as he assisted the women onto the truck. To Nicla, he seemed similar in nature to the kind German soldier. With a smile, he helped her aboard. Nicla turned to help Tina climb in. They sat next to each other on one of the benches that ran along the sides of the open truck.

The soldier stood in the street at the back of the truck and addressed the women. "I'm going to drive you around town before I take you to the port, so you can take it all in and keep it in your heart." He made a sweeping gesture, starting from his eyes, that ended at his chest. His words were meaningless to Nicla, but his gestures were eloquent.

The soldier drove them slowly all around the city. As they passed the canal, so many memories flooded Nicla's mind – some happy, like boating with Luca or eating sea urchins with Tony. But there were painful memories – the German soldier pointing his gun at her from the bridge, and Claudio's last mission on that same bridge. They passed streets where she had laughed and held hands with Claudio, and narrow alleys where they had kissed. Those were innocent days. She felt much older now.

At one point, Nicla was able to look down the street where she once lived. As she feared, her home was still in ruins. The street had been cleared, and children were playing where Nicla and her mother had knelt, embracing one another after her father's death in the bombing. *I'm going to America Babbo,* she spoke softly to her father. *You are with me, in my heart.* Neither Nicla's tears, nor her quiet declaration were conspicuous. All the women on the truck were sobbing loudly, holding handkerchiefs to their faces, and calling out parting laments. The two babies were fast asleep.

When they arrived at the port, Nicla saw the ship which was to take them to their new lives in America. She was astonished. It was an ocean liner. She marveled at the smokestacks and lines of lifeboats. Nicla had never been in a vessel larger than a small motorboat. She wondered what it would be like traveling on this immense ship.

In the street, near the docks, were several buses which had brought war brides from other towns. The women had begun queuing in front of a small office for a final review of their papers. Tina was at Nicla's side.

Suddenly a ruckus erupted toward the front of the line. The column of women moved over as one of the war brides was being escorted by two soldiers away from the office. She was crying hysterically. "I must get on the ship! My husband is in America! Stop!" She struggled against the grip of the soldiers holding her arms. "Let me go!" The soldiers understood none of her pleas.

They did however, as a result of their time stationed in Italy, understand the epithets she pronounced upon them.

Tina gazed wide-eyed at Nicla. "What do you think happened?"

"I don't know. Maybe something was wrong with her papers." Nicla stared pensively toward the office. "I won't be happy till we're on that ship."

"I won't be happy till my husband finds me on the dock in America."

"Don't worry, *carina*. Your Blue Prince will be there." Nicla fixed Tina's hair. "You're a little diamond. He'll come for you."

Tina hugged Nicla.

"We just have to get past this office." Nicla recalled the German checkpoint where Luca wore the chauffeur's uniform and used Vivi's identification. Through her dress, she touched the medal of the Virgin pinned to her bra.

When they arrived inside the office, a bald sergeant with a cigar in his mouth sat at a desk. He took Nicla's papers and looked up at her. She thought perhaps she should smile, but wanting to resemble her photo as much as possible, she refrained. He squinted his eyes slightly as he drew a puff from his cigar. Allowing the smoke to drift slowly from his mouth, he fixed Nicla in his gaze. Her anxiety rose. *Does it end here?* she thought. Had she come all this way for nothing?

She gave him a nervous smile. He looked back at her papers. Putting the stub of a cigar back in his mouth, he picked up a rubber stamp and brought it down heavily on her papers. With a tilt of his head toward the door, he sent her on her way. Tina was similarly approved.

Each carrying their bags, the other women were led by two soldiers to the gangway. Nicla looked up at the side of the great ocean liner. It was so tall. She wondered how something so massive stayed afloat. Stepping aboard was no different from walking into a building. It was strange to be on water with no rocking sensation. She wondered if it might be different on the high seas.

A young lady in Red Cross uniform escorted them through the narrow hallways of the ship. From behind, Tina squeezed Nicla's arm. Nicla turned her head and smiled. "The rooms will be bigger. You'll see." She did feel a bit claustrophobic.

They were brought to a large room. It had been a lounge for passengers. Now it was a dormitory for war brides. Cots were arranged in neat rows. Bags lay next to most, attesting that someone had laid claim. Small playpens of tubular steel and netting were pushed up against many of the cots. One woman sat with a bare-bottomed baby on her knee applying some talc before wrapping the child in a diaper.

Nicla and Tina found two open cots next to one another. On the cot to Nicla's other side sat a raven-haired woman going through her bags on the floor. She turned and looked contemptuously at Nicla. "You better not snore."

Nicla was taken aback. "No. I do not snore." She fixed the woman in her gaze. The woman's eyebrows seemed to be permanently fixed in an angry position. Clearly a country girl, she was strong and voluptuous. Nicla could imagine her heaving a basket of washed clothes up onto her head and walking from the town fountain to her home in the hills.

"Good," replied the woman. "And don't touch any of my things."

"Don't worry. I wouldn't want to."

The woman glared at her. They held each other's stare for a moment. "Alright," the shapely one pronounced slowly. "Then we shouldn't have any problem." She went back to sorting through her bags.

Nicla tried to place the woman's dialect. It sounded Neapolitan. The ship had obviously made ports coming up the Tyrrhenian coast from the South. She turned to Tina who was gaping.

"Don't worry," Nicla whispered close in Tina's ear. "We'll just mind our own business. She won't bother us." Nicla turned to see the woman stride confidently away.

"I don't know." Tina whispered back. "She scares me."

"I've been through a lot scarier things. Hey. Didn't you just go through the same war I did?

"Yes. That's true. Nothing compares to an air raid, does it?" Tina half grinned. "But I think your experience was different from mine. You're not afraid of anything."

"Oh, I'm plenty afraid. I just learned to fake being brave." She took Tina's hand. "Come on. Let's go up on deck. We're going to be pulling out soon I think."

When they arrived on the main deck, the ship was already starting to move. All they could see were the backs of women straining for a spot along the rail. They were all waiving and calling to people on the docks. Nicla and Tina found a crevice to squeeze into. Nicla's eyes swept across the throngs ashore.

"I see my mother!" cried Tina. "Mamma!" She waived furiously. "Mamma!" She repeated over and over, tears running down her cheeks. "She doesn't see me!"

"I'm sure she sees you. You can't tell where her eyes are looking from here." Nicla rubbed Tina's back. "She sees you."

Nicla, instead, saw no one from her family. *They must be here,* she thought, and continued to scan the crowd. But the ship moved farther out in the harbor and the people ashore became smaller. She hoped her mother had been there and had at least seen *her.* It was a slim hope, but she held onto it.

As the ship made way out of the harbor, the women on deck began to thin out as some went below. Nicla and Tina remained. They were passing Molo Nuovo. Two young men with fishing poles stood up as the ship passed.

"Hey!" one of them called. Nicla could barely hear him from the distance. "Where are you going! I can take care of you, right here!"

"I'll bet you can!" shouted back a vivacious passenger, eliciting an eruption of laughter from the women still on deck.

Looking at Molo Nuovo, Nicla thought back on the day she spent with Luca – how he swam while she sat on the rocks. She remembered him coming up from beneath the waves in front of her and throwing back his wet hair. She could still see his smile and the sun gleam on his shoulders. *He could be someone's Blue Prince,* she had thought. *He could have been mine,* she admitted to herself.

"What's wrong?" Tina touched Nicla's hand on the rail.

"Just thinking back."

"On good times, I hope."

"Some, yes." Nicla tried to smile. If she were certain Tony was well, it would be easy to smile. But she knew something wasn't right.

"Come," Tina put her arm through Nicla's. "Let's go to the front of the ship."

As they walked past wooden benches and lounge chairs, shuffleboard lines and the usual amenities of a cruise ship, Nicla was surprised that everywhere she looked, diapers hung from makeshift clotheslines. One woman sat on a lounge chair breastfeeding her baby.

When they reached the bow, Nicla and Tina walked up to the rail. The breeze pushed back Nicla's hair. They were heading out to the open sea. "Look." Tina pointed to the horizon. "Our husbands are waiting for us over there." She turned to Nicla. "It won't be long. Then you'll be happy."

Nicla closed her eyes. The wind felt good. She hoped it would chase the negative thoughts from her mind. How many times, growing up, she had surveyed the horizon with fancies of adventures that lay beyond. Now she was trying to convince herself that the man she loved would be waiting for her when she transcended that boundary. The cloudless sky offered no clues.

❧ ·•◆•· ☙

Sitting on their cots facing each other, Nicla and Tina prepared for bed. The lights were turned low. With her hands free under her nightgown, Nicla slipped off her bra. Poking her arms out, she folded the bra, one cup nestled inside the other. Pinned to one strap, the medal of the Virgin caught what little light streamed into the room and gleamed. Nicla kissed the medal and whispered a prayer most intently, before tucking the bra under her dress already folded on her suitcase.

"What's wrong?" whispered Tina. "Something is worrying you. I know it."

Nicla studied Tina's face. She wondered how someone so innocent looking could be so perceptive.

"Alright," Nicla sighed. Her shoulders dropped. "I'll tell you. I haven't heard from Tony in more than a month." She struggled to hold back tears. "I'm worried something is wrong."

"Oh," Tina moaned.

"He won't be there," came a derisive voice from another cot. It was the shapely woman. "More than a month? And you haven't heard from him? You won't see *him* on the dock."

"Don't worry." Tina spoke, trying to ignore the woman. "I'm sure there's a good reason. The mail has been terrible."

"Is he good looking?" the woman interjected.

"Yes... but what does that have to do with it?" Nicla retorted. "And what business is that of yours?"

"All you girls marry for love. These young guys, they don't care about love. And they *don't* want to get married."

"And you know about these things?" Nicla mocked.

"Yes. I do. My guy is a grown man with his own business. You should see his house. I have the picture." She flipped her thumb towards her bags. "Maybe he's not going to win any beauty contests, but I know he'll be waiting for me when I get there."

"Good for you," remarked Tina contemptuously. Nicla turned, surprised, to look at her formerly timid friend.

"Well, anyway," the woman continued dismissively, "He won't show up. You'll see." She got under her covers and rolled over, away from Nicla.

"Don't listen to her," Tina whispered. "He loves you. And you're beautiful. Of course he'll be there." She moved her cot closer to Nicla's. "Tell me all about how you met." Tina placed her cheek on her pillow with both hands beneath it.

"Are you sure you don't want me to tell you the fable of Buchettino?"

"No. I heard that one enough growing up. Tell me about you and Tony."

"Fine." Nicla laid herself down, facing Tina, and began recounting her story in a whisper. As she told it, the images in her mind became more vivid. They reminded her how intense her love affair had been. It reaffirmed her faith in Tony – despite how the curvaceous woman had assailed it. The farther she went into the retelling, the more Nicla lost herself and began to relive it. She never knew when the story telling ended and her dreams began.

The next morning, Nicla woke late. Tina was already up and dressed. "That was a beautiful story." She sat down at the foot of Nicla's cot. "But you fell asleep. You have to finish it tonight."

"Thank you. That story helped me more than you know."

"You don't have to thank me. *You* told the story. Did you really hit the ball far with the bat? I bet those American nurses thought you were something."

Nicla laughed. "They were amused, I can tell you that. But they were more interested in Tony than me." She sat up and reached for her clothes on top of her bags. As she did so, she noticed her dress was not folded as she had left it. She took her bra out from under it. "My medal! Someone took my medal!"

"What? What medal?"

"*La Madonna di Montenero*! She was pinned to my bra." Nicla held out the garment in both hands.

Tina grabbed Nicla's dress from atop the bag. "Maybe it's snagged on this."

There was no medal.

At the moment, the Neapolitan woman walked in drying her hair with a towel. "The sink in the supply room is big enough to wash your hair," she announced and sat on her cot. The glares from Tina and Nicla could not be ignored. "What's the matter with you two?"

Tina rushed over. The voluptuous woman stood up to meet her. Tina looked up under her chin. "You took Nicla's medal didn't you?" She poked the woman in the chest.

"What are you talking about? Get away from me." The taller woman shoved Tina onto Nicla's cot and turned to reach for something under her own pillow. Tina leapt back at her. The woman spun around, swinging a small knife. It caught the inside of Tina's forearm. A scream went up from the women who had gathered around.

Nicla dove at the knife-wielding arm. She squeezed the limb with both her hands as the woman raised it above her head.

"*Aiuto*! Help!" Nicla shouted desperately. Two of the nearby women also grabbed the raised arm.

"What the hell is going on!" bellowed a sailor entering the room. He bounded over and began wrenching the knife out of the woman's raised hand. As he did, Tina grabbed at the woman's shoulder. Her dress tore down enough to reveal the gleaming medal of the Madonna pinned to her bra. The onlookers gasped.

The woman relinquished the knife. "That's right," she sneered. "Take a good look. All of you." She unhooked the medal with her free hand and threw it at Nicla. Turning, she scowled at the women around her.

"You think you're all better than me? Because you didn't have to do what I did to keep from starving?"

With a tug, the sailor began leading her away with the knife in one of his hands and the woman's elbow in the other.

Looking back over her shoulder, she continued, "You learn quick how to use one of these when the men don't pay up." She grabbed at the knife in the sailor's hand who held it at length.

"Hypocrites! Like you all didn't do things!" she exclaimed as the sailor pulled her out of the door.

As the other women murmured about what had transpired, Nicla turned to Tina. She was sitting on Nicla's cot holding a handkerchief against her forearm.

"Let me see that." Nicla took her arm.

"It's just a small cut." Tina lifted the handkerchief.

Nicla examined the wound. It was not deep.

"Here," Nicla took the handkerchief from Tina's hand and replaced it with her medal. She closed Tina's hand around it and began tying the handkerchief around Tina's forearm. "How did you know enough to tear at *that* shoulder?"

"I don't know. Something told me."

"Or some-*one*." Nicla tapped Tina's hand which held the medal.

Tina smiled, then became serious. "Why would that woman do it? She bragged about how her husband had money."

Nicla furled her brow. She finished tying the dressing. "I don't think any of us will ever feel completely safe again."

"We will. When we're with our husbands."

Nicla gazed fondly on Tina's innocent face. *How can you forget the bombs, the rats in the shelters, and the smell of death?* she wanted to ask her. But Nicla only smiled and brushed a lock from Tina's forehead. "That's right, *bella*. Everything will be alright then."

Chapter 32

F or more than two weeks, Nicla's Atlantic crossing stretched into an interminable blur of worry and seasickness. The malady was not peculiar to her. The deck hands were so busy cleaning up after the sick women, they hardly attended to their normal tasks. During rough seas however, their duties of weathering the storm took precedence, and the ship became overpoweringly foul.

Sometimes, on clear days, Nicla's foreboding about Tony was interrupted by the sight of an iceberg. They were so beautiful and fascinating that Nicla would linger at the ship's rail and marvel at them.

One gargantuan sculpture resembled a cathedral. It had jagged points across the top, like the Duomo of Milan, but in the sun, it shined brilliant white as no manmade structure Nicla had ever seen. The face of this ice cathedral was missing. Deep inside, the air itself glowed in shades of blue.

Nicla imagined walking down the aisle in this ethereal temple. Marching across the spectrum of blues, she envisioned the faces of the Partisans from her own wedding. Indigo darkness cloaked the altar where she was reunited with Tony. There, a single candle barely lit their faces. They recited their vows. But as they declared their devotion, the candle flickered, and Tony began to recede into the darkness. Nicla found herself once more at the railing of the ship with her unanswered questions about Tony's fate. There would be no peace, she concluded, until they were together once more.

On the fifteenth day of the voyage, word spread around the ship that they would be reaching New York the next morning. Nicla went to bed that night afire with anticipation and apprehension. After tossing and turning for hours, she drifted into a fitful sleep. She began to dream.

Floating high in the air, the city of Livorno began to materialize below. Nicla could see a garage. A figure was pumping gas into an automobile and a smaller figure chasing a ball. She knew who they were. Unable to see within the house, Nicla cried out, "Mamma!" but she continued to soar past.

Moving out toward the countryside, a pond came into view. She recognized it from her rendezvous with Tony. No lovers lay at its shore with whom it could share its hidden beauty. She saw how the thick brush and tall grass closed it off from the rest of the world. It was clear that more than the reckless desire of youth had made them so bold in their intimacy there. It was paradise.

Nicla tried to summon up memories, hoping that figures of Tony and she would appear beside the pond. To her excitement, they began to take shape. But before being fully realized, she was lifted higher, and the amorphous duo on the blanket faded away.

Nicla was moving swiftly now, away from land and out across the ocean. As in her previous dream, she saw a man in a small rowboat. This time, the boat was moving out to sea, away from her. He faced her as he rowed, but Nicla could not make out his features. Everything else about him – his physique, his movements – told Nicla this was Tony. She struggled vainly to will herself into moving faster, but there was no controlling her speed. She called out to him, but it was useless. He was getting farther from her. The sky towards the horizon darkened. A bank of clouds, like an immense black sheet across the ocean, covered the little craft.

"No!" Nicla wailed. She heard thunder from the storm raging beneath the swirling blackness. "Stop! It's too much for him!"

Suddenly, as if a stone had been dropped in a gigantic pond, the clouds drew away in rings. The eye of the storm widened. Nicla could see tall waves rising, cresting, and smashing down on the ocean's surface. There, in the trough between the waves, she saw Tony's boat - capsized.

"No!" She screamed. Frantically, she scanned the surface of the water. It was so convulsed that she could hardly see beyond the next wave. She felt herself being pulled higher, up into the sky.

"Wait!" She reached down. "Tony!" But she continued to rise.

"Nicla!" came a faint voice from afar. "Nicla. Wake up."

It was Tina.

Nicla bolted upright and threw her arms around Tina. "Oh no, no. Please don't be true!" she moaned.

"What was it?"

"It's too terrible," she sobbed, burying her head in Tina's shoulder.

"Don't cry." Tina stroked Nicla's hair. "It was only a dream. It's not true." She leaned back and put her hands on Nicla's shoulders. "Come on." She guided Nicla back onto her pillow. "You go back to sleep. Tomorrow you'll see Tony, and everything will be alright." She smiled and brushed a tear from Nicla's cheek. "No more crying, now. Alright?"

Nicla nodded halfheartedly. "Thank you. I'll be fine now." She knew she wouldn't, but she squeezed Tina's hand, and rolled over. Her eyes did not close again that night.

Eventually, Nicla saw the first, dim light of dawn streaming through the portholes. She rose, dressed quietly, and made her way up to the main deck.

It was foggy. Looking out from the rail, Nicla could not see very far. She wondered how close they were to their destination. She moved toward the front of the ship. A deck hand was standing watch. He tipped his cap.

Standing at the bow railing, Nicla remembered Tina's words – how, out ahead of them, their husbands would be waiting, and everything would be alright. Nicla wondered how close she was to finding out.

As the minutes passed, the fog began to disperse. Something was slowly taking shape through the gray haze - the Statue of Liberty. Nicla's heart leapt. As if to echo her sentiments, the ship's horn blared. Startled, Nicla grabbed the rail.

Regaining her equilibrium, Nicla marveled as the colossal lady was revealed in the fading mist. The drapes of her garments reminded Nicla of the Virgin, and her crown a halo. Her raised arm and torch seemed to be welcoming Nicla.

Through the material of her own dress, Nicla felt for the medal of the Madonna of Montenero. Pinching it between the cloth, pulling it to her lips, she leaned her head and kissed it.

"I made it," she whispered. "You brought me through everything. I know it. Please, pray to God for me, that Tony will be on that dock." Just then, Nicla imagined her own mother all those miles across the ocean. *She must be praying too,* she thought.

"Nicla! Here you are!" It was Tina. Nicla turned to see that many passengers were now on deck, brought up by the booming horn. "You see!" Tina cried, "We're here!" She hugged Nicla tightly. "Our dreams are coming true."

Dreams? The word conjured Nicla's nightmare just hours ago. The specter of Tony's overturned boat sent a chill through Nicla's soul. She fought to stay in the aura of Tina's innocent face, but in her mind, she was back on the rolling sea calling out Tony's name.

"Nicla?" Tina grasped her by the shoulders. "Don't you understand? Everything is alright. Look." She waved her hand at the reveling passengers. "You see?" Taking Nicla's face in her hands, she leaned forward and declared with deep assurance, "You're *going* to see your husband."

Nicla studied Tina's face – so guileless and full of hope. "Yes," Nicla managed with a half-smile. "Let's go get ready."

At the New York docks, the "War Brides Ship," as it was christened by the newspapers, had arrived. The haze of the dawn had been vanquished by the sun. The bluest sky reigned. Nicla and Tina stood with their bags among throngs of women on the main deck. They were all shouting and waving down at the pier. Some held babies aloft for husbands below who had never seen their own children.

Nicla looked down at the sea of men cheering and waving back up at the women on the ship. It reminded her of the crowd at Palio horse race. How would she find Tony amidst this chaos?

"You have my address, don't you?" Tina shouted over the noise of the crowd.

"Yes," Nicla nodded.

"I'm afraid we might get separated down there. You'll hold my hand?"

Nicla took Tina's hand and squeezed. "You'll be holding your husband's hand soon." They both turned to scan the crowd again as they moved toward the hatch to lower decks.

"There he is!" Tina screamed, pointing to the multitude. "There's Sean!"

Nicla could not tell Sean from any of the others waving on the dock. "Oh, yes. Hello!" She waved, nonetheless.

Tony was nowhere to be seen.

Soon they were coming down the gangway onto the pier. Nicla could not believe the tumult raised by the mass of humanity. Shouts of joy, embraces, passionate kisses, and tears were swirling through the raucous assemblage. She looked all around for Tony but couldn't see over the pandemonium.

"Sean!" Tina cried. "He's going the wrong way! He doesn't see me!"

"Go after him!" Nicla exclaimed.

"Come with me."

Nicla grabbed Tina and hugged her. "I have your address, *bella*. Go!" She gave Tina a gently push. "Hurry!"

Tina leapt up and kissed Nicla's cheek before turning to disappear through the crush. Nicla stood alone.

For what seemed like an eternity, Nicla alternated between staying put and wandering though the turmoil. *Guide me to him, Holy Mother*, she prayed. At that moment, Nicla's eye caught an older woman. She stood alone some twenty paces away. Dressed in black, her hair in a bun, she was looking at Nicla.

As Nicla studied her, a thought, like a shock of electricity, took Nicla's breath. *It's Tony's mother!*

Before Nicla could get a better look, several reuniting couples danced between her and the woman. As they passed, Nicla caught fleeting glimpses of the older lady. Nicla took some halting steps toward her. The way between them was clear now. This was the woman she envisioned when Tony spoke of his mother.

To Nicla's dismay, she could see tears flowing down the woman's cheek. To her horror, the woman seemed to be reaching out to her.

Please, Nicla whispered to herself, *Madre di Dio, don't let her tell me anything bad.* The woman took a step toward Nicla, opening her mouth to speak. Nicla became weak in her knees.

Suddenly Nicla was jolted by a push in the back. A soldier escorting his new bride and child squeezed past Nicla, and up to the old woman. They placed the woman's new grandchild in her outstretched arms. They all embraced.

Nicla was still trying to comprehend the turnabout she had just experienced when she felt a hand slip into hers. She spun around.

"Tony!"

There he was, looking at her with that familiar smile turned up at one corner. Nicla threw her arms around him and squeezed with all her might. She leaned back to look at him and convince herself she wasn't dreaming. Throwing herself against his chest, she hugged as if she would never let go. He was all right. He was alive.

She leaned back again, her cheeks wet with tears. "What happened? Why didn't you write?"

"There was an accident. I was in the hospital in bad shape. I couldn't write. When I was able to, I did. You didn't get it?"

"Hospital? Are you alright?" Nicla ran her hands up and down Tony's arms.

"I'm fine. Full recovery. See?" Tony patted his chest with both hands. "Come here." He put his hand around the small of Nicla's back and pulled her near. "This is the cure I needed."

Nicla put her head against Tony's chest again. "I worried so much for you. People said you left me. But I knew something must have happened."

Tony took Nicla's face in his hands. "It's alright. The important thing is we're together. The war and all that misery is behind us. Remember I asked you to have faith that I'd make you happy the rest of your life? Well, that starts now."

Nicla gazed upon the man that had lifted her in his arms, off the street, when she was at her most hopeless and brought her back to life. He had saved her. He was her Blue Prince.

But Nicla knew she had also saved herself. By the grace of God and her own inner strength she had overcome all. Her long journey was over and a new one, full of promise and dreams she had never thought possible, was beginning.

Made in the USA
Middletown, DE
02 October 2023